DUEL OF THE MONSTERS
Volume 2

Pete Rawlik

Matthew Dennion

Zach Cole

Dustin Dreyling

Tyler Shepard

D.G. Valdron

Robert E. Wronski, Jr.

Cody Bratsch

Brion Halloway

Patrick Rahall

Christofer Nigro

Preface Dialogue:
Christofer Nigro

Cover Art:
Illustration and design by Jimi Bautista and finalized by Elden Ardiente

Interior Artists

Preface featuring Vue X Monroe:
Małgorzata Mika

"Bigfoot vs. Killer Grizzly":
Illustration by Glenn Lugapo. Final art and title design by Elden Ardiente

"Mr. Hyde vs. The Phantom of the Opera":
Illustration and title design by Małgorzata Mika

"Lich vs. Zombies":
Illustration by Myke Guisinga. Title design by Elden Ardiente

"Wendigo vs. Lizard Man":
Illustration and title design by Ferdie Misa

"Sea Serpent vs. Kraken":
Illustration and title design by Elden Ardiente

"Man-Beast vs. Swamp Monster":
Illustration by Glenn Lugapo. Final art and title
design by Elden Ardiente

"Invisible Woman vs. Insectoid Alien":
Illustration and title design by Ferdie Misa

"Werewolf vs. Gargoyle":
Illustration by Zach Cole. Title design by Elden
Ardiente

"Man-Made Monster vs. Great Ape":
Illustration by Glenn Lugapo. Final art and title
design by Elden Ardiente

"Vampire vs. Velociraptor":
Illustration by Jim Faustino. Title design by Elden
Ardiente

"Cactus Cat vs. Hidebehind":
Illustration and title design by Ferdie Misa

DEDICATIONS

This volume is once again dedicated to the memory of my beloved grandparents, Gertrude "Trudie" Nigro and Thomas J. Nigro, both of whom had a major hand in raising me. It is in their honor that I continually strive forward and seek to make them proud. I also dedicate this work to the respective crews of Wild Hunt Press and Lungga Creatives who have worked so hard at my side to make these publications a reality and not just a pleasant daydream.

Table of Contents

PREFACE

Vue X Monroe created by Stu Niven

Christofer Nigro
Preface
Duel of the Monsters Volume 2

At the Mansion of the Macabre...

Greetings, fiend-lovers! I'm Vue X Monroe, known to many as Master of the Synths and purveyor of death. As a clown, I may be good for a few laughs, but only at the expense of others. Hah!

I come to you from the rec room of the Mansion of the Macabre to bring you info on the yarns you're about to encounter in this second volume of *Duel of the Monsters.* I'm not really sure why or how I came to be here, but what I do know is that this manse is my kind of place! Alright, maybe a distant second to a few other places. You know, like cemeteries, slaughterhouses, crematoriums, the local crack house (maybe in your very own neighborhood – look for me there the next time you visit for a fix!), a few choice boulevards here and there like Skid Row. Pretty much anywhere your sorry ass is apt find death in its myriad grisly forms, you just might find me there to help deliver you or someone else into her waiting arms... and your soul into the arms of Satan.

You see, death is sort of my thing. It just happens to be one of the greatest forces in the universe, the ultimate finality for mere mortals like yourself, the sister to the other totally awesome universal forces like entropy, oblivion, and decay... I think you get the gist. In fact, feeding on these necromantic energies is exactly how I acquired my good looks. As for my relationship to a certain lord of Hell... well, let's just say he's known as a seriously good maker of *deals,* and he offered me one hell of a contract. I'll spare telling you what I signed it in, though; never say I'm without some degree of mercy. Hah! Hah!

Now, before you think I'm too much of a bad guy, let it be known that I'll be so generous (or, sadistic; you decide!) as to play a kick ass dirge that I composed just for you as your physical body succumbs to the inevitable and your soul is carted off to Hell. Or, I can perform one of the classics for you; my personal rendition of Chopin's funeral march is totally bitchin'. Hah!

But where are my manners? With my introduction out of the way, it's time for me to mention the tales you will encounter in this tome!

You will start off with a clash of the hirsute horrors as a Bigfoot and a Killer Grizzly face off to prove which of the two is "King of the Forest," courtesy of Christofer Nigro. That author seems like my kind of guy, and I really hope I get to meet him one day! Bwah-hah-hah!

Secondly, we have an untold tale of two infamous and decidedly monstrous gents spawned during the Victorian era, Mr. Hyde and the Phantom of the Opera, as they have a nasty difference of opinion in "Vile Intentions," by Matthew Dennion. You should read this guy's books, as they are filled with copious amounts of death and mutilation! Hell, I get empowered every time I turn the page of one of Mr. Dennion's tomes!

Next up we have a dread undead entity known in legend as a Lich running up against undead nasties of a Zombie sort, in "A Night at the Monastery," brought to you by Pete Rawlik. This writer dude has done a stand-up of job of chronicling the gruesome life and work of one Herbert West, and he continues that awesome scientist's life story here. I'm getting euphoric just thinking about it, as Dr. West is a favorite of mine for a few reasons that should be obvious to your sorry asses by now. Heh.

After this tale you will be privy to what happens when a human-eating supernatural beast known as a Wendigo suddenly has his world intruded upon. No, not by an annoying relative who drops by unannounced, but an equally deadly hominid – one of the scaley rather than furry sort – that is known in popular lore as a Lizard Man. This yarn of woe, "War of the Appetites," is brought to you by Dustin Dreyling. And not to give too many spoilers here, but your ass can rest assured it's gonna be filled with superb amounts of bloodshed and death! My kinda story!

After that, you're gonna take a voyage to the bottom of the sea – a grand place to find death, I should add – as Brion Halloway brings us "Raging Waters," where a massive ass sea serpent decides not to share the briny waters with an equally massive ass kraken. If you should ever happen to drown in the sea (trust me, it can happen!), you might just get a firsthand view of awesome battles to the death between the dark depth's most dangerous residents.

Then you will follow one of those annoyingly persistent investigative reporters (I've gotten to kill more than a few of them!) in "A Battle in the Green" as he tracks down a much-feared Man-Beast when the deadly bruiser seeks shelter in a bayou… only for both to find out that it's home to a mighty Swamp Monster that lacks any semblance of hospitality to visitors. This short but bitterly sweet tale of obsession and bestial combat comes your way courtesy of Robert E. Wronski, Jr. That fellow knows a thing or three about crossovers, so expect to find some awaiting you here.

Next up we have a serial killer that can't be seen pitted against an extraterrestrial monstrosity as both the Invisible Woman and Insectoid Alien become rivals when the two begin separately stalking a group of hapless college girls in "When Killers Cross Paths," as scribed by Patrick Rahall. If you are a fan of the depredations of the notorious Griffin family and the bloody havoc wreaked by creatures from beyond this world, then I gotta highly recommend Mr. Rahall's horror tale to you. Your nightmares deserve nothing less!

After this, you will find yourself reading another short but evil tale as a tortured Werewolf seeks refuge in what the furry fellow *thinks* is an abandoned cathedral… only to find out that it's tenanted by a Gargoyle as the titular "Guardian of the Church." This one was penned by Zach Cole, an author who knows quite a bit about werewolves and other things that go bump in the night.

Next on the bloody roster is a truly twisted love story containing a deadly donnybrook between creatures as an intelligent Great Ape faces off against a patchwork Man-Made Monster over a certain lovely lass's ass in "The Masterpiece Creation." This one is composed by D.G. Valdron, so you can hedge a bet on your pitifully short life that you're gonna be in for a shocker of an ending that will put the authors of the classic EC & Warren horror tales to shame.

After that tale you will witness a merry mixture of blood and gore from both humans and monsters alike in "Bloodthirsty." For this vicious yarn, soldier guys on a secret military installation are caught between the unlikely but awesome battle of an undead Vampire and a genetically bred Velociraptor. This one is brought to you by Tyler Shepard, and you will be thrilled by a really chilling ending that results from this clash between two very different species of monsters.

Finally, you get a dosage of whimsy – along with another dose of that stoner dude Bill Chan – in a fun little flash fiction once again featuring two of the "Fearsome Critters" from 19th century lumberjack folklore courtesy of Cody Bratsch. For this little tale, a prickly Cactus Cat runs afoul of an elusive Hidebehind in "The Drop," and death must come to one of them... and, I'm excited to mention, possibly for poor Mr. Chan as well. I mean, his luck is bound to run out eventually, just as it one day will for all you pathetic mortals, am I right? Bwah-hah-hah!

So, my future prey, turn the pages, be thrilled by tales of monstrous mashups and mayhem, and be sure to visit me at the local crack house (or the cemetery, if that's more your thing). But if you're more of a homebody, then worry not, because one day I might just come to visit you right where you live! Hah! Hah! See ya then!

END

Christofer Nigro
Bigfoot vs. Killer Grizzly: King of the Forest
Duel of the Monsters Volume 2

BIGFOOT VS. KILLER GRIZZLY: KING OF THE FOREST – Christofer Nigro

Christofer Nigro
Bigfoot vs. Killer Grizzly: King of the Forest
Duel of the Monsters Volume 2

Christofer Nigro
Bigfoot vs. Killer Grizzly: King of the Forest
Duel of the Monsters Volume 2

Many thanks to JJ Lindsey for assistance on the final epilogue in this story

Kootenai National Forest, Montana

Calvin Stewart was a very disgruntled forest ranger this day. He understood that mysterious disappearances and deaths tended to occur in the middle of National Forests like the one he had been employed to look after for over a decade. Any number of factors could be involved, as a large wilderness area was a dangerous place that hikers and campers should always be aware of. Usually, however, if you stayed at certified camping grounds, followed established trails, and observed various precautions, one was apt to live to tell the tale about a fun trip.

However, some disappearances and deaths were on the *strange* side. As in, a hint towards something unusual going on within the camouflage provided by the numerous species of trees that added to the plethora of normal dangers. These additional factors seemed to come and go periodically, and Stewart's studies of the forest did not overlook certain phenomena that appeared to correlate with these deadly mystery occurrences.

For instance, two months earlier a decidedly odd meteorite had landed in the middle of the woods. It was one of those strange rocks from the stars that mysteriously failed to burn up completely upon sailing through the atmosphere at hundreds of miles per hour and managing to land as a large, nearly intact ferrous mass. It was also the type of aerolite that gave off strange radiations, of the sort that conventional science was not comfortable with even acknowledging what possible effects it may have on the surrounding flora and fauna.

It was the same type of landing that preceded dangerous aberrant behavior on the part of the wildlife, such as that incidents involving attacks on humans by swarms of disparate bird species that occurred in Cornwall during the 1950s, again in Bodega Bay a decade later; and yet again during the 1990s on a small East Coast atoll. Then there was that incident during the 1970s in Yellowstone National Park involving

Christofer Nigro
Bigfoot vs. Killer Grizzly: King of the Forest
Duel of the Monsters Volume 2

an unusually large, cunning, and powerful grizzly bear; followed by another incident later in that same decade involving multiple animal species, not just avians or bears. That latter event was attributed in the tabloids to an excess of fluorocarbons streaming in from man-made holes in the ozone layer, but the rumors of one of those meteor landings deep in the woods persisted.

Finally, the ranger could scarcely forget another such incident from earlier in the '70s decade, where sections of Jefferson City, Missouri located near a bayou were overcome by a plethora of aberrantly behaving insects, reptiles, avians, and amphibians. That mass assault by nature was attributed to pollution and pesticides wrought by the allegedly corrupt patriarch of the wealthy Crockett family, though such catalysts were rumored to be preceded by yet another meteor with odd radiations that landed in the swamp during the closing months of 1971.

Bearing all this in mind, Stewart realized that he would never convince the government to close off the national park to tourists. Moreover, he would be out of a job if he did that. Hence, he was at times concerned that he failed to try as hard as he should for that important but selfish reason. Nevertheless, he looked around as often as possible for evidence or reports of erratic animal behavior – particularly of the big carnivores like the grizzly bears believed to be the "Guardians of Kootenai" by local Native American tribes. The ranger also tried keeping himself informed of the occasional sightings of bizarre animals that science has not yet officially discovered, including disturbing tales of huge bipedal primates that witnesses insisted were not misidentified grizzlies.

Stewart found himself especially unnerved this particular summer morning, as he always was when he saw a large SUV carrying a family into the station lot just outside the forest. He was instructed not to scare paying tourists away, but he had recently found what he had identified as grizzly tracks near the camps, which was atypical of the species. This implied one or more of them were getting bolder than usual, which in turn implied that the alleged meteor landing of several months earlier may finally be having an effect. If it was truly one of

Christofer Nigro
Bigfoot vs. Killer Grizzly: King of the Forest
Duel of the Monsters Volume 2

those meteorites, the effect of its radiation on the woodland fauna could spell a lot of trouble for unsuspecting campers.

The ranger ran up to the family he saw emerging from the spacious vehicle to register at the station. Emerging from the SUV was a middle-aged father, his similarly aged wife, a teen daughter, a tween son, and an elderly woman that was likely the mother of either the dad or the mom.

"Excuse me," he said upon approaching who he presumed to be the husband and wife. "I'm Ranger Stewart. Are you going to be camping in the woods?"

"Hello, Ranger," the man said, holding out his hand. "I'm Bill Lindrick. And we most certainly are going to camp in the woods. To me, there's nothing like a nice summer outing in the forest to bring a family closer together."

"What my dad means is that we're stuck here with him all weekend to do the 'bonding' thing," his ten-year-old son quipped in frustration.

"Kenny!" his mother, Astrid, griped while swatting her boy on the shoulder. "Don't talk about your father like that to the ranger. He just wants us to do things together as a family. Why is that such a bad thing to you?"

"It's a 'bad' thing to him, Mom, because he had to miss that comic book convention," his seventeen-year-old sister interjected.

"Shut up, Ellie," Ken retorted. "You didn't want to be here any more than I did. You'd rather be having 'fun time' with Lenny in his car at the park. I heard you bitching about having to come here instead of going out with Lenny over the phone to one of those slutty friends of yours."

"You little prick!" Ellie lamented as she shoved her smaller sibling. "I did not! And you shouldn't be listening in on my fucking conversations anyways!"

"Watch your mouth, Ellie!" Bill exclaimed. "I can't believe how you and your brother are acting this weekend! And in front of the ranger! You're embarrassing the shit out of me and your mom!"

Stewart could not help but notice that the elderly woman accompanying them seemed oddly uninterested in the family squabble.

Christofer Nigro
Bigfoot vs. Killer Grizzly: King of the Forest
Duel of the Monsters Volume 2

She simply looked around in a somewhat vacuous manner, as if not truly understanding where she was or what was going on.

"Um, folks," the ranger said in the hope of ending the argument so he could have the discussion he wanted with them. "Before you decide to set up camp in the woods, I wanted to give you a heads-up. There's been evidence of grizzly activity lately. At least one bear has been approaching the lot here, which means it may not be apt to avoid areas of human habitation. And that would go triple for one of the temporary sort set up in the middle of the woods."

"Wow, *bears!"* Ken stated excitedly. "I always wanted to see one of those! Maybe this won't be such a boring weekend after all."

"Yea, maybe it'll eat you!" Ellie snapped. "How cool would that be?"

"Listen!" Stewart interposed with a louder tone. "That actually wasn't very funny, young lady. Bears can be unpredictable, especially when... well, there are certain factors at work in the woods."

"What kind of factors?" Bill's wife asked.

"Astrid, stop worrying the kids," her husband requested. "I'm sure the ranger means well, but what he doesn't understand is that I've been an outdoorsman most of my life. I'm well acquainted with bears and how to deal with them if they come around."

"Things may be a bit different this time, Mr. Lindrick," Stewart insisted. "So, I'm just suggesting..."

"I understand what you're suggesting, sir," Bill replied in a stern manner. "But I told you, I have a lot of experience in the woods and I'm trying to teach my family to appreciate the great outdoors. I'm well equipped with a shotgun and a can of bear spray. And besides, my mother is with us, and we want to... well, spend as much time with her as we can."

"I thought I noticed your mom looking a bit, well... listless," Stewart noted. "Not to pry or anything, but... is there something the matter with her?"

Bill moved in a bit closer and spoke in a lower voice. "My mother has Alzheimer's. Her memory is starting to go. We don't know how

Christofer Nigro
Bigfoot vs. Killer Grizzly: King of the Forest
Duel of the Monsters Volume 2

much longer she'll get to enjoy outings like this with the family, and…"

"I understand," the ranger interrupted, "and I'm sorry to hear that, Mr. Lindrick. But considering the circumstances, maybe it's not a good idea to bring her into the woods. She could be in a lot of danger if…"

"Ranger Stewart, you've been sort of vague about what type of 'circumstances' there are to be concerned about here," Bill snapped. "So far, you just said bears have been acting bolder than usual, right? Well, I told you that I've got a lot of experience in the woods, and I'm well equipped to deal with shit like that. I can look after my family, including my mother. Hell, she's always been a tough old bird and I'll bet that despite her condition, she'll outlive us all."

The ranger wished he could believe that. He also sulked, knowing that if he explained his pet theory, Bill Lindrick would only scoff at the idea of worrying about the effects of a big rock landing in the middle of the forest months ago. Moreover, seeing what he had of the Lindrick boy's personality, Stewart worried that such a revelation would only encourage him to run deep into the forest to try and find the meteorite.

"Isn't that right, Mom?" Bill called to his mother, Vicki. "Aren't you a tough old bird?"

The old woman did not respond. Instead, she just glared intently at a section of the woods to her left.

"Mom?" Bill repeated a bit louder. "I'm talkin' to you!"

The senior lady finally turned around. "Oh, sorry there, son. I just thought I saw your brother Edward looking at us from behind those trees. He's gotten so big!"

Ellie and Ken rolled their eyes simultaneously, and the girl mumbled a quiet, "Oh, geez."

"Quiet, you two!" Astrid scolded the kids under her breath.

"Alright, Mr. Lindrick," the ranger said, trying to control his frustration. "Just please keep an eye on your mom at all times. Make sure she's always walking in front of everyone else during a hike,

Christofer Nigro
Bigfoot vs. Killer Grizzly: King of the Forest
Duel of the Monsters Volume 2

never at the end of the line. Also be sure that she's never left unattended at the camp, or when using one of the latrines and…"

"I know how to look after my family," Bill stated in an irritated fashion. "That includes my mom. We'll be heading down the main trail now, if that's all right with you, Ranger Stewart."

The forest guard paused for a second before responding. "Yes, okay. Please take my card here and call me on your cell phone if you need me. Like I said, just stick to all the trails and don't venture too far into the woods."

"He's worse than Grandma used to be before she started losing her-" Ken stopped himself before finishing the sentence.

"Let's go!" Bill demanded and the family headed towards the main trail leading out of the lot and into the woods.

They were soon out of the range of sight for Stewart and the registration cabin employees. The ranger could not help but notice the sparse number of vehicles parked there that day. He resolved to journey through the woods and track the family to keep tabs on them.

As Stewart disappeared into the forest, he failed to notice the dark human-like yet not human face with the piercing yellow eyes glaring out the left side of the woods where Grandma Vicki had been looking. The head and torso of this being was covered with matted reddish-brown hair, and the man-beast displayed a set of large, sharpened teeth as he growled in rage. People were again violating the sanctity of his home! This time, however, he was not going to tolerate their presence.

The furtive man-monster had spent his entire life eluding human detection, but as of today he felt the odd but unmistakable urge to parlay that surreptitious attribute into a far more aggressive form of behavior.

***

Dr. Hiram Coleman inspected the eighteen-inch man-like footprints embedded in the mud. He was certain they were not bear tracks, which he and his group had found plenty of in a field close by. The

Christofer Nigro
Bigfoot vs. Killer Grizzly: King of the Forest
Duel of the Monsters Volume 2

opportunity to compare the two made it clear that the same animal had not left both sets of tracks.

"Look at this print," the cryptozoologist said to his two companions, the dedicated naturalist Karen Sundham and expert hunter & tracker Brett Halverson. "You see it does not resemble those of the bear tracks you identified earlier, Karen."

"I can see that, Hiram," she concurred. "I know that's not the track of a bear, as it looks rather human… except for its immense size. Still, it's not necessarily the print of a Bigfoot."

"What else might you think it is, dear?" the older, veteran investigator queried. "Or, how about you, Brett? You've tracked many a bear during your life. Do these prints resemble an ursine track?"

"No, they don't," the gruff man said while straightening his cowboy hat. "I admit that, okay? Maybe it was some big man walking around."

"Oh, it was a big man-*like* fellow, that's for certain," Hiram conjectured with a smug certainty. "But it was not of the species we belong to. And the recent landing of that meteor suggests we might be dealing with a specimen that is of that mutant sub-species of Sasquatch that, unlike the mainstream type, is not docile and shy of human contact. It is the type that actively hunts and kills humans who encroach upon the territory in which it conceals its existence, the true apex predator of this planet."

"There he goes again," Brett grumbled. "Look, this here rifle of mine will take down anything, including a grizzly. I'm not worried 'bout no mythical hairy man."

"I'm inclined to agree with Brett," Karen said. "And to be frank, Hiram, I'm much more concerned about those actual bear prints we saw back there. They were unusually big, and that suggests it may actually be one of that rare, very large sub-species of grizzly that considers humans a viable source of prey. If so, then *it* would be the king of the forest, not any type of hairy man."

"One of those mutant Bigfoot critters might argue that point, my dear lady," Hiram opined with a smirk. "The species is said to kill

Christofer Nigro
Bigfoot vs. Killer Grizzly: King of the Forest
Duel of the Monsters Volume 2

bears, including grizzlies, when they have a hankering for meat. They are the apex predator, the real kings of the forest."

"If such a mutant iteration of grizzly is roaming the woods," Karen pontificated, "then it would be the actual apex predator of this forest, and a threat to all humans… or anything like a human. Reports of past encounters with such bears attest to that, including the incident that occurred during the 1970s; or the one that the legendary Marshall Cole dealt with in Wyoming during the 19th century. Those ursine specimens can reach up to fifteen tall and 1,600 lbs. They were able to kill a horned bull with no major effort, and they appeared to kill both humans and their livestock for the sheer sport of it… or, perhaps for territorial reasons."

"You two scientist-types can argue all you want," Brett stated while clicking the chamber of his rifle, "but I'm going to get ready in case that bear shows up."

"We are here, sir, to acquire a sighting and any evidence of Bigfoot activity in these woods," Hiram reminded his armed comrade. "Bears, even a mutant iteration of errant behavior, are already well documented by science. But a large primate or hominid species that has developed such an elusive propensity for concealing itself in large, wooded areas would be an incredible discovery to the scientific community. Books on paleontology and primatology would need to be re-written, and they would partially be composed by the three of us.

"We would be famous and would make a major contribution to the world. It would prove that not only do large species with highly developed elusive capabilities exist undiscovered by science in the 21st century, but it would also demonstrate how incomplete the fossil record on hominid species actually is."

"Don't cream your pants just yet, Doc," the veteran hunter said. "I was hired to keep you safe while tracking this thing down, and that's what I'm gonna do. I have no idea what made that print there, but if we can find further spoor, I'll track it, I promise you. Right now, though, I want to keep us ahead of that bear whose prints we saw back over there. The lady is right in that they were some of the biggest grizzly tracks I ever saw, and I don't want it running into us."

Christofer Nigro
Bigfoot vs. Killer Grizzly: King of the Forest
Duel of the Monsters Volume 2

As Brett began tracking the huge human-like prints, they were unaware of another entity likewise tracking the mysterious hominid that was concealed in the foliage just a few yards away. The head of an enormous grizzly bear emerged unseen from the thickets and sniffed the air, picking up the scent of these other intruders into his territory. The huge animal snarled, its sharp rows of teeth backed up by incredible jaw strength salivated at the thrill of the slaughter it would now be seeking to carry out.

***

Ranger Stewart trekked slowly through the woods he was familiar with. His hand was on the firearm in his belt holster as he scanned for signs of bear tracks. He found several in a field that were unusually large, and in a location frequented by human hikers that bears normally avoided. This alarmed him, and he decided to seek the area where the Lindrick family would set up their camp. He wanted to make sure the family was okay, since despite Bill's boasting of being an experienced outdoorsman the ranger was certain he was facing a bear unlike any other he may have encountered before.

That was when a large boulder suddenly landed just a few feet from him. The forest guard drew his pistol and looked around. That rock was at least 400 lbs., much too heavy for a human mischief-maker to lift, let alone toss such a distance. Further, bears did not lift and throw boulders.

Jesus, could it be? Not one of them, too!

Stewart carefully looked all around him, scanning the lush greenery that surrounded the glade he was in. He specifically looked for a face that, from a distance, may have reminded a person of a fellow human, or a very large man-shaped silhouette. Nothing was visible. Should he heed the obvious warning he was given and retreat? That would be the wise thing to do.

No. I have a job to protect people who visit this forest. I need to find the Lindrick family. I'll call for help once I do.

Christofer Nigro
Bigfoot vs. Killer Grizzly: King of the Forest
Duel of the Monsters Volume 2

And so, the ranger carried on, keeping his gun drawn and his eyes alert for signs of not only an extremely dangerous specimen of grizzly, but also for an equally terrifying beast that was the subject of legend.

***

Bill Lindrick and his wife struggled to set up two small tents in a clearing the family had come across. He thought it was a perfect place to settle for the weekend just before gathering firewood to cook a lunch the old-fashioned way.

"I can't believe Dad wouldn't let us bring a grill," Ken complained. "We're really gonna cook steaks on a stick hanging over a campfire?"

"Look on the bright side, dude," his sister Ellie remarked out of their parents' earshot. "At least he isn't expecting us to kill whatever we're gonna eat. I'm glad Mom at least convinced him to bring steaks, hot dogs, and etcetera."

"Yeah, I suppose so," her brother concurred. "But wait, where is Grandma going?"

The boy pointed as his older sister observed the elderly Vicki heading towards a section of trees while glaring intently at something.

"Arg! Not again," the girl groaned. "Dad just had to bring her, knowing what condition she's in. I feel bad for her, but he and Mom shouldn't have turned their back on her. That ranger warned them not to do that! You wait here, I'll go get her."

"Fine," her sibling replied. "I wanna check out that big hill over there anyways."

Ellie rushed over to her meandering grandmother and gently but firmly grabbed her arm.

"Grandma, what are you doing over here?" the girl asked the old woman.

"Well, I thought I saw something in those bushes there," Vicki said. "I just went to see if it was who I thought it was."

"Oh, Grammy. Did you think you saw Uncle Edward again?" Ellie enquired.

"Who?" was Vicki's only response.

Christofer Nigro
Bigfoot vs. Killer Grizzly: King of the Forest
Duel of the Monsters Volume 2

"Hey, sis, look!" Ken shouted from several yards away.

Ellie and Vicki turned to see the young boy standing atop a seven-foot knoll.

"Oh, geez," his sister lamented. "Will you get down from there before Mom and Dad see you and shit ten bricks each?"

"Ha! Ha! No freakin' way!" Ken hollered while waving his arms around with glee. "I like it up here! Look at me, I'm king of the hill!"

All mirth was abruptly nullified when an enormous male grizzly suddenly stood on his hind legs behind Ken and bit into his right shoulder blade. The boy screamed in agony and horror as the giant ursine lifted him effortlessly off the mound in his jaws. The bear then grasped the hapless tween in the animal's knife-like claws and tore the entire upper part of Ken's body away from his lower abdomen. Several of the boy's organs and an enormous deluge of blood spattered on the hill as his lower extremities rolled down the mound's grassy surface.

Ellie screamed in terror while Vicki simply gaped her mouth open with no sound being emitted. The girl instinctively pushed her elderly grandmother towards the tent that her parents were haphazardly trying to assemble.

Hearing the screams of their kids both Bill and Astrid ran over just in time to see the upper portion of the twelve-foot bear ripping their son's head, arms, and torso to pieces in a fit of brutal anger. Astrid released a scream of her own just before her eyes rolled upwards and she fainted onto the grass.

"Dad!" Ellie shrieked as she ran into her father's arms. "It killed Kenny!"

"That bastard!" Bill shouted. "Ellie, get out of the fucking way! I need to aim my rifle!"

The man felt he had no choice but to push his panicked daughter down to the ground so he could wield his firearm. As he properly aimed the weapon all he could see was a flash of brown as the bear disappeared behind the hill. The sight of his son's detached lower extremities covered in the boy's eviscerated bowels and a pool of blood sent him over the edge of rage. As a result, he fired three shots

Christofer Nigro
Bigfoot vs. Killer Grizzly: King of the Forest
Duel of the Monsters Volume 2

in the direction of where he sighted the bear despite only perforating the hillock that shielded the animal.

"You mother fucking son of a bitch!" Bill hollered while tears streamed down his face. "You son of a bitch! I'll kill you, kill you!"

"Bill…" Vicki said while tapping his shoulder. "Astrid fell down. And I think she can't get up."

Bill brushed his mentally decayed mother aside and grabbed his hysterical daughter by the shoulders. He shook her violently.

"Ellie!" he shouted in her reddened, tear-soaked face. "Get a fucking grip! You have to tend to your mother and grandma! We gotta get them out of these woods! We gotta find that ranger! Now for God's sake, help your mother up!"

"He's dead!" the girl screamed as she pounded her fists on her burly father's chest. "Dad, he's dead! Kenny is dead! That bear…!"

"I know, dear! I know!" the man hollered back while continuing his attempt to shake his daughter back to her senses. "But we have to get a grip until we can get out of these woods! That bear is still around! I have to pay attention with my rifle! Wake your mom and help her and your grandma out of here! Down that trail there! Okay? You got that?"

Bill struggled to hold back his tears and retain an outward appearance of composure as he grabbed a few rounds of ammo from his pocket and reloaded his rifle.

***

Karen Sundham stood looking about for any signs of the bear tracking her group. For a moment her eyes became transfixed upon the sight of the beautiful Scotchman Peaks on the distant horizon. It was then that Dr. Hiram Coleman courted her attention.

"Karen, dear, I know you're concerned about the bear," the cryptozoologist said, "but you need to keep your eyes on the real prize, and potential threat, we're seeking here. I just found a whole line of tracks that cannot be from anything *but* a Bigfoot. Come and see, please."

Christofer Nigro
Bigfoot vs. Killer Grizzly: King of the Forest
Duel of the Monsters Volume 2

The naturalist with the long black hair had no intention of forgetting about the bear in favor of a hominid she believed was most likely a mere myth. However, when she examined the trail of prints at the Doc's request, she could not help but notice both their unnerving size and their eerie resemblance to a bare human track. The toes were oddly straight in a way that a human's were not, but otherwise, only the length and width of the prints deviated from that of a man.

"They don't look anthropoid at all, Hiram," Karen opined upon close inspection. "Apes leave a print quite distinct from a human despite also having five toes. But they aren't nearly this large, and they do not walk upright for more than a few steps at a time. Whatever was walking here was fully bipedal, as there are no knuckle tracks around it in the soil."

"No man could possibly be that big," the hunter Brett Halverson added, "or that heavy. Look how deep they're sunk into that hard ass soil. It's not like the mud back there where we found the other track like it. Not only that, but who the hell would be walking barefoot out here with all the pebbles and shit all over the ground?"

"So, do either of you still doubt the reality of the Bigfoot species?" Hiram queried with a proud smirk.

"I have no idea what the damn thing is," Brett replied. "I only know that I've got a bad feeling about it. And I got another bad feeling about the size of those bear tracks we found back there."

"I must agree with Brett that we seem to have two very different but very large animals out and about here," Karen added. "One of them is clearly a bear, but I suspect it's one of those very dangerous mutant specimens. The other is something I admit that I can't identify, but like Brett I'm getting a really bad feeling about it. The track looks somewhat human, but it can't possibly have been made by a person."

Brett prepared his heavy-duty hunting rifle for firing, looking for any possible target around him. He could not shake the feeling that something was hunting *them* just as they were tracking a reputed Bigfoot. The veteran tracker was determined to get whatever it was before it could get anyone in the group… namely himself.

Christofer Nigro
Bigfoot vs. Killer Grizzly: King of the Forest
Duel of the Monsters Volume 2

A sudden sound behind a growth of thickets several yards to their right caused him to spin his long firearm in that direction. Karen and Hiram gasped in tandem and looked as well. They could see the vague outline of a human-like figure trying to conceal itself in the shrubbery. They were even more shocked, however, when the silhouette suddenly aimed a revolver back at them in response to Brett's gesture.

"Don't shoot!" hollered Ranger Calvin Stewart from within the thickets. "I'm a forest ranger. I was hiding here since I'm tracking something, and I had no idea who you people are or what you're doing here. And I still don't."

"You can lower the rifle, Brett," Hiram said as both he and Karen breathed a loud sigh of relief. "It would seem we have some additional firepower at our beck and call."

"Who are you people?" Stewart inquired more firmly as he slowly lowered his gun.

"I am Dr. Hiram Coleman," the Doc introduced himself. "I am a cryptozoologist investigating Bigfoot sightings, and I believe we have picked up the trail of one. This lovely lady is Karen Sundham, a talented naturalist; and this grim looking fellow is Brett Halverson, a hunter of the highest esteem."

"It's interesting to meet all of you," the ranger said. "But you all may be in grave danger."

"We know that already," Karen replied. "But now that you're here, I definitely feel safer."

Suddenly an extremely long and muscular hair-covered humanoid arm suddenly sprung from concealment in the nearby flora and grasped the naturalist by her throat. The enormous human-shaped hand effortlessly lifted her over four feet off the ground and repeatedly smashed her face against a lodgepole pine. Within seconds her once lovely visage was nothing but a mass of shapeless pulp as a large bloody stain in the size and shape of her face dribbled crimson down the bark of the tree. The enraged Bigfoot then simply tossed the woman's lifeless body away as he screeched angrily at the other three human interlopers.

Christofer Nigro
Bigfoot vs. Killer Grizzly: King of the Forest
Duel of the Monsters Volume 2

"My God!" Stewart shouted as he drew his revolver and fired at the hirsute man-like monstrosity.

"Karen dear!" Hiram yelled as he ran toward the naturalist's unmoving body.

"Jesus mother fucking Christ!" was Brett's exclamation as he likewise fired into the green shrubbery where the vicious Bigfoot was now only partially hidden.

The echoing cacophony of the two firearms continued for several seconds before it became obvious that the Bigfoot had disappeared into the woods.

"Oh, dear, I am so sorry," Hiram cried as he turned the woman's corpse over to see her face smashed beyond all recognition. "But… your death was not in vain. We proved the existence of the species."

"Did you hit the damn thing?" Brett asked the ranger once they both ceased firing.

"I can't tell," Stewart replied. "I think we may have, but I'm not sure how bad it's injured."

"We need to kill that son of a bitch!" the hunter decreed. "It killed someone I was hired to protect. Her loss is on me, and I'm going to get that fucker!"

"We can't worry about retribution right now," Stewart insisted. "There's a family out there camping, and it's my job to get them out safely. Along with you and the crypto guy here."

"You do what you gotta do," Brett retorted, "and I'll do what I gotta do."

"No, you won't," the ranger said while walking directly up to the incensed tracker. "I have legal authority in these woods, and you're not going to run around hunting such a dangerous creature on your own. Not to mention that bear being around too. What you can do, however, is help me get that family to safety. You're armed and experienced and frankly, I need your help. It may take too long for other help to come."

"Fuck that!" Brett exclaimed while reloading his high-caliber hunting rifle. "I'm not the law. I have my own job to do. And I need to make restitution to this dead lady there for screwing things up!"

Christofer Nigro
Bigfoot vs. Killer Grizzly: King of the Forest
Duel of the Monsters Volume 2

"Well, I am the law here," Stewart declared as he cocked the hammer of his gun and aimed it directly at the hunter's forehead. "And I say you either help me do the right thing or get the hell out of my forest; or, refuse to do either and I shoot you dead as a dangerous armed criminal. You have five seconds to decide."

"Brett, my boy, let's do as the ranger says," Hiram suggested calmly as he put a hand on the hunter's shoulder. "After all, you are still on my dime, that family needs help, and, well… I would be most grateful to catch sight of that magnificent Sasquatch again."

Brett gritted his teeth before looking Hiram in the eye and then back at Stewart again. "Okay, okay. Fine. I'll go help you get that family out of here. But I'm gonna kill that sum'bitch if I see it again. Don't either of you try to stop me if I do."

***

The trio of Stewart, Brett, and Hiram tread cautiously through the thick verdure of the woods, the former two with firearms drawn and alert for any sudden sound or movement within the shrubbery. The realization that there was not just one but two savage predators separately hunting them caused the men to be extremely on edge. Moreover, Stewart was quite concerned about the Lindrick family, who were now in extreme danger and led by a patriarch who was too stubborn to acknowledge that.

"Did you hear that, man?" Brett asked the ranger. "I hear some human voices down that way. Like some deranged woman yelling."

"Yes, I hear it," Stewart replied. "It's less than a hundred meters down that way. It has to be the Lindrick family. Let's head over there!"

"Yes, let us do that," Hiram agreed. "There is a chance they may have seen the hominid!"

"Shut up, Coleman!" Stewart admonished the overzealous cryptozoologist.

Christofer Nigro
Bigfoot vs. Killer Grizzly: King of the Forest
Duel of the Monsters Volume 2

Just down the ridge where the three men had made a beeline for, a now conscious Astrid Lindrick was furiously screaming at and pummeling her husband.

"It's your fault, you son of a bitch!" she bellowed as Bill Lindrick attempted to block his wife's onslaught of punches. "It's your fault our boy is dead! You made us come out here! You and your fucking obsession with this outdoor bullshit! Did you see what that animal did to Kenny? *Did you see?*"

"Astrid, stop!" Bill pleaded. "I saw what that bear did to him! You think it didn't affect me? I know it was my fault, but I'm sorry. I didn't mean for this to happen! You have to know that! I couldn't have foreseen something like this!"

"Oh, no?" Astrid said as she continued the assault on her beleaguered spouse. "The ranger warned us! But you didn't listen! *You didn't listen!* And our boy was torn apart right in front of us! All because you had to be such a know-it-all son of a bitch!"

"I know, sweetheart, I know," her husband contended as tears finally streamed from his eyes. "But we can't do this now. We have to get the hell out of these woods! That animal is still out there somewhere!"

Ellie simply leaned against a nearby tree crying. It was the elderly Vicki who decided to get proactive. The family matriarch stepped forward and wedged herself between the grief-stricken couple.

"Astrid, please stop," she implored gently but firmly. "My son was wrong, and he admitted it. That's all he can really do, even though it's not nearly enough. But you are going to need each other more than ever now. And I will do what I can for you both, just like always."

Astrid broke down and embraced her mother-in-law. "This isn't happening; it's not happening…"

The elder of the family held her daughter-in-law tightly as the woman literally cried into her shoulder.

Just then Bill's sobbing was interrupted by the sound of something moving through the brush to his left. Reacting with a desperate determination to protect the three surviving members of his family the man aimed his rife and took a shot in that direction. He heard the

Christofer Nigro
Bigfoot vs. Killer Grizzly: King of the Forest
Duel of the Monsters Volume 2

bullet strike a tree, followed by the shouts of a gruff, unfamiliar male voice.

"Hey! What the fuck now!" the just out of sight Brett exclaimed.

"Dad!" Ellie screamed. "It's a person!"

Recognizing the girl's voice from back at the station, Stewart called out. "Bill! Hold your fire! It's me, Ranger Stewart! And some help!"

"For God's sake, stop shooting!" Astrid yelled. "It's the ranger! He's here and he brought help!"

Stewart, Brett, and Hiram emerged from the woods to see the emotionally devastated family. The ranger noted that a member of the clan was missing, and his stomach filled with acid as he surmised what must have happened.

"Ranger Stewart!" Ellie cried as she ran into his arms. "Kenny's dead! A bear killed him! A big fucking grizzly!"

"Dear God," the forest ranger said solemnly as he tried to comfort the traumatized girl. "I… am so sorry."

"Did any of you folks happen to see a large hairy hominid?" Hiram asked the family members.

The ranger turned and berated the scientist. "Coleman! You shut the hell up!"

The tense situation was then violently interrupted when a 300-pound boulder was hurled out the left side of the greenery and thudded to the ground less than an inch from where Bill Lindrick was standing.

"Bill!" Astrid screamed.

"Jesus!" the family patriarch bellowed. "What in the hell?"

"The bear is back!" Ellie proclaimed.

That incorrect presumption was followed by a horrific screeching sound emanating from the direction the rock was thrown. It vibrated clear through every person standing there, sounding like a combination of a cougar's cry and a woman screaming in terror or agony.

"Bears don't throw rocks!" Bill stated as he raised his rifle. "And they don't make sounds like that! What the hell is out there?"

"It's the Bigfoot!" Hiram uttered with a smile.

"Huh?" was Bill's response.

Christofer Nigro
Bigfoot vs. Killer Grizzly: King of the Forest
Duel of the Monsters Volume 2

"Shit, we gotta get out of here!" Brett exclaimed as he too aimed his rifle towards the flora concealing their right side. "That first throw was just a warning shot!"

Barely a second later a second boulder flew out of the concealment of the shrubbery and struck Astrid in the head. She slumped down on the grass without making a sound.

"Mom!" Ellie screamed as Stewart and Brett opened fire into the thickets on the right in tandem. Bill ran to his wife while his mother looked on with a somewhat confused expression.

The husband and father turned his fallen wife over to check her condition. She was twitching and gurgling with her eyes open wide and blood pouring out of a large gash in her cranium.

"Oh God, Astrid!" Bill muttered as he lifted his quivering wife. "C'mon, sweetie, I'll help get you out of here! Just hang on, and I'll get you out of these woods so you can see a doctor!"

"The hominid is remarkably aggressive and territorial," Hiram observed aloud. "It is most definitely of the mutant sub-species of Bigfoot that is every bit as ultra-elusive and cunning as the mainstream species… but has abandoned the latter's reserved nature for this more extreme behavior. It fights to displace humanity from our position at the top of the planetary food chain rather than passively yielding it to us."

"Shut the fuck up, Coleman, before I turn this rifle on you next!" Brett shouted as he continued to scan the right side of the woods. "Stewart, we gotta get out of here!"

Suddenly another boulder was hurled from the same direction, smashing into the yellow pine tree directly above Hiram.

"Jesus, get back, man!" Brett barked while pushing the scientist behind that same tree for cover.

Vicki looked in the vicinity of the shrubbery where the large rock came from and squinted as if seeing a familiar face.

"Edward, is that you?" she queried.

The physically spry old woman then ran directly into the woods.

"Mom!" Bill yelled. "Don't go in there!"

Christofer Nigro
Bigfoot vs. Killer Grizzly: King of the Forest
Duel of the Monsters Volume 2

"Damn it!" Stewart exclaimed. "Watch out for the rest of the family, Brett. I have to go after her!"

"Don't be a damn fool, Stewart!" Brett yelled back. "The old biddy ran right towards that thing! She's a goner! There's nothing you can do, man!"

Ellie slumped against a tree and began crying hysterically again while Bill ran to console her. Just as Stewart began heading towards the woods to retrieve Vicki he was stunned by the sound of another piercing high-pitched screech from the hidden Bigfoot. This was followed by another scream, this one clearly from Vicki. That was followed in turn by the sound of a loud thudding noise, after which the elderly lady abruptly went silent.

"Mom, nooooo!" Bill hollered as he ran from his crying daughter to the right side of the woods into which his mom had disappeared.

"Bill, get away from there!" Stewart yelled.

"Dad, please come back!" Ellie shouted.

"You son of a bitch!" Bill hollered into the woods with his rifle drawn. "Stop hiding in those trees like a fucking coward! Come out and face me!"

Unfortunately for Bill Lindrick, the Bigfoot immediately responded by leaping out of the concealing foliage mere inches from the bereaved man. The savage hirsute humanoid towered over the '5'11" tall Lindrick by over four feet and chilled him into immobility by a blood-curdling shriek at close range. Bill could only stare trembling in fear while the horrid hominid grabbed the rifle from his grasp and broke it over its knee like a mere stick in a manner that mirrored a human action of contempt.

"Oh, hell!" Brett bellowed as he and Stewart simultaneously drew their firearms.

Ellie simply screamed in horror.

For his part, Hiram smiled and said, "How incredible. It took the challenge."

With one quick swipe the Bigfoot effortlessly lifted Bill into the air and struck him across the face, shattering his jaw and sending several of his teeth flying out in a spray of crumpled enamel.

Christofer Nigro
Bigfoot vs. Killer Grizzly: King of the Forest
Duel of the Monsters Volume 2

Brett nervously aimed and took a shot with his high-caliber rifle. Blood and bits of bone exploded from Bill's left leg as the lead projectile accidentally struck the man as he was held aloft by the Bigfoot. The man was unable to emit an audible scream of pain due to the severe dislocation of his jaw.

"Fuck!" Brett cursed in frustration.

The Bigfoot then pulled Bill towards its copper-skinned, vaguely human-like face where it bit the hapless man's nose clean off. The man-beast chewed the nasal cartilage while hurling the gravely maimed Lindrick patriarch directly at Brett. It had correctly identified the latter's rifle as a far greater threat than the ranger's more modest pistol.

Bill's thrown form slammed into Brett, knocking the hunter down and causing him to drop his heavy-duty firearm. Ellie squealed in horror and sunk to the ground in a fetal position, still not convinced that the past hour's events were not just a horrific nightmare.

Stewart fired several shots from his revolver at the Bigfoot, but the smaller-caliber bullets penetrated no more than a quarter of an inch into the creature's extremely dense hide and muscle fiber. The hominid shrieked at the sting of the metal slugs, but otherwise shrugged the salvo off.

Brett hastily pushed Bill's now unmoving body off him while spitting the man's blood and his mouth.

"Damn Jesus!" the tracker shouted as he reached for his rife.

He was not to retrieve the weapon, however, because Hiram stepped forward and lifted the rifle before the hunter could reach it. The older man then promptly hurled it into a clump of nearby thickets.

"I am sorry, Brett," Hiram said, "but I cannot allow you to do that. This specimen is magnificent, and it must be preserved for later capture and tagging."

"Are you fucking kidding me, Coleman?" Brett rejoined. "I swear I'm gonna kill you!"

Stewart pointed his revolver at the scientist. "Dr. Coleman, stand back and put your hands on your head!"

Christofer Nigro
Bigfoot vs. Killer Grizzly: King of the Forest
Duel of the Monsters Volume 2

"You are truly magnificent!" Coleman said to the Bigfoot while cautiously approaching the beast. "You are what man was before evolving into a weaker form. And what we can be again while retaining our civilized traits if we simply study you!"

The Bigfoot cocked its large hairy head and looked quizzically at the approaching Hiram Coleman.

"You are incredible!" the scientist continued ranting. "The apex predator of this land. The true king of the forest whose supremacy none can challenge!"

Hiram Coleman ironically had his bold declaration contested when he suddenly heard a deep growling from directly behind him. The scientist turned to find himself looking at a furry barrel chest. He then looked up to see the gaping fanged muzzle of the largest grizzly bear that he had ever seen the likes of.

Hiram had time to utter a single scream of terror as the bear hoisted him over ten feet off the ground in its mighty paws. The ursine powerhouse then bit clear into the scientist's skull, crunching it like a squeezed eggshell.

"Shit!" Brett hollered. "The bear is back!"

Stewart opened fire on the animal, but as with the Bigfoot, its tough hide proved too thick for this lower caliber of bullets to penetrate far enough to inflict anything like a serious wound. The bear then tossed Hiram's lifeless body, which now sported only half a head, to the side.

The ursa major had spotted the Bigfoot standing several feet away and roared a challenge. The hominid recognized what it considered a true threat to its hegemony of the forest and raised its clenched fists while shrieking a loud, piercing counter-challenge.

The bear angrily charged at the Bigfoot on all fours, while the hominid rushed forth to meet the bulky opponent's attack. Brett was by now back on his feet and he grabbed the still-crying Ellie by her arm and pulled her along with him.

"C'mon, girl!" he said. "We've all gotta get the hell out of here while those two are distracted with ripping each other apart!"

"Ranger Stewart, please don't leave my mother!" Ellie shouted at him.

Christofer Nigro
Bigfoot vs. Killer Grizzly: King of the Forest
Duel of the Monsters Volume 2

"I won't!" Stewart yelled back while lifting the insensate body of Astrid Lindrick over his shoulders. "Follow me! I'll lead us back to the station! We can find help there!"

As Ellie and the now unarmed Brett followed Stewart down the trail leading out of the woods, the ranger carefully balanced the body of Astrid on his one shoulder as he pulled a communications radio from his belt.

"Danny!" he shouted into the device. "This is an emergency, and I have to make it brief! So, listen up! I need you and Nick to get your rifles and prepare a service truck to evacuate us and three other people from the area! Phone the local sheriff's office, tell them we have two dangerous animals in pursuit of us! A bear… and something else!

"Yes, you heard me right! Just arm yourselves and prepare the vehicle! We'll be arriving in less than fifteen minutes! Over and out!"

Meanwhile, behind the fleeing humans, the Killer Grizzly and the Bigfoot slammed into each other, with the bear latching its mighty jaws onto the Sasquatch's right arm. The ursine's razor sharp teeth penetrated deep into the Bigfoot's uber-thick dermis and the hominid shrieked in pain. It responded by side-punching its opponent's head with its free hand, the blow knocking the bear away from its arm. The Bigfoot then delivered a blow to the bruin's head, followed by another to its jaw. The mighty ursine was painfully rattled more than it had ever thought possible. But much to the Bigfoot's consternation, however, the grizzly did not fall.

After shaking off the blows from the Bigfoot's piledriver fists, the bear stood back up on two legs and swiped its opponent with its razor-sharp claws. The hominid again screeched in agony as the four-inch talons ripped nearly half of its face off. The pain-wracked Bigfoot backed off and put its hairless palm over the profusely bleeding wounds in an instinctual attempt to staunch the blood loss.

The bear took advantage of such a distraction to rush forward again and smash its head into the Bigfoot's chest. Despite how strong and resilient the hairy hominid was, being rammed by a 1,600-pound grizzly knocked the Sasquatch back several feet until it slammed into a fir tree.

Christofer Nigro
Bigfoot vs. Killer Grizzly: King of the Forest
Duel of the Monsters Volume 2

The bear next charged the shaken hominid with its outstretched paws slashing. The Bigfoot blocked the first swipe with a right forearm, only to have the claws cut deeply into the hair-covered flesh. The enraged Bigfoot unleashed several more haymakers with its enormous fists that again thoroughly rattled the bear, causing the mighty animal to pause for a moment to spit blood and a few extricated teeth.

The Bigfoot reached behind it and easily broke a thick branch off the tree it was pinned against. The beast-man then used the branch as a weapon against its ursine opponent. The bear growled in pain as it was struck several times by the makeshift wooden bludgeon, an onslaught that effectively beat the animal back.

Sensing that it was time for a temporary retreat to regroup, the bear turned and darted back into the forest. The Bigfoot considered pursuing and finishing off this rival for supremacy of the forest until it turned and noticed the human interlopers retreating. The hominid screeched a chilling utterance while lifting its new weapon of choice and began pursuing the fleeing people.

***

Danny and Nick, the two-armed employees of the Forest Service station, were standing by with rifles drawn and a government-owned truck taken out of the garage. They soon witnessed the strange and startling sight of Stewart emerge from the woods with an apparently unconscious woman over his shoulders, followed by a man they did not recognize pulling a teen girl they could identify as the Lindrick girl.

"Calvin, what the hell is going on here?" an alarmed Danny asked the ranger.

"Nick, get in the passenger side of the truck!" Stewart ordered. "Danny, take this woman and get her into the back seat alongside these two. She's badly injured, so be careful with her. I'm going to drive! *Hurry!*"

Christofer Nigro
Bigfoot vs. Killer Grizzly: King of the Forest
Duel of the Monsters Volume 2

Danny took hold of Astrid's limp body as ordered and he quickly checked her condition.

"Calvin… I'm sorry, man, but this woman is dead," Danny lamented.

"Noooooo! Mom!" Ellie screamed.

Brett pushed the hysterical teen into the back seat of the vehicle. "Have your grief fit *inside* the truck, girl! We gotta get out of here!"

The hunter then slid into the spacious back of the vehicle beside Ellie, doing his best to ignore the girl's bereavement tantrum.

Stewart looked at Astrid's blank open eyes, ashen gray pallor, and the trickle of blood flowing from her mouth to join the fluid seeping from her head wound. He knew immediately that Danny's diagnosis was sadly accurate.

"Okay… leave her on the ground for now," the ranger said solemnly. "We can have medical units retrieve her body later."

"Noooo!" Ellie screamed again. "Don't leave Mom!"

"She's gone, kid!" Brett screamed back at her. "Face up to it, okay? We won't be doing either her or ourselves any good if we try lagging her body along with us!"

Before Stewart could jump into the driver's side of the truck, an ear-shattering shriek from the edge of the woods indicated that the Bigfoot had finally caught up to them.

"Holy shit!" Danny exclaimed as he struggled to overcome a state of abject terror to aim his rifle and fire.

"Damn it all, Stewart!" Brett yelled. "Get in the truck and start the fucking engine already!"

Danny never got his chance to shoot as the over ten-foot-tall hair-covered humanoid threw the makeshift wooden club it carried at the Forest Service employee standing about thirty feet away. The wooden cudgel struck Danny in the crown of the head, causing him to drop his rifle and fall to the ground.

"Danny!" Stewart hollered when he was half inside the truck.

The stricken man tried to push himself past the pain of his fractured skull to get to his feet and enter the truck. However, the Bigfoot was upon him too swiftly for that. The creature lifted Astrid's lifeless form

Christofer Nigro
Bigfoot vs. Killer Grizzly: King of the Forest
Duel of the Monsters Volume 2

and used the cadaver as a flesh and blood sledgehammer by smashing her face into Danny's own. Both of their faces were instantly pulverized on contact with each other, and Danny joined Astrid in the realm beyond life.

Ellie began screaming again as Stewart pushed himself completely into the driver's side and slammed the door shut. Within a quick second he had the key in the ignition and the engine of the truck was started.

"Hurry the hell up, Stewart!" Brett bellowed as he brandished the revolver he kept in his belt as a supplement to his now lost rifle. "That thing is gonna be on top of this truck in seconds!"

"That guy is right, Calvin!" Nick said from the driver's side. "We've got to get out of here before…"

The Forest Service employee was cut off as he suddenly heard a low, ominous growl come at him from just outside the open passenger window. It was accompanied by the pungent stench of what was unmistakably the breath of a grizzly bear.

Nick barely had time to scream before the killer ursine snatched him out the window with its razor-hewn claws. The bear then bit into the side of the man's neck, its teeth sinking deeply into the flesh. It then violently shook Nick about like a leaf in the wind, a move that culminated in the sickening sound of his neck snapping.

"That's the fuckhead that killed my brother!" Ellie shouted as she boldly grabbed the pistol out of Brett's hand.

"Hey, now!" the tracker shouted back as he attempted to retrieve his weapon.

The girl fired several shots at the bear, with the slugs penetrating the back window, a few of which whizzed past Brett, scarcely missing him.

"Stop it, girl!" he berated her. "You're wasting ammo and you almost hit me…!"

This complaint was cut off when the driver's door was partially caved in by a sudden punch from the Bigfoot.

"Goddamn it!" Stewart said as the blow jilted him and thwarted his attempt to start the engine.

Christofer Nigro
Bigfoot vs. Killer Grizzly: King of the Forest
Duel of the Monsters Volume 2

If the bear was hit by any of Ellie's shots, the animal showed no signs of being disabled as it rammed its head into the car from the passenger side. Between the assault on opposite ends by both powerful creatures the truck was beginning to crumple like tinfoil.

The Bigfoot then brought both of its piledriver fists down on the roof, causing it to collapse inwards and nearly crush both Brett and Ellie.

"Shit and hell!" the trapper yelled while Ellie screamed and futilely pulled the trigger of the now empty revolver.

"I can't get it started!" Stewart warned. "The truck's been too badly damaged!"

The death knell for the government-commissioned vehicle came when the bear put its massive paws underneath the fenders and lifted the two-ton truck over with minimal effort. It landed on its side, jarring and panicking the three people trapped inside while further damaging the vehicle.

After this, the bear caught sight of its main quarry and rival, the equally large Bigfoot. They roared and shrieked another challenge at each other, respectively. The bear then clambered over the devastated truck and again charged at the Bigfoot.

This time, though, the mighty hominid was better prepared for its opponent. The Bigfoot unleashed a series of punches that stunned the bear and sent the animal reeling on its back. Never before had the ursine terror been knocked off its feet like that. However, the Bigfoot's Neanderthalic face took on something akin to a startled expression as the bear rose again and roared at its foe, baring all its sharpened teeth set within a jaw bearing tremendous crushing power. Many living creatures had fallen before the hominid's blows in the past, but never before had one gotten back up again.

The bear ignored the series of fractures in its facial bones and lunged at the Bigfoot. Once more its jaws clamped down on the Sasquatch's right wrist with incredible force, penetrating the rhino-thick skin and crushing the dense carpal bones beneath. The Bigfoot emitted a shrill shriek of pain and began pounding at the bear with its free fist. Try as it might, the ursine attacker could not sustain its grip

Christofer Nigro
Bigfoot vs. Killer Grizzly: King of the Forest
Duel of the Monsters Volume 2

under such an offensive and within seconds the hairy humanoid was free.

The Bigfoot's rage enabled it to ignore its injured right wrist and raise its left fist to deliver another punishing blow to the bear. The beastly bruin recovered quicker than expected, however, and slashed at its foe. Its claws tore a hand-sized gash in the ten-foot humanoid's side. This excruciating wound caused the Bigfoot to stumble backwards, and the bear rushed towards its pain-wracked foe.

The grizzly brought its full bulk down on the injured manimal, sending it down to the pavement of the station lot. The Bigfoot shrieked and struggled on, pummeling the bear in the sides of its rib cage and skull. This volley of blows delivered great punishment to the bear's skeletal structure. Nevertheless, the bones ultimately held long enough for the animal to bite into the man-beast's throat.

The bear tore into the Bigfoot's thick, near-nonexistent neck and tore out everything that was inside. The hominid attempted to shriek in agonized defiance, but only succeeded in releasing a scratchy squeal as streams of blood bubbled out of both its gaping throat wound and its mouth. Within moments the Bigfoot's struggle ceased and the great hairy man-monster went still.

Having proven itself king of the forest, the triumphant Killer Grizzly raised its bleeding head and emitted a resounding victory roar into the sunny blue sky. Its rival defeated, the bear now sought to relieve its gnawing hunger pangs.

To this end, the ursa major sunk the claws of both paws into the slain Bigfoot's massive gut and tore it open the way a person might unzipper a Ziploc storage bag. The animal slavered at the sight of the glistening organs and pinkish dermis that were now exposed. It began eating voraciously, savoring the taste of each strip of flesh and chunk of organ devoured.

This distracted the bear from the thrashed vehicle. Hence, it did not see Brett's leg kick the damaged back passenger door open. The tracker pulled himself out of the wreckage just before reaching back in to extricate both a stunned Ellie and frazzled forest ranger.

Christofer Nigro
Bigfoot vs. Killer Grizzly: King of the Forest
Duel of the Monsters Volume 2

"Stewart, get back to your senses!" the hunter demanded. "You've gotta lead me and the girl out of here now, while that fucking grizzly is busy stuffing its face!"

The ranger did indeed shrug off the pain of a mild concussion as he led his two fellow survivors away.

"Follow me!" he stated. "This trail leads around to the other end of the woods. We should be safe there for a while as the bear gorges itself. The sheriff department should be arriving soon, and they'll find us if we stay put in that area."

The haggard hunter and the still-crying girl thus followed the ranger down the designated path, leaving the ravenously feeding grizzly behind them.

***

About forty minutes later, the three survivors were in the spot that Stewart had led them to, anxiously awaiting the hopeful arrival of sheriff deputies.

Brett leaned against a large rock as Ellie silently sat in a nearby glade of grass with deeply reddened eyes. The ranger stood and surveyed the surrounding woods with his re-loaded pistol in hand.

It was then that he heard the rustling sound of something moving towards them in the nearby green foilage. Stewart pointed his gun, prepared to empty the entire chamber in the hope of getting lucky and hitting some vital and vulnerable spot on the bear.

"Stewart, wait!" Brett yelled while jumping off his stone chair. "Whatever's coming isn't making enough of a ruckus to be anything near the size of a bear. I think it could be a person!"

Stewart listened to those wise words and lowered his gun as whoever was in the woods continued to approach. Moments later, a rather confused-looking Vicki Lindrick emerged from the thickets.

"Grandma!" Ellie shouted and ran into the older woman's arms. "You're alive!"

"Of course, I am, dear," the old lady replied as she held her granddaughter tightly. "Sorry if I scared you before when I ran into the

36

Christofer Nigro
Bigfoot vs. Killer Grizzly: King of the Forest
Duel of the Monsters Volume 2

woods and screamed. I just thought I saw your Uncle Edward, but it wasn't him. Instead, some beast shrieked at me, so I screamed back, and it tossed a big rock at me. It hit a tree I was standing near, and I went quiet so it wouldn't know I was there. Then I got lost and wandered around until I heard you people over here and followed your voices."

"See, I told you, ranger guy," Brett said. "It was only the old lady."

Stewart ignored his comrade and approached Vicki to give her the bad news he felt it was his responsibility to do.

"Mrs. Lindrick... I'm sorry to have to tell you this, but your son Bill is dead."

Vicki's simple response was, *"Who?"*

***

The monster hunter stood within the northern section of the woods, in a trail leading deep into the green verdure. The man wore a black leather jacket over a dark T-shirt with blue jeans and heavy work boots, his usual raiment for such missions. He carried a high-powered rifle that had taken down many monstrous beings in the past. Standing about six feet in height, his hair was on the long side and his build thin but athletic. He closely inspected the huge man-like prints that were situated near a trail commonly used by hikers in the Kootenai National Forest.

Oh yeah, definitely Bigfoot tracks. No hoaxer made these with some cardboard cutouts. Looks like a mutant, too, which means probably a killer. Haven't had to deal with one of these in a long while; this'll probably be a couple days work finding it and putting it down.

"Well," Dale said to himself while peering into the dark woods. "Best get to it, then."

He then proceeded down the trail, his rifle raised and his combat-hardened senses alert for the first sign of his adversary, or for people in danger. Little was Dale aware that he did indeed have a major battle

Christofer Nigro
Bigfoot vs. Killer Grizzly: King of the Forest
Duel of the Monsters Volume 2

with a hirsute predator of humans ahead of him that day... just not the one he was expecting.

END

Matthew Dennion
Mr. Hyde vs. The Phantom of the Opera: Vile Intentions
Duel of the Monsters Volume 2

MR. HYDE VS. THE PHANTOM OF THE OPERA: VILE INTENTIONS – Matthew Dennion

Matthew Dennion
Mr. Hyde vs. The Phantom of the Opera: Vile Intentions
Duel of the Monsters Volume 2

Mr. Hyde vs. The Phantom of The Opera:

Vile Intentions

Matthew Dennion

Matthew Dennion
Mr. Hyde vs. The Phantom of the Opera: Vile Intentions
Duel of the Monsters Volume 2

Dr. Henry Jekyll fought back tears as he sat in the audience while the beautiful Christine Daae reached the climax to the first act of the opera. The young woman had stepped in for the injured lead in the role and the reports of her performances were that she was a prodigy. Ms. Daae came from relative obscurity to being the talk of the Parisian social scene. During an interview with one of the leading newspapers in the city, Christine had credited her recent improvement to the Angel of Music. She claimed the angel would come to her then instruct and inspire her to reach new heights with her voice.

Jekyll had his eyes fixed on the young woman. Her beauty was truly captivating. As he took in the features of her face and to a greater extent, her body, he imagined a future where he and the young singer were married and lived together in London. In his dream, Jekyll saw himself working as a physician during the day and then attending Christine's performances at night. Then of course, he imagined the two of them walking back to their home for the evening, and the acts they would engage in there.

From the dark corner of his mind, a thought erupted. He could hear a voice in his head saying that there was no need for him to marry Christine – he could make her into a kept woman. The doctor could use his wealth to pay for her stay in a flat and then call on her when he wanted to visit the local clubs, or to engage in other pleasurable activities. He had done this before with other women; or, rather, his other self had.

Jekyll turned his head away from the alluring Christine and toward the other people in the crowd. He saw happy couples of all ages sitting in the opera holding hands, smiling, and sneaking kisses when they thought no one else was looking. To Henry's left was a young couple who kissed passionately after Christine had reached her crescendo. He could see that the young couple were filled with lust and desire for each other.

To his right, he saw an older couple holding hands and smiling. While this pair lacked the intensity of the young lovers, the doctor could see that these people had been in love for a very long time. The latter

41

Matthew Dennion
Mr. Hyde vs. The Phantom of the Opera: Vile Intentions
Duel of the Monsters Volume 2

duo had clearly spent many years together and would spend whatever time they had left enjoying each other's company.

Henry shook his head as he reminded himself that love of any kind would be denied to him. He would never find himself in the embrace of a young woman like the man to his left. His other self may find himself in such a position, but it would be unlikely that it was a loving embrace. The physician's darker persona had taken to forcing himself on women when he wanted them, removing any form of consent, let alone love or attraction from the interaction.

The doctor looked back at the older couple as he thought that the beast within him would never let him be in such a long and loving relationship as those two. Hyde would kill a woman, either through abuse or simple spite toward his "better" side, before Henry could ever settle down with anyone.

Jekyll's sadness turned to rage as he thought about the steps Edward Hyde had taken to destroy his life. One by one Hyde had destroyed all of Jekyll's hopes and dreams. The monster took the doctor's desires and turned them into perverted nightmares.

Jekyll shook his head and whispered to himself, "No more. Today I use your own methods and desires against you."

He then looked back toward Christine as the curtain fell and he focused on the lust he had for the young woman. As the crowd stood up for the intermission and walked outside to smoke or to get a drink at the bar, Henry made his way toward the side of the stage.

As he approached the backstage area, an usher held up his hand. "I'm sorry, *Monsieur*. Only performers and employees of the opera house are permitted beyond this point."

Jekyll shrugged. "Very well."

The physician began turning around while surreptitiously balling his hand into a fist. Jekyll then struck the usher in the jaw, knocking him unconscious. The doctor took a quick look around to make sure that no one had seen what he did. Once he was sure the act went unnoticed, he dragged the unconscious usher to a nearby closet and threw him into it.

Jekyll then purloined the man's overcoat and hat and put them on himself so that he could walk around the backstage area unnoticed in

Matthew Dennion
Mr. Hyde vs. The Phantom of the Opera: Vile Intentions
Duel of the Monsters Volume 2

the guise of the usher. Having operated as a prominent doctor he took little time to remember the names or faces of many of the nurses and attendants who he had worked with in his career. He assumed that the people of opera would have the same attitude toward a lowly usher.

As Jekyll made his way through the backstage area, he found that his assumption was correct. He passed by numerous performers and stagehands, all of whom ignored him. When he reached the dressing room of Christine Daae, the physician placed his ear against the door. He could hear the young woman's voice, as well as a soft but strangely menacing male voice speaking to her. The doctor listened to the grim voice giving Christine instruction for a few more moments before he knocked on the door.

When the young singer opened the door, Jekyll was once more struck by her beauty. Normally, he would try to be a gentleman and look the young woman in the eyes so as not to offend her. Today, however, was not a normal day. Today he needed to feed his more base desires as much as he possibly could.

Jekyll immediately fixed his gaze on the young woman's voluptuous breasts as he spoke to her in near perfect French. "Excuse me, *Mademoiselle,* but wardrobe says they need to see you right away."

Noticing that the attendant was staring at her chest, the diva placed her hand over her breasts and replied, "Thank you, *Monsieur.* I shall go to them immediately; and I shall thank you to look at my face if you ever address me again in the future."

Christine then pushed her way past the false usher and headed to the wardrobe area. As the singer's door was closing, Jekyll used his foot to halt its progress. He then slipped into her room, reached into his pants pocket, and pulled out a vial containing some form of liquid.

The doctor looked around the chamber, held the vial up, said "Cheers," and drank its contents.

Jekyll then began walking around Christine's room as he felt his heart rate increasing. He stopped by her dressing shade and ran his hand over some of the clothing that was draped across it. He then spoke aloud to seemingly no one.

Matthew Dennion
Mr. Hyde vs. The Phantom of the Opera: Vile Intentions
Duel of the Monsters Volume 2

"I know that you can see and hear me. I heard you talking to Ms. Daae before I knocked on the door."

Jekyll began to sweat as he continued to pace about the room and speak aloud.

"Most people think that Ms. Daae's tutor, the so-called 'Angel of Music,' is either some trainer she meets up with outside of Paris; or, a clever ruse on her part to add an air of mystery to her performances and thus draw more people to see her."

The doctor took off the usher's coat and hat and then undid his tie before continuing his spiel.

"I am aware that most people would be mistaken. Most people would also be unaware of the reports of a Phantom-like character lurking in the tunnels beneath Paris. Aside from the occasional glimpse of a masked man grabbing food from a street vendor's cart, there is really nothing else to report about the supposed Phantom.

"When the occasional person would disappear, there would be whispers that the Phantom had taken him but no one in authority gave those rumors any credence. The Phantom is seen as little more than an urban legend created by the lower classes to keep them entertained and largely ignored by the press and the police."

The doctor dropped his tie on the floor as he grabbed Christine's overcoat, brought it up to his nose, and smelled it. As he pulled the garment away a devious smile crept across his face.

Jekyll shook his head. "Of course, most people are not esteemed doctors. Most people would not put a second thought to one of the numerous circuses that came to London with a gallery of freaks in a sideshow. The young boy who was a part of that freakshow with his horribly deformed face would be lost in the shuffle of freaks they had seen over the years. Likely, they would consider him to be a hoax."

Jekyll shrugged and continued his patter. "They would think he was a normal-looking young man covered with make-up, maybe even something extreme like piano wire being used to disjoint his nose – but again, most people would be wrong."

Jekyll continued to sweat profusely as he undid the buttons on his shirt to reveal an unusually hairy chest. "I know differently, though, eh?

Matthew Dennion
Mr. Hyde vs. The Phantom of the Opera: Vile Intentions
Duel of the Monsters Volume 2

The young man from the circus was much more intelligent than those he worked with gave him credit for. During his travels he would read anything he could procure, particularly discarded medical journals. The freak learned of my work in bodily transformations."

Jekyll threw his shirt to the floor. "I recall when that young boy from the freak show came to my laboratory in the middle of the night. I remember him begging me to help him find a cure for his deformity. He wanted me to help extract the evil that afflicted his outer body from his soul. He wanted me to give him a chance at a normal life.

"Sadly, the freak was poor. He had no money, but he told me he had other skills. Those skills included being a musical prodigy and an accomplished assassin."

Jekyll's hands began to shake, and his devious smile turned into a scowl as he shouted, "Does this sound familiar to you? Do you remember how I said I had no desire to kill anyone but that I would accept your payment in the form of music? Do you remember how beautifully you sang for me that week as you came to my laboratory every night? Do you remember how magnificently you played your violin as I drew your blood and ran test after test?

"When I read the reports of Christine's 'Angel of Music' and heard the rumors of this Phantom in Paris it was easy enough to realize that these reports were not only of one and the same person, but they were also describing the young man I had treated all those years ago."

Jekyll slammed his fists onto Christine's dresser as he screamed, "I will not be able to contain him for much longer, Erik! Come out now if you wish to prevent any harm from coming to Christine!"

The long mirror on the wall in the back of the room slid open and the Phantom of the Opera stepped out from behind it. He was wearing a cloak with a wide hat and a ghostly white mask over his face.

Erik stared at the shaking form of Henry Jekyll and spoke in a wispy monotone replete with subtle menace. "I remember our encounters, Doctor Jekyll. I also remember that even after two weeks of tests and working with me you were unable to help me with my condition." Erik shook his head. "I had always thought of you as a kind man. Why do you come here now and threaten Ms. Daae?"

Matthew Dennion
Mr. Hyde vs. The Phantom of the Opera: Vile Intentions
Duel of the Monsters Volume 2

Jekyll unleashed a chilling laugh as his voice grew deeper. "Because even though I was unable to help you, you were able to help me!" The doctor sat down and struggled to pull his feet out of shoes that were suddenly much too small for them. "The enzymes in your blood, the evil as you called it that infected your outer body, helped to lay the foundation for my work. By studying those enzymes and combining them with other chemicals, I was able to synthesize the formula that I thought would allow me to expunge the evil from within me, and eventually from all mankind!"

Erik continued to stare at the doctor as his brow expanded and his canine teeth extended until they appeared more like the fangs of an ape than the teeth of a man.

After pulling off his shoes – to reveal hairy and vaguely simian feet – and tossing them aside, the bestial man glared at the Phantom. "The formula did not work as I had planned, though. Instead of expunging the evil from within me, it separated it from my consciousness. My most base desires have been given the freedom to operate without my rational mind offsetting them."

The doctor looked down at his hands as hair began sprouting on them and his nails began to grow into long thick claws. Tears formed on Jeykll's elongated face as he started to cry.

"I've unleashed a monster on the world who calls himself Edward Hyde. When I ingest the formula you saw me imbibe, I change into him and he then carries out my most foul desires – the desires we all have but keep ourselves from acting on. Hyde destroys property, kills people, engages in cannibalism, and rapes women as he wants."

The rapidly transforming Jekyll looked down in disgust, "And I have directed his attention, as well as my desires, toward Christine Daae."

Anger flared into Erik's eyes as he moved across the room with lighting speed and wrapped his hands around Jekyll's neck. "Why? Why, damn you? Why would you set this beast after Christine?"

Jekyll sobbed, "Because when I read her story about the 'Angel of Music' torturing her and I read about the Phantom in Paris, I knew it had to be you. I remembered what you had said about your skills as an assassin and I knew that of all the people in the world, only you had the

Matthew Dennion
Mr. Hyde vs. The Phantom of the Opera: Vile Intentions
Duel of the Monsters Volume 2

skill needed to kill Hyde. I also knew that you must love Christine, or why else would you go through this charade to help her?"

Jekyll's voice became more desperate – and increasingly more guttural. "The only way to stop Hyde is for us to die. I knew if I set him after Christine that you would have no choice but to slay him."

Erik tore off his mask and let his top hat drop to the floor to expose his grotesque, skull-like visage. He glared into the doctor's face and spoke in an icily sinister tone.

"Still, there is no need to place Christine in danger! In all my tortured years of life on this cursed planet, you are one of the few people who was kind to me! If you really needed me to kill you, all you had to do was ask. I would have done it quickly and painlessly. Why would you take the risk of placing an innocent person like Christine in danger?"

Jekyll's body began to further change as his neck and shoulders doubled in size and forcing Erik to release the grip on the doctor's throat. He looked at the Phantom as tears once more ran down his increasingly hirsute face while again resuming his tirade.

"You do not understand. Hyde's power is growing. While I cannot control him, he can influence me. He knows that I want to die but he also knows I am too much of a coward to actually experience death myself. Hence, he knows I need to get someone to kill us both when he is free. He would never simply let me contrive a situation like this unless there was something in it for him."

Jekyll had by this point reached a height of nearly seven feet tall with rippling muscles protruding from his powerful simian body. "Hyde is a sadist. When he realized what I was coming here to do he did not attempt to stop me; to the contrary, he chided me on. He relishes the idea of pummeling you to death for trying to kill him. He will beat you within an inch of your life and then... then he will..."

Jekyll threw his head back in an agonized spasm, and when it came back down it was now the horrific face of Edward Hyde staring at the Phantom. For the first time in his life, Erik shuddered as he beheld Hyde's huge, hulking figure, a personage even more horrifying in appearance than he was.

Matthew Dennion
Mr. Hyde vs. The Phantom of the Opera: Vile Intentions
Duel of the Monsters Volume 2

Hyde leaned toward the Phantom and spoke in a grinding voice. "I will ravage and then devour that girl in front of you. It will not be quick, either. I will make you watch as I violate that girl repeatedly in ways you can scarcely even imagine. Then when she is no longer coherent enough to have fun with, I shall eat her alive!"

Hyde laughed. "Then we shall see what happens to you. If you prove to be a simple deformed freak with no skills, I will just snap your neck. Knowing what Henry does of you, however, I do not think that will be the case.

"If you present the good sport that Henry thinks you will, I shall let you live. The thought of you going forward with all of that anger building up inside you is like a fine wine to me. Your continued sorrow will bring me joy that you cannot imagine. Think of the games we can have! You, chasing me across the world seeking revenge, only to have me thrash you again and make you watch as I do to some other girl what I am going to do to Christine."

Hyde released another sadistic chuckle. "Oh, thank you, Henry. You have brought me here with the thought of killing me when in truth all you have done is present me with the greatest gift you could have possibly conceived!" Hyde then smiled at Erik. "You have given me my own personal pet to torture."

The Phantom shook his head. "You shall not leave this building alive, monster. Nor shall you touch a hair on Christine's head."

Erik sprang toward the gargantuan Hyde, but the monster swatted him aside like a fly, sending the skull-faced assassin crashing into the wall. The Phantom slid down to the floor, his head ringing from the blow. He then heard Christine begin to sing her concerto in the second act of the opera. The Phantom used her voice to clear his mind and focus on the threat to her.

Hyde smiled his hideous sneer and said, "I can't grab the girl off the stage during a performance, but aside from being rude, that would draw too much attention to me."

The brutish man jumped over to the mirror through which the Phantom had entered the room.

Matthew Dennion
Mr. Hyde vs. The Phantom of the Opera: Vile Intentions
Duel of the Monsters Volume 2

The maniac sniffed the air coming from the corridor behind the glass and then grinned as he turned toward Erik. "You have had some fun times down here together, haven't you? I can smell the death in this place." He nodded. "Yes, you will present good sport to me."

Hyde turned and bowed to the Phantom. "Come, good sir. Why should we make a mess of Ms. Daae's room? Let us have our fun in your underground lair. I will come back for Christine after her performance is done."

Hyde was laughing as he leapt into the darkness behind the mirror. Erik lifted himself off the ground, recovered his mask and hat, and ran over to the mirror passageway.

He peered into the hallway and snarled, "Fool, you have entered my domain, where I alone am master."

The former sideshow performer then dropped his hat and mask in the corridor and sprinted into the dark passage that led to his underground kingdom. The Phantom ran through the dark access strip that led to the Paris underground. The assassin shifted through the shadowy tunnels of his kingdom with the speed of jungle cat hunting prey. Despite the near total lack of light, Erik was well versed in traversing the tunnels. He was able to move through dimly lighted corridors as if they were lit up like the Eiffel Tower.

The beast had already demonstrated that he was physically much stronger than Erik. The speed and agility that Hyde had displayed when moving through Christine's room also suggested the monster was quicker than he was. The assassin knew that he would have to rely on his legendary cunning to defeat this creature. Erik was well aware that Hyde may have taken this advantage away from him as well. He had seen the gleam in the monster's eye when he spoke of what he would do to Christine.

The Phantom had no doubt that Hyde fully intended to carry out what he said. The thought of those acts being inflicted upon his beloved Christine dominated Erik's mind. No matter how hard he tried he could not push the thoughts completely aside and make tracking down and killing Hyde his sole focus.

Matthew Dennion
Mr. Hyde vs. The Phantom of the Opera: Vile Intentions
Duel of the Monsters Volume 2

The deformed assassin entered a large man-made cavern that served as part of the city's drainage system running all the way to the river. The upper part of the grotto was completely shrouded in shadow and its floor had a thin covering of stagnant water. Erik knew this area well. It was near his personal torture chamber filled with mirrors. The former circus performer was staring into the darkness at the web of pipes above him when he heard booming laughter echoing over him.

"The high ceiling and pipes make it difficult to see up here, and the echo off the walls will make it nearly impossible to decipher where my voice is coming from." Hyde laughed again as Erik spun in a slow circle trying to find a way to determine where his beastly opponent was. "My more animalistic features allow me to see in the dark better than any human could. The truth is, though, even with my eyes shut my nose and ears could tell me exactly where you are."

Hyde leapt down from the darkness and struck the Phantom, sending him flying into the stone wall of the cavern. As Erik rose to his feet, he grabbed his side and was certain that Hyde's blow had cracked if not outright broken several of his ribs.

Hyde cackled, "That is the difference between you and I. You are simply a man who looks like a monster. But me, I truly *am* a monster."

Erik stood up and through the dim moonlight that made its way into the cavern he saw the hulking form of Hyde coming toward him. The Phantom charged the brute. When he was a few steps away from Hyde, the assassin ducked under a blow from the monster and then delivered a series of strikes – first to each of Hyde's knees, then to his ribs, and finally to the creature's face. The Phantom's final blow managed to turn Hyde's head to the side, but the ruthless maniac was otherwise unaffected by the assassin's attack.

Hyde wrapped his massive arms around Erik and then pinned him to his burly chest in a bear hug. Erik could feel his spine being crushed to the point of snapping as his foe's fetid breath wafted into his face.

Hyde squeezed the Phantom a little harder as he mocked him. "Yes, this will do nicely. Breaking your back but at the same time being careful not to sever your spinal cord. That way you can watch helplessly as I have my fun with dear Christine."

Matthew Dennion
Mr. Hyde vs. The Phantom of the Opera: Vile Intentions
Duel of the Monsters Volume 2

The man-beast then shook his head while saying, "My God, you are ugly. Let me ask you something, which you must have considered yourself while consumed with thoughts of taking Christine as I am going to.

"Well, maybe you would not go so far as to suck the marrow from her succulent bones as I would, but having your way with her must have crossed your mind, right? I mean, look at you! You make me look handsome by comparison. You love the girl but deep down you know that no woman, let alone a beauty like that, could ever love or accept a hideous creature such as yourself."

For a brief moment, Erik's struggles to break free from Hyde's grip stopped as his adversary's words swirled around his mind. The Phantom's face was suddenly filled with remorse as he looked down toward the murky ground.

Hyde smiled when he saw Erik's reaction. He applied a little more pressure to the Phantom's spine as he continued to psychologically break the hardened assassin.

"Ahh, there it is," Hyde remarked. "That dark little secret that you like to keep hidden from yourself. You have thoughts of taking the girl, of forcing yourself on her." Hyde laughed. "You are almost comically pathetic. You are just like me, but unlike me you are unable to accept your power and your status as an outcast. None of them will ever see you as human and worthy of being loved. You shall always be a freak to them.

"I accept this fact about myself and make the masses pay for their arrogance and bigotry, but you? *You* skulk around in the dark and teach little girls how to sing behind a mirror. You should really be thanking me for what I am about to do to you. After what I do to your little singer, at least you shall have purpose in life as you try to hunt me down. That is more than you have now, here in your modern-day cave."

Tears began to fill Erik's eyes as Hyde made him face the dark desires within his own mind. The sadness and disappointment the Phantom felt in himself changed into anger as he thought about Hyde performing those acts on the woman he loved. Erik pulled back his thick and oddly shaped skull and then drove it into Hyde's long flat nose.

Matthew Dennion
Mr. Hyde vs. The Phantom of the Opera: Vile Intentions
Duel of the Monsters Volume 2

There was a sickening crack as the assassin headbutted the brutish man and broke the cartilage of his foe's proboscis.

The Gargantua dropped Erik and grabbed his bleeding nose. With his opponent stunned, the assassin grabbed Hyde's right leg and pulled it out from under him. This caused the brute to fall onto his back and splash down in the filthy water that had failed to drain into the river.

The Phantom then leapt onto Hyde's burly chest and being raining down blows into the monster's face as he screamed, "You shall not touch a hair on Christine's head! You are going to die down here in the muck and rot of the sewer where you belong!"

Erik's repeated blows drove the monster's head into the stone on which it rested. The Phantom had connected with nearly a dozen bashes before Hyde wrapped his massive hand around skull-faced assassin's head. The creature then stood up as he lifted Erik in the air like a rag doll. Hyde growled and slammed his smaller opponent into the ground.

The Phantom's entire body shook as it bounced off the hard floor of the tunnel. Before he could stand up, Hyde kicked Erik in his injured ribs, a blow that sent the assassin tumbling across the floor of the cavern.

The Phantom was just starting the painful process of standing up as Hyde approached him and howled, "That bloody hurt!"

"That is going to cost you and the girl," the bestial man continued. "Now know that the last thing I will take from your dearly beloved is her eyes. You shall be able to see her looking at you, longing for your aid as you sit there powerless to do anything to help her."

Hyde nodded. "Trust me that staring into the eyes of someone being tortured is not an experience you will ever forget. Of course, I doubt that the memory will bring you the pleasure it will provide to me."

The assassin ignored the pain in his ribs and quickly scurried between Hyde's massive legs to then leap onto the giant's back. Erik screamed as he pulled a rope which he had tied into the deadly Punjab lasso – his dreaded signature weapon of death – from within his cloak and wrapped it round Hyde's throat.

"Christine is mine!" the Phantom bellowed. "Neither you nor anyone else will have her! She is mine and mine alone!"

Matthew Dennion
Mr. Hyde vs. The Phantom of the Opera: Vile Intentions
Duel of the Monsters Volume 2

Erik squeezed the brute's neck with all his considerable strength. Hyde shook violently as the Phantom cut off the beast-man's supply of oxygen. Hyde tried to reach back and grab Erik, but the Parisian assassin's flexible body and quick reflexes allowed him to avoid his adversary's steely grip. Hyde's legs began to shake, and he fell to one knee. When his feet touched the floor, Erik whispered into his opponent's ear.

"As the darkness claims you, know that this is exactly what your other-self wanted. He wanted you to die so that he would be rid of you and pass onto the next life painlessly. I can sense how much you hate him. How you do not fear your own death as much as you fear knowing that Jekyll got the better of you. That the events he conspired to set up your death did just that. Die knowing it was not me who killed you, but that weakling Jekyll."

Hyde roared in response to the assassin's words. The bulky madman forced himself to stand up and then he threw his body backwards to bring the entirety of his substantial weight crashing down onto the Phantom.

Erik felt as if a mountain gorilla had thrown itself on top of him and the impact of the blow forced him to release the cord he had tied around Hyde's throat. The Phantom was only saved as his coughing foe rolled off the assassin in an attempt to catch his breath.

Hyde was on his knees hacking while Erik crawled away from the maniac. As the former circus performer continued to scuttle away, he realized that he may have finally turned the tide of the battle. Erik's adversary was superior to him in every possible way, and until this point the monster's taunts and threats had given him the psychological edge; but now the assassin had found the chink in Hyde's armor. As much as the brute hated Jekyll, he also feared how vulnerable the doctor made him.

The Phantom forced himself to stand. He looked around at his location in the cavern and began walking backwards as he yelled at Hyde.

"I see you for what you truly are! You portray yourself as a monster and murderer but what you really are is a coward and a fool! If you hurt

Matthew Dennion
Mr. Hyde vs. The Phantom of the Opera: Vile Intentions
Duel of the Monsters Volume 2

Christine, you are right that I will avenge her death, but I shan't play your game!

"I *will not* come after you! I will come after Jekyll! I will track you down and wait for you to change back into that pathetic doctor! Then I shall take him and trap him down here in my lair! He will be stuck here until the day he dies, and you will be trapped inside of him. Every day I will look upon him and laugh knowing that both you and Jekyll are in a living hell for daring to threaten my Christine!"

Hyde's face was flushed with anger as he howled at the Phantom. "I will grind your bones into the muck. You can die knowing Christine will be my toy and then my meal!"

"Even with your enhanced prowess you will never be able to catch me in my domain," Erick retorted. "I shall wait until you revert back to Jekyll. After I subdue him, I will deprive the doctor of ever indulging himself in the formula that sets you free!"

The Phantom then sprinted into a nearby corridor as the animalistic Hyde began to leap after him. Erik ran as fast as he could. With each step he took he could hear Hyde gaining ground. The former circus performer thought of his beloved singer, and he pushed his body as hard as he could. The assassin knew he was only a few steps from his mirror filled torture chamber. He felt that if he could reach the space, he would have a chance of defeating the hulking Hyde.

The Phantom ran into the chamber with Hyde right behind him. As Erik entered the compartment, he felt the ground shake behind him as his foe's massive form landed just out of arm's reach.

Hyde reached for the Phantom, but the smaller man dropped to the floor, grabbed a handful of mud, and then threw it into the brute's face.

Hyde roared in frustration as he hastily cleaned the sludge out of his eyes. With his adversary temporarily blinded, the Phantom closed the steel door to his chamber. He then ran to the middle of the room, opened the secret panel providing egress to the room, and slid out of it.

Hyde cleared his vision to see his horrific visage staring back at him from countless angles in the Phantom's hall of mirrors.

Erik activated the mechanism that sent waves of stifling heat into the torture chamber. Within seconds, the room temperature increased by

Matthew Dennion
Mr. Hyde vs. The Phantom of the Opera: Vile Intentions
Duel of the Monsters Volume 2

thirty degrees Fahrenheit. When he felt the surge of heat, Hyde began frantically searching the room for an escape route. The simian maniac began smashing mirrors only to find an impenetrable wall of rock behind them. Sweat poured off the brutish man's body as he roared at the walls of the chamber.

The Phantom quickly moved to an area where he could observe the torture room unseen by the monstrous Hyde. He increased the temperature in the room by another fifty degrees as he questioned his prisoner.

"While that bloated body of yours gives you increased strength and speed it must also increase the amount of body heat you give off. I would imagine that rehydrating after a battle like the one we had would be vital for you. I suspect with the heat you are now experiencing it will take only a few minutes at best before you lose consciousness."

Hyde wiped a pint of sweat off his huge brow as he fell to one knee. The madman looked at the countless mirrors surrounding him and threatened, "You had better kill me, freak! Or, I will come back for your beloved singer."

Hyde fell face first to the floor. He was panting heavily as Erik entered the chamber and walked over to him.

"No, you will not. I have defeated you once and I can do so again. If you or Jekyll ever come near Christine again, I will carry out my promise to trap the doctor down here and entrap you within him for the rest of your cursed lives."

Hyde laughed once more. "You think you have won? Really, my ugly friend, for a moment I thought you might be an intelligent foe, but you are just as daft and pitiable as the rest of the rabble. What was it that you came to Henry for all those years ago? For a solution that could turn a monster back into a man, right?

"Now know that he has perfected that formula. Also know that my hold over Henry has grown to the point where I can influence him even when I am buried deep within his mind. Know that no matter what happens, I will *never* let him give you the formula."

The brutal killer then turned his head toward the mirrors on the wall nearest him. "Enjoy looking at your reflection in all of these mirrors. I

Matthew Dennion
Mr. Hyde vs. The Phantom of the Opera: Vile Intentions
Duel of the Monsters Volume 2

am sure when you finally show Christine your dashing good looks it will be love at first sight."

Hyde laughed and shrugged. "I suppose, of course, that you could always kidnap her just as I was going to and show that you really are a monster." Hyde smiled, showing his pronounced canines. "Do you really think Henry tricked me into coming here? Or, do you think this was all an opportunity for me to torture someone no matter what the outcome?"

Erik's shoulder's fell and he sighed as Hyde's body shrank down and started to return to its original form of Henry Jekyll. The doctor rolled over to see the Phantom standing above him.

The assassin reached down, grabbed the exhausted Jekyll by the throat, and lifted him into the air. The former sideshow attraction then brought doctor within inches of his misshapen face.

Jekyll wheezed, "Please kill me and free me from Hyde's curse."

Erik snarled, "Years ago you tried to help me. Had you simply come to me, explained the situation, and asked me to kill you, I would have done so. Instead, you saw fit to give into Hyde's whims and threaten Christine."

The Phantom looked into Jekyll's eyes before continuing. "Is what Hyde said true? Can he prevent you from giving me the formula that will change me into a human?"

Jekyll nodded. "The formula would not be the same as mine, as your change would only be physical and not psychological. I am confident that I could develop a formula that would work for you, but I can already feel Hyde clawing at the back of my mind for simply thinking about it."

The Phantom dropped Hyde to the floor. "Go. You have one of the two things I desire in life, and your other self will deny it to me. The second thing I desire you have threatened in ways even a soul as dark as mine could not imagine. Now, leave my sight. If I ever see you again, I shall do as I promised and trap you here and Hyde with you."

Erik then lifted the secret panel on the floor to free Jekyll. As the doctor walked past him, he gave the Phantom a demented smile. The smirk was not from Jekyll, but rather Hyde gloating over his victory.

Matthew Dennion
Mr. Hyde vs. The Phantom of the Opera: Vile Intentions
Duel of the Monsters Volume 2

Paris's deadliest assassin walked over to one of his mirrors and looked at his disfigured face. He took a deep breath as he admitted to himself that he had not let Jekyll/Hyde depart out of mercy or convenience. The Phantom let them leave because even if he had Jekyll trapped and Hyde buried in his mind, every time he walked past his captive, Erik would have seen the gleam in Jekyll's eyes that was Hyde.

The latter would have watched as Erik's desire for Christine drove him to consider kidnapping the singer himself. Then whether she came with him willingly or he kidnapped her, the demented Hyde would watch through Jekyll's eyes.

If Christine rejected him, it would bring the madman untold pleasure to see Erik's soul crushed. If he forced himself on Christine, Hyde would still have his intentions toward Christine carried out by proxy. Even worse, he would see them carried out by a man who loved her, and the depravity of that act would likely bring Hyde even more joy then if he had carried out the act himself. The demented madman would see Christine betrayed by her teacher and he would see Erik struggle with the guilt of his act.

The Phantom began to tear up while he pondered the most likely outcome of his infatuation. As a tear trailed down his deformed face, Erik closed his eyes and heard Hyde mocking him: "Do you really believe you have won?"

END

Pete Rawlik
Lich vs. Zombies: A Night at the Monastery
Duel of the Monsters Volume 2

LICH VS. ZOMBIES: A NIGHT AT THE MONASTERY – Pete Rawlik

Pete Rawlik
Lich vs. Zombies: A Night at the Monastery
Duel of the Monsters Volume 2

Pete Rawlik
Lich vs. Zombies: A Night at the Monastery
Duel of the Monsters Volume 2

January 1919

There was something familiar in the air. It was a smell in the wind, a sound echoing down from the mountains; it was a feeling he had experienced before, though he couldn't exactly put his finger on it. He knew it was important, it was there in the pit of his stomach, gnawing at his psyche. But Doctor Herbert West had other things on his mind, so he ignored it. He was on the hills outside the small Portuguese village of Bouzano, not far from the River Guadiana and beyond that, the border with Spain. It was a picturesque town of red tile roofs and quiet streets that all ran to a central plaza with a renaissance fountain.

He had resided at the place for a week and had found it quite pleasant. The food was tasty, if spicier than he was accustomed; the Port was excellent, the coffee robust, and the bed in his hotel room was very comfortable. The only annoyance was the pack of children that seemed to have the run of the town. The youngsters appeared to eschew the town library where West had been doing his research, and for that the scientist was grateful.

Normally, West had no use for the parochial libraries of small towns. They rarely carried medical texts and were less likely to have a subscription to any journals of relevance. Indeed, he had no use for small towns in general, unless it was to supply the raw materials for his experiments in reanimation – but even this was something he preferred to explore in more metropolitan areas. Cities were large, chaotic places where it was easy to steal a dead body or ten, and just as easy to dispose of them. And West had a need for bodies, as his work demanded it.

His first attempts to bring back the deceased had used a crude formula, and the results had been just as crude. That had been two decades prior, however. Since then, he and his assistant had made vast improvements and had recently achieved a modicum of success: they brought back not only the dismembered head of a colleague, but the headless body as well. This last achievement had given credence to one of his theories concerning the dispersed location of the human will. West was on the verge of perfecting his formula and that allowed him the luxury to explore certain avenues of research that he would have

Pete Rawlik
Lich vs. Zombies: A Night at the Monastery
Duel of the Monsters Volume 2

previously ignored. Thus, his assistant was in Bavaria searching for a town that was not shown on any map, and he was here in the ruins of the Monastery of Berzano, an edifice crouched in the low mountains outside Bouzano.

West had first read about Berzano a year before, in a copy of *Cultes des Goules* by the Comte d'Erlette and it had intrigued him. As the legend went, in the early 14th Century a sect of Templar Knights had dominated the area along the Guadiana River, with a stronghold not only at Berzano, but another by where the waterway met the sea, effectively controlling trade in the region. In 1315, reports of Templar blasphemy in France reached Portugal. Enflamed by rumors and several local tragedies, the villagers of Bouzano became convinced that the Templars worshipped a demon. The creature took the form of a gigantic frog with sharp teeth, claws, and a spiked crest, and was named either Bahamut or Behemoth.

For years the knights would terrify the countryside, conducting secret rites to satisfy the bloodlust of their god, or so the locals claimed. Emboldened by the anti-Templar sentiment, the residents of Bouzano rose up and put torch to the order. As with all legends there were conflicting accounts. One source claimed that the knights were hung, and their eyes pecked out by crows; another placed the blame on seagulls; but most claimed that it had been the villagers themselves that had blinded the knights, burning their eyes out, before then burning them alive until there was nothing but ash.

Regardless of the method of their execution and blinding, one common thread ran through the accounts: the knights had been defiant to the end, claiming that it did not matter what the villagers did, for the knights could not be killed. With their dying words they claimed they had discovered the secret to eternal life. It was this claim that had brought West to the little town that sat in the valley, with the ruined monastery looming like the crumbling bones of a dead titan.

It was his intent to explore the ruin but not before doing his due diligence. Which is why he had spent the last few days perusing the local bookstore and library. At the latter he had met an educated gentleman and student of medieval history named Pedro, who was working on a thesis concerning the legends of the area. He and West

Pete Rawlik
Lich vs. Zombies: A Night at the Monastery
Duel of the Monsters Volume 2

quickly became friendly, and each helped the other without knowing exactly what they were studying.

Most interesting had been the book of fairy tales Pedro had shown him. It was a slim, gruesome volume, written for children and illustrated with morbid pen and ink drawings, particularly of the fat frog demon that the Templars had worshipped, and in the background was the suggestion of serpentine symbols. West wished to see these alchemical inscriptions in person, in the flesh as it were, assuming they still existed. He hoped there was some truth to the legend and not merely a story of blind ghosts wandering the night, manufactured to frighten children.

It had taken him nearly three hours to walk up the hills to the monastery. Given the short winter days, and the routine trip, that would leave little time to explore the ruins. It would have been faster with a vehicle, but there were none in the village. The only alternative, and one which West had refused, was to travel by horseback. He found the animals particularly loathsome and unreliable. So, he had walked. It had been worth the trip.

The ruins were wholly unremarkable, and typical of those that spotted the European landscape. They were based around a simple kind of architecture that integrated large, quarried blocks with the native landscape to form crude buildings, rooms, and passages, and then finished them off with finer bits of rock gathered from the local surroundings. In its current state it was difficult to tell where a building ended and the mountain began, or even what had once been indoors as opposed to outdoors – though there were some obvious clues in the context of various spaces.

This was particularly true of the area that appeared to have been used as a cemetery, a bleak and rocky patch of land that had fallen into disrepair. Patches of vegetation had made inroads amongst the crumbling gravestones and shattered stone footpaths, but there was limited soil, and these had all withered and turned dry, brown, and gray.

Most of the headstones were little more than shattered pieces of rock, but a handful were still intact, and these retained the form of a looped cross or ankh. It was a symbol the Templars had brought back with them from their ventures in Egypt, where it was associated with Osiris, the god of the dead and of resurrection. Some texts described Osiris as the

Pete Rawlik
Lich vs. Zombies: A Night at the Monastery
Duel of the Monsters Volume 2

Lord of Silence and as *He Who is Permanently Youthful*. Thus, the ankh and the god it was associated with were fitting symbols for a sect that believed they had achieved immortality.

The existence of the ankh headstones bothered West. It was clear to him that the stone carvings were the final resting places for the Knights that had been killed in the peasant uprising of 1315. But if the Order had all been executed and burned to ash, who had buried the remains? And who had spent the time and money to install these rather sect-specific monuments? And how was it that they had survived unmolested by their enemies for more than 500 years? They were mysteries that intrigued West, but he had no answers. Hence, he relegated his observations to memory, to be researched if and when the opportunity presented itself.

More intriguing were the queer serpentine symbols that had been carved into the walls of the monastery. They were not unlike things he had seen elsewhere and were particularly reminiscent of symbols he had observed in the letters of several gentlemen who had fled Salem after they had been accused of witchcraft. There they had been referred to as the Dragon's Head and the Dragon's Tail and were also associated with death and resurrection.

To his dismay, the stone idol that had once occupied the central dais of the great hall was no longer intact, shattered it seemed by either an onslaught of vengeful hammers, or the simple passage of time. All that remained was the great base which had apparently been made out of sturdier stuff than the idol itself. This too was decorated with strange symbols that struck a chord in West's memory. He was certain he had seen them before, not only in the letters of those men from Salem, but also perhaps in the copy of *Cultes des Goules* he had studied.

It was as he began his finer inspection of these inscriptions that Pedro arrived, wild-eyed and out of breath.

"Please Doctor, you will come with me. We need to go somewhere safe."

Pedro's English was much better than even some of those who spoke it as their primary language. He was a young man, somewhere in his late twenties, with a crop of curly black hair, a thick mustache, and dark brooding eyes. He was not quite six feet tall but was broad in the shoulders and legs like tree-trunks.

Pete Rawlik
Lich vs. Zombies: A Night at the Monastery
Duel of the Monsters Volume 2

"*O Paladino* – Henrique Mitchell de Paiva Cabral Couceiro – has seized control of Porto and declared the *Monarquia do Norte*. I am sorry, Doctor, but it seems Portugal is in the midst of a revolution!"

And there it was. West knew what he had smelled on the wind and echoing through the mountains. He knew what it was that clawed in his gut and gnawed at the back of his mind. It was the monster that stalked all of mankind and brought with it the specter of Death.

West picked up his medical bag with the vials of reagent that clinked inside. It was as if they knew that soon they would soon be needed and were growing impatient at their own idleness. He stroked the bag as if it were a cat begging to pounce and he were trying to ease its restless nature, but he knew better. He knew that things were inevitable. Against all decorum he smiled in anticipation of what was to come. War was on its way.

Pedro grabbed the doctor by the arm of his coat and pulled him out of the ruined hall and through the winding maze of the crumbling outbuildings. It was late afternoon and the mountains to the east were just biting into the sun. By the time they reached the village it would be dark, and Pedro wanted to be behind closed doors as soon as possible. The young man seemed to despise the idea of monarchist troops entering the country.

"We have been a republic for nearly a decade now, having overthrown the last vestiges of the constitutional monarchy and exiling Manuel II. The soldiers that come now to reinstate him, they may be led by members of the old guard, but I doubt the rank and file have ever served Portugal. It will not surprise me to learn that they are simply the adult children of those in exile, given guns and a uniform and ordered by their fathers into action, but with no actual experience themselves."

He looked at West with sadness in his eyes, and then glanced at his watch. "We can make our way across the field to the south and then follow the railway into town. It would be best to stay off the roads and avoid any soldiers."

But it was already too late. Just as the pair reached the main gate, they heard voices and the sound of boots on the gravel road. They hid behind the wall and watched as three men in uniform came marching up the slope.

Pete Rawlik
Lich vs. Zombies: A Night at the Monastery
Duel of the Monsters Volume 2

Pedro recognized the regalia immediately. "Officers wearing the colors of the Portuguese Empire! We must hide."

It was West's turn to grab Pedro by the sleeve and drag him back into the ruins. "I know a place!" His voice was almost a whisper.

In moments they were back in what remained of the main building, in a crumbling gallery overlooking the cemetery. It had been West's intent to allow the soldiers to pass, and then sneak down and head back to town. But the soldiers had not passed. Instead, they had stopped and set about clearing the decaying brush away from several of the plots. It was only when they opened their bags and removed the contents that West understood what was happening.

"Those robes bear the same symbol as the graves," murmured Pedro. "The Knights said they had discovered the secret of immortality; these must be some that survived the purge all those centuries ago."

"Don't be ridiculous," West said and shook his head in disappointment. "Some members probably escaped and passed on their traditions either to their direct or spiritual heirs." Pedro didn't seem to understand. West sighed in frustration. "They're more likely to be descendants of the Knights, or just contemporary members of the same sect."

This Pedro understood, and while West shrunk back against the stone to stay concealed, his friend strained to overhear what was being said by the trio as they obviously prepared themselves for some kind of ritual.

Pedro's eyes grew wide. "They say that *Carnamagos* – whoever that is – was very specific about how to prepare the ground. They're spreading some kind of dust upon the graves." He paused as a single voice seemed to issue commands. "The one in charge reminds the others that they must wait for nightfall to begin the ceremony."

Unseen, Herbert West nodded his head. "Of course, no sorcery is ever done by the light of day." With his right hand he held a flask of reagent, while his left carefully drew back on his third syringe. "We might as well get comfortable, as it seems we shall be here for a bit."

His syringes prepared, he secreted them back in his bag, and then removed a small book from the side pocket. "I find the poetry of Phillip

Pete Rawlik
Lich vs. Zombies: A Night at the Monastery
Duel of the Monsters Volume 2

Hastane oddly appropriate for the situation, and there seems to be no better way to occupy my time. At least, until the sun sets."

And with that the doctor who was also a madman settled in to bide his time.

***

The sun set, as it was bound to do, and the mountain to the west cast a long shadow across the valley and crept up into the hills, before finally swallowing the crumbling monastery in its umbral embrace. The soldiers lit torches so that they could see what they were doing, and in turn this allowed West and Pedro to see as well. The former had seen members of other secret societies, illegal boxing clubs, and even other cultists – it was an occupational hazard – and these were some of the most inept he had ever bore witness to. This lot generally seemed unprepared. They fumbled through what he assumed was their grimoire and argued over how to position various sacred objects in the crude magical circle they had created. One would have thought that such details would have been worked out beforehand.

Pedro translated snippets. "The tall one is reciting a warning from the book. 'Do not call up what you cannot readily put down.' What does that mean?" And then later, "They're pledging that the Knights they raise here will lead to a swift restoration of the monarchy. It's almost as if they are trying to convince themselves that the restoration of the king would justify their blasphemous actions." He turned and looked at West. "Doctor, are you not appalled by these profane actions?"

West shrugged. "Men are always pious, until they find the tenets of their own religion in conflict with their desires for money, power, and women. It is why the Catholic Church instituted confession and penance. They would rather have devotees that are rich and powerful and forgiven, than the poor and powerless who are faithful."

Pedro stared at West, suddenly realizing that they did not share some of the same beliefs, but before he could say anything there came a mournful sound from the soldiers below. It was disorganized at first, a kind of poorly coordinated chanting with the voices overlapping and drowning each other out. But eventually the three found their rhythm

Pete Rawlik
Lich vs. Zombies: A Night at the Monastery
Duel of the Monsters Volume 2

and the words (if they could even be said to be words) resolved themselves into something that West could at least attempt to write down in his notebook. He wrote the following:

Y'AI 'NG'NGAH
YOG-SOTHOTH
H'EE—L'GEB
F'AI THRODOG
UAAAH!

With the synchronous chanting there came from the sky a terrible wind that carried with it a sulfurous stench. West grabbed his notebook and satchel and cowered behind a rock wall. Pedro brought his knees up over his ears and whispered a prayer. All around them a maelstrom of debris churned, throwing itself against the walls of the decrepit fortress. Storm clouds appeared out of nowhere, blotting out the moon and stars; they too swirled in a vast vortex of darkness, roiling with thunder.

There followed a mighty crescendo that shook the very foundations of the ruin and even brought a small boulder or two tumbling from their resting place. This Brobdingnagian climax brought the whole process to an end. The clouds receded, the wind died, the debris fell to the ground, and with great caution West and his companion braved to see what had occurred below.

The three soldiers stood in ceremonial robes, positioned on the circle they had created, forming an equilateral triangle. In the center stood a fourth figure, but West would be hard pressed to call it a man. It stood upright, and wore a cloak long gone grey and moldering with age. Beneath this was a tabard emblazoned with a faded red ankh within a flaming annulus. At its side hung a scabbard and sword which seemed just as corrupted by age as the rest of the figure. The worst of it, though, was the face that had turned the same festering grey as its clothing.

But it was not the visage of a man, at least not a living one.; It had a shrunken, desiccated look to it, with only the remnants of any kind of musculature, such that what remained was tight to the underlying bone and pulled back in a rictus grin. Given its state, the skull and little flesh

Pete Rawlik
Lich vs. Zombies: A Night at the Monastery
Duel of the Monsters Volume 2

that was left on it could have easily passed as some kind of primate, but the garments marked it as a man, and West refused to speculate further.

In unison the three soldiers knelt down before the decayed thing and spoke words that West could not understand but seemed to be highly respectful.

Pedro translated for his companion. "They are welcoming that thing back into the world and asking it for help in restoring the monarchy to power."

The thing stood there for a moment and then in utter silence it drew forth its sword and raised it up towards the sky. It appeared to be saluting its compatriots, but then one of them rose and took a step forward. The sword came down in a frightful stroke, severing the arm of the one who had moved. One of the others yelled in protest and was rewarded with a backhanded swing that caught the offender in the neck and sent the severed head arcing through the air, spraying blood across the stone graves. The third one panicked and fumbled through his garment for his firearm. He fired twice point blank. West saw the bullets make small holes in the thing's chest, but to no avail. It lunged at the soldier and the robe-bedecked man fell back onto the hard ground. The monster's mouth latched itself to the man's neck. He screamed in agony.

West could see the creature's cheeks inflating and deflating regularly like the pale belly of a bloated toad. It was sucking the blood out of the man, and whatever life force he possessed along with it. The soldier was still alive, though; still conscious, and still a man. Unable to overthrow the monster and fully aware that bullets had no effect on it, the poor man did the only thing he could to ease his suffering. He brought the gun up to his own temple, closed his eyes, and pulled the trigger.

Pedro opened his mouth and took a deep breath. He was going to scream in horror, but West clamped his hand down over the man's mouth.

"Shh," the doctor whispered. "I don't think it knows we are here."

The two watched in abject terror as the monstrous lich continued to feed, draining the body for the fluid it needed for sustenance. When the loathsome creature was finished it rose up on to its feet and then stumbled about with its arms outstretched. It took careful steps, but they

Pete Rawlik
Lich vs. Zombies: A Night at the Monastery
Duel of the Monsters Volume 2

were slow and in a methodical manner that suggested that there was a method to its madness.

"It's looking for something," said Pedro.

"Yes," nodded West, "the other bodies, but it can't find them. It's blind. That might work to our advantage."

"How is that?"

"Of that I'm not sure, but it's always best to note the weakness of your foes."

"Is it our enemy? It killed the soldiers. Doesn't that make it our ally?"

West was not convinced. "I don't think this thing has political affiliations. It's not against the Monarchists, I think it might be against life itself."

"You're saying that thing isn't alive?"

West thought for a moment. "No. It's not alive, at least not in the way we think of life."

The thing ceased searching for the soldiers it had killed and began taking purposeful strides out of the graveyard.

"Where is it going?" wondered Pedro.

"I would assume that it's heading toward Berzano. It's still probably in the same place it was more than six centuries ago."

"We need to kill it before it gets there." There was a sense of panic in Pedro's eyes. "Can we kill it?"

"Perhaps, perhaps not; but it is imperative that we try." West paused and gathered his thoughts. "There will be risks." He looked down at the carnage that had engulfed the boneyard. There were the bodies of the soldiers, their supplies, and their weapons. They were scattered, but still recoverable. "Almost everything I need is here. I just need one more thing."

"What is that, Doctor West?" Pedro was almost begging.

"I need time, Pedro. A half hour, at least And then I should be ready to deal with our enemy."

Pedro checked his watch, appearing resolved to the task. "A half an hour, Doctor. I'll be coming with that thing right behind me. You had best be prepared."

West smiled. "Trust me, we will be ready."

Pete Rawlik
Lich vs. Zombies: A Night at the Monastery
Duel of the Monsters Volume 2

Pedro didn't even bother to ask what West had meant by 'we. He just made his way down the stone steps, through the graves, and after the blood-sucking monstrosity that was set on terrorizing his hometown.

West followed, at least down into the graves. He held his medical bag close to his chest as he picked through the shattered remnants of the soldiers' equipment, and the soldiers themselves. He found the dismembered arm and laid it out on top of the body it had come from.

"Where did that head get to?"

In his bag West's syringes jangled as if in anticipation.

Out on the hill, the wind whipped through Pedro's jacket as he did his best to follow the monster and not alert it to his presence. He kept well back but made sure that he could always see the thing. It was not terribly fast, but it moved with more assurance than Pedro would have expected from a creature without sight. It also relied greatly on its sword, using the thing as a kind of cane to identify large objects in its path.

Unfortunately, West had been correct concerning the location of the town. Little had changed in the last few centuries, not even the trails that led down from the mountain. Only the railway was new, but that was a good distance from the foothills across a field of sedges killed by the winter frost.

The lich moved like an old dog who had slept in comfort for too long and was now being forced to make its way out to the yard. It had to be done, and it would be done; it would just take time and effort, and it was not a pretty process. And God protect anybody who got in its way.

Pedro almost laughed at that notion and paused a moment to contemplate the spiritual ramifications of the living dead actually existing. On the one hand it suggested that necromancy was real, that there were ways that a long dead body could be returned to life, or a semblance thereof. Pedro was unsure what was motivating that body, as it could have been the spirit of the Knight, or some other force – a demon, for lack of a better term.

This existence of magic in the world should have given him some comfort in his faith, but it did not. His faith, as it had been taught to him, promulgated an all-powerful God that protected mankind from spiritual

Pete Rawlik
Lich vs. Zombies: A Night at the Monastery
Duel of the Monsters Volume 2

evil. That the simple rite he witnessed could break what he assumed were God's laws shook his faith.

Pedro followed the creature for twenty minutes, winding down the steep descent with careful, well-placed steps that minimized the sound of boots on gravel. He also made sure to avoid any debris or dried detritus that might crunch or snap under his weight. He felt confident that he could easily dodge the thing, but he had already seen it kill three men and he was not a fool. Hence, he was not taking any unnecessary chances.

At least not until he had to.

The thought of not helping to stop the creature crossed his mind. There was nothing in Berzano for him, not really. He could make a run for the railway and follow it east, follow it all the way to Lisbon, and once there he could find employment, perhaps in another library or even a museum. He was an intelligent man, an educated man, and finding a job would be easy.

But with his intelligence and his education there came also a sense of conscience, of duty, of compassion. He was, after all, a child of the Republic, and with that he held certain responsibilities to his fellow countrymen. The young man could run, he could leave the town to deal with the monster on its own, but he could never live with himself afterwards.

Pedro checked his watch… it was time. He carefully picked up a rock and ran full speed toward the resurrected knight. The determined young man flung the chunk of granite with all his might and smacked the creature in the back. The rock fell to the ground, and the monster turned its face pulled back in rage.

Pedro slid to a stop, sending a spray of pebbles towards his adversary. The lich lunged forward with its sword, but the young man scrambled back and easily avoided the attack. He turned back towards the ruin, realizing his need to make enough noise for the monster to follow him. It was then he thought back to a song he had learned during his studies in Vercelli, and he sang the chorus as he climbed the foothills back to where he hoped West was waiting.

"Bella ciao, Bella ciao, Bella ciao, ciao, ciao!"

Sword drawn, the blind fiend followed, silent but clearly enraged.

Pete Rawlik
Lich vs. Zombies: A Night at the Monastery
Duel of the Monsters Volume 2

West had just put his syringes back in their case when Pedro came running back into the yard.

The doctor checked his watch. "Good man. You're right on time."

"The knight isn't that far behind me," Pedro explained between breaths. "What's our plan? What do we do?"

"Do?" West retorted mounting the steps back up into the gallery. "We don't do anything but hide and wait."

Pedro was obviously bewildered but followed the older man's lead. From the relative safety of the gallery he watched as the sword-wielding brute entered the courtyard. It was then that he noticed that two of the bodies had been moved from where they had died. West had propped them up against opposite walls of the ruins. He had sewed the head back on to the one body, and the arm back on to the other.

Pedro wondered what the point was. Aesthetically, the family might certainly appreciate the fact that their loved ones were whole, but that was more of a task for an undertaker, not something to waste precious time on when they were being hunted by a monster. He was about to say something to West, berate the man for squandering the few minutes they had, when something caught his eye.

One of the bodies had moved.

It was a subtle motion, just the twitch of a hand, but it was undeniable. The dead body, the one that had lost its head, was moving. Its hands were twitching, its arms jerking, its legs gently kicking, not unlike a newborn. Pedro then looked over at the other body and that one was moving in a similar manner.

He turned to look at West to find an expression of glee on his face. "What sorcery is this?"

West shot back with a look of anger and pride. "Not sorcery... *science!* You are looking at the culmination of decades of study and experimentation. I and I alone have succeeded in discovering the secret of reanimating the dead." There was a hint of megalomania in the good doctor's voice.

Pedro was not having any of it. He stood up and pointed at the undead knight that was making its way through the graves. "I would suggest someone else may have beat you to it!"

Pete Rawlik
Lich vs. Zombies: A Night at the Monastery
Duel of the Monsters Volume 2

West took his feet and pointed angrily with a raised voice. "I don't know what that is, but it isn't life!"

The ghoul's head swiveled around and took notice of the argument. It changed course and began marching towards the bottom of the stone stairs.

"Now look what you've done!" snapped Pedro.

West looked down at the boneyard smugly. "Indeed, look at what I have done!"

There came from both sides of the boneyard a great wailing, of living things broadcasting their agony. The sounds were coming from the two bodies that had once been dead but now, through West's weird science, were alive once more. They stumbled to their feet, clawing up the walls, using them for support, for it was obvious that they were unsteady on their feet, like infants first learning to walk.

But they weren't infants, they were full grown men, and from their anguished screams they seemed to be in agony. The knight had changed direction and was now approaching the soldier who had once been beheaded, drawn in by the terrible cries.

"Why are they screaming like that?" asked Pedro.

West did not flinch at the query. "I'm not sure, but I've seen this before. I suspect that coming back to life must be very painful. Pooled blood pushing through veins. Muscles uncramping. The circuits of the central nervous system electrifying again. Like an old machine turned on for the first time, the accumulated dust making things creak." West nodded. "They'll be fine, more than capable of doing what we need them to do."

Step by step the lich knight moved closer to the mewling reanimate. It slowly raised its sword, fully intent on bringing the blade down once more on the creature's head.

"It has been my experience that following a momentary adjustment period, reanimated subjects are preternaturally fast," West added.

The blade swung down, but instead of burying itself in the flesh of its target, it hung in the air, gripped between both palms of the reanimate's hands, as if in a vise.

"And strong."

Pete Rawlik
Lich vs. Zombies: A Night at the Monastery
Duel of the Monsters Volume 2

The reanimate zombie reached and grabbed his attacker by the grey, soil-caked garment it wore and threw it across the room. The hurled lich impacted against the far wall and crumpled to the ground.

"And violent."

The one reanimated soldier charged across the grounds, obviously intent on tackling its enemy. But the knight was wiser than the young soldier had been. It curled into a ball and at the last moment raised its sword. The roaring reanimate skewered itself. The long blade nearly exploded out of the man's back with the still beating heart impaled on its tip.

"Unfortunately, most also tend to be relatively stupid. I think it's brain damage, a side-effect of prolonged oxygen deprivation." West scratched his head. "Oh, well. I'll figure it out eventually."

"Eventually!" Exclaimed Pedro. "What are we going to do about that zombie knight?"

West cocked his head in puzzlement. "Are we thinking it's a zombie? More of a mummified vampire, I think."

"That is not the point!"

"My friend, you've forgotten about the other one."

The second reanimate enveloped the knight in its limbs and yanked the skeletal entity from where it had crouched, forcing it to leave its sword behind. The mummy-like lich twisted and kicked, but without any leverage it could not break the reanimate's hold. The two monsters both paused for a second and seemed to be at an impasse, each pondering what to do next. Then the still barely human creature took a deep breath, flexed its muscles, and began to scream, while at the same time making its grasp around the knight tighter and tighter. The latter monstrosity squirmed and kicked, but to no avail.

"I've seen something like this before," said Pedro. "When I was in America, they called it free-style wrestling. I saw Frank Gotch take on George Hackenschmidt in Chicago back in 1911."

"I've never been a fan of athletics," remarked West. "Well, perhaps boxing."

The undead knight seemed to be desperate. It didn't need to breath, that much was obvious, but it still seemed genuinely distressed, panicked even, as the arms wrapped around it closed even tighter. Then

Pete Rawlik
Lich vs. Zombies: A Night at the Monastery
Duel of the Monsters Volume 2

inevitably, something inside the reconstituted soldier snapped with a very audible crack. The lich went still for a moment, but only a moment. Then it began to struggle again, this time with renewed vigor.

The vampiric creature was like a fish caught in the paws of a cat. It wiggled back and forth violently, its mouth gasping in obvious agony. Its neck was straining in what seemed like an impossible length and direction. Then something else cracked, and the body of the gray dusty thing went still and limp.

Then the most curious thing happened. The knight's body, which had been as solid and corporeal as anything else – and had been adorned with clothing, boots, and even armor – suddenly began to crumble. It was as if the gray-blue mold that had covered it and had in fact been the entirety of its body and accoutrements, had suddenly become dry and brittle and then just disintegrated. It fell in pieces from where the reanimate had crushed its chest, down to the rocky ground, and there it just broke into little more than ash or dust.

Confused by the sudden disappearance of its enemy the reanimate roared in frustration. It flexed its arms and shook its body, casting the last of the bits of the knight into the air, where they tumbled down to join their fellows in small drifting piles. These little heaps of detritus lingered for a moment, but then the breeze came up and even these remnants were lost to the winds, scattered amongst the crags and nooks and crannies of the ruined graveyard that had spawned it.

The reanimate continued to roar in irritation, stalking about like some great predator suddenly denied its prey.

Pedro nudged West. "It seems you've traded one problem for another."

"Indeed," nodded West. "Technically, I suppose this would be counted as a success, but it's obviously not my best work."

He raised a pistol, and Pedro recognized it as belonging to one of the soldiers. The doctor aimed, squeezed the trigger, and a single shot sped through the night air to find its mark between the thing's eyes. The reanimate zombie tumbled to the ground, convulsed for a moment or two, and then finally lay still.

"A good shot," noted Pedro.

Pete Rawlik
Lich vs. Zombies: A Night at the Monastery
Duel of the Monsters Volume 2

West grinned. "I've had some practice. Early in my experiments I was inexperienced and ended up taking six shots before a similar thing was put down. I thought it prudent to learn how better to dispatch my mistakes." He checked the number of shots still left in the gun. "A bullet to the brain or severing the head from the body is usually sufficient, though there are some outlying behaviors."

"Whatever happened to the third soldier?" pondered Pedro.

"Hmm? Oh, the one that had been fed on by the knight. I tried to reanimate him, but he didn't respond to treatment. It happens sometimes." West looked around at the carnage that surrounded them. "What will you tell the authorities?"

"What can I tell them? Three soldiers – supporters of the monarchy – were attacked in the ruins by a man dressed as a knight. The knight killed them and then vanished into the mountains. I certainly can't tell them the truth now, can I?" Pedro laughed briefly.

"No, and I would appreciate if the name of Doctor Herbert West was kept out of any records, official or not."

"What doctor?"

West put his arm around his companion, and the two of them slowly made their way out of the gallery. The doctor picked up the grimoire and handed it to Pedro. The young scholar reluctantly took it and secreted the volume in his coat pocket. They made their way down the hill and followed the trail back to Bouzano. That night the two drank sangria and ate pastry till both succumbed to sleep. Neither mentioned what they had been through.

The next morning both received telegrams. Pedro's was from his professor back in Lisbon, asking him to return on the next train. The administration was fearful of the coming revolution and wished to prepare and protect the various university archives and holdings. Across the country students, professors, and alumni were returning to protect the institution they had studied at. West's telegram was from his fellow researcher who had found the Bavarian village they were searching for and contained the name of the nearest town with a rail station.

Late that morning West and Pedro bid farewell to each other and boarded separate trains, heading in separate directions. The last thing Pedro did was drop a note to the local authorities suggesting they

Pete Rawlik
Lich vs. Zombies: A Night at the Monastery
Duel of the Monsters Volume 2

investigate the ruined monastery. The written message was delivered later that afternoon but given the political situation it was not given any priority.

As revolutions go, it was a sad affair. Manuel II refused to lend his support to the forces of Henrique Mitchell de Paiva Cabral Couceiro and the *Monarquia do Norte* never was able to seize control of the country. In less than a month, restoration forces silently surrendered to the Republicans and order was restored.

Finally, in late February a detail traveled up to the ruined monastery and discovered what was left there. Bodies were recovered and shipped home to grieving families in Spain. It was assumed that the men had died in an unreported skirmish during the attempted coup. No one amongst the small band that went to the ruins knew that there should have been three bodies. No one among them had ever been there before, and none noticed that the rocky ground in the graveyard had been disturbed.

Only a scholar of medieval studies would have realized that there was a new grave amongst the old, but of course Pedro was not there, and had no intention of ever returning. He wrote his thesis on the Knights of Berzano, but never mentioned what happened that night he and Herbert West had spent in the ruins.

It wasn't until much later that he finally picked up the book they had confiscated from the soldiers. It took months for him to translate the Greek that was contained in the *Testament of Carnamagos*, and even longer to put the knowledge within to practical use.

But that is another story.

END

Dustin Dreyling
Wendigo vs. Lizard Man: War of the Appetites
Duel of the Monsters Volume 2

WENDIGO VS. LIZARD MAN: WAR OF THE APPETITES – Dustin Dreyling

Dustin Dreyling
Wendigo vs. Lizard Man: War of the Appetites
Duel of the Monsters Volume 2

Dustin Dreyling
Wendigo vs. Lizard Man: War of the Appetites
Duel of the Monsters Volume 2

"Whoa, look at that, Teddy!" Kristen exclaimed, pointing at the truck laying torn open on the side of the road.

Her husband slowed down as they neared the wreck, pushing his glasses up his nose as he gawked at the incapacitated utility vehicle. It had crashed into the shallow ditch and the driver's side door hung askew. The back doors hung open precariously on ruined hinges and the twin pieces of metal had been torn into repeatedly in several places by some unknown sharpness.

"What do you think did that?" Kristen asked.

The side of the truck was labeled with the name of a laundry delivering service neither of them had heard of: Clean and Clean Again.

"I really don't think that's a laundry truck," Kristen's facial muscles wrinkled in her disbelief.

Teddy nodded and grunted his agreement as he came to a complete stop next to the wreck. He put the Lincoln town car into park and sighed with the apprehension of what they might find. Kristen got out immediately, not waiting for him to unbuckle his seat belt. By the time he caught up to her at the back of the Sprinter van, her jaw looked like a corpse from the movie *The Ring*.

Blood painted the inside of the cargo area like some abstract hippie artist had gone nuts with crimson. Incredible violence had unfolded inside the vehicle, and it had occurred somewhat recently. The fluid dripped intermittently from splotches on the ceiling, while trails of it ran down the walls to form several congealing puddles on the floor.

The thing that really unnerved Teddy, however, was the mangled cage torn to pieces inside. It was the kind of pen one would keep a large animal – like a tiger or a bear. Whatever had been inside the cage had clearly escaped and eliminated some of its captors in the process.

"What the hell did this, hon?" Kristen asked as she absentmindedly fingered a series of tears in the passenger's side door.

"Kristen, don't touch anything! You don't want your prints all over this thing," Teddy cautioned his wife. "Besides, you're going to infect yourself with God knows what if you cut yourself on that door!"

The petite young woman tore her hand away like it had gotten burned and held it to her chest, a small whimper escaping her as she did so. She

Dustin Dreyling
Wendigo vs. Lizard Man: War of the Appetites
Duel of the Monsters Volume 2

looked at her finger, making sure she had not invited disease into her body by touching the damaged door. Satisfied that such a thing was averted, her hand returned to her chest, and she looked back at Teddy.

"Teddy... what were they keeping in here?" Kristen asked and noticed what her man was already investigating.

He was eyeballing a wide smear of blood that started by the ruined cage and ended at the rear opening of the cargo van. The smell of the drying substance was nauseating, and Kristen nearly lost her breakfast when the sickening scent reached her olfactories.

"It looks like someone was dragged off into the woods," Teddy said calmly.

He pointed to the splashes of gore that trailed from the back of the truck into the thick pine forest that was the dominant foliage in this part of Minnesota. Kristen spotted a pile of guts ten feet from the truck, partially hidden by long grass, and promptly coated the shoulder of the back road with her own half-digested pancakes and eggs.

Then she showed the organ pile to her husband as she grabbed his shoulder with a grip like a vise. He winced in pain at her clutch before he too retched all over the place at the ghastly sight. The ill man barely had time to finish before Kristen was pulling him away from the smelly area.

"Let's get the fuck out of here, Teddy!" Panic and fear had crept into her voice, and it made Teddy's blood run cold. "We can call the cops once we're anywhere but here!"

They ran to the Town Car and quickly got in, and he wasted no time in starting the aging boat of a car. Teddy locked all the doors before he peeled out from the shoulder, heading towards their destination with a manic determination. Neither of them had cell reception in this neck of the woods, which made alerting the authorities impossible until they came across a landline.

The couple drove for about ten minutes before an old gas station appeared on the right side of the road. Ancient signs for everything from gas to soda pop covered the tiny building's exterior. The largest was a faded Dr. Pepper sign asking, *"Wouldn't you like to be a Pepper, too?"* Teddy pulled into the lot slowly, his nerves frayed and causing things to appear as if they were in slow motion.

Dustin Dreyling
Wendigo vs. Lizard Man: War of the Appetites
Duel of the Monsters Volume 2

A single pickup truck was parked next to the big white propane tank in front of the little shack that contained the apparatus for filling compressed cylinders. Flammable warnings covered the tiny box of a metal shed with a rusting door. A sun-weathered "fire extinguisher inside" sticker screamed for attention in the top right corner, wrinkled from the rust pitting that was no doubt underneath. The ancient main building and small island of gas pumps were likewise embracing dilapidation… or antique status.

"What a shithole," Teddy said as he pulled up in front of the pump farthest from the propane tank and killed the engine.

They both got out and hurried inside the small convenience store. An elderly man with one of the most wrinkled faces Kristen had ever seen sat behind the counter, staring at them like they were space aliens coming to abduct him. The concern in his eyes radiated the distrust he had of these two city slickers before him as they frantically explained what they had seen along the side of the road. The man listened quietly to their ravings, then dismissed them with a wave of his hand.

"Are you kids on the Mary Jane or something?" he spat, incredulous with their story. "I know that garbage is legal in Colorado, but this is Minnesota. We don't do drugs around here. I hope you ain't bringing the 'Rona in here, either. Prolly hand me a death sentence, if ya did."

"Mister, you gotta call the cops!" Teddy said in his most commanding tone, ignoring the old guy's delusional statement. "Somebody was murdered back there! By something horrible!"

"Some*thing?*" the elderly man asked, his question dripping with sarcasm. "What, like the *Boogeyman*? Grow up, kids. You damn millennials are ruining this country."

"Look, pal," Kristen said. "Someone is either hurt or dead ten miles back, and the last thing we need is this shit baby boomer attitude from you! We aren't even millennials! Now, will you please call the cops?"

"I'll do no such thing, you little twat," the old guy growled, his face reddening with anger. "Now get out of here before you make me mad!" He pointed back at the rack of rifles and shotguns on the wall behind the counter, looking very possibly locked and loaded.

"Let's get out of here, Kristen. We can call the cops when we get to the ranch," Teddy said as he tugged on her arm.

Dustin Dreyling
Wendigo vs. Lizard Man: War of the Appetites
Duel of the Monsters Volume 2

Kristen was extremely upset. Tears had begun to run down her face from the frustration of dealing with this relic of a man from a different time and place. She looked at Teddy and nodded, and together they hurried out of the store.

Once they were back in the Town Car, Kristen checked the bars on her cell phone before buckling her seat belt. Teddy, already buckled, put the car in drive and pulled out of the decrepit station, resuming their route to the Patrick family ranch, which surely had a landline. They would be certain to mention the uncooperative asshole at the gas station that time forgot, as well.

***

"Gawddamn kids," the old man said, watching out the window as their car pulled back onto the road and carried the hopheads away from his business. "What a horrible thing to joke about."

A loud crash came from the back room of the tiny building, causing him to reflexively grab a shotgun off the wall before he went to investigate the noise.

It was probably those damn hopheads, they must have doubled back on foot, he thought, simple logic escaping him in his anger and decades of loving all three wise men – Jim, Jack, and Johnny. *I'll give them a good scare with this .12 gauge!*

He grabbed the doorknob and stopped, mid-turn. A hissing noise on the other side pricked up his ears, causing him to grip the pump on his gun tighter. He jacked a round of birdshot into the weapon, the sound deafening in the silence of the little room. A smell like rotten eggs and piss suddenly hit him like a ton of bricks, and the old guy retched as he stumbled back from the door a few feet to steady himself against the counter.

The door to the back room blew open, the latch splintering into fragments as it was hit by the force on the other side. He reeled back in surprise, raising his free arm to protect his face from the flying chunks of wood. When he looked up, his eyes nearly popped out of his head at what stood in the doorway.

Dustin Dreyling
Wendigo vs. Lizard Man: War of the Appetites
Duel of the Monsters Volume 2

The old man squealed in fear as something evil – something that could not be one of God's creations – stepped through the busted wood frame. The thing's jaws drooled as it stared hungrily at its next meal. Scaly claws wrapped around the old man's throat, cutting off the air from his lungs. The shotgun clattered uselessly to the floor as his strength gave out and the green abomination pulled his head towards its serrated teeth that were already covered in blood.

***

Less than an hour later, they both had nearly forgotten about the wreck and the blood and guts all over everything. Of course, there was the ridiculous, stereotypical old man straight out of a crappy movie from the twentieth century. The surrealness of it made it so easy for the couple to disengage, especially with their usually distant friends waiting just down the road for them.

Teddy turned down the long drive for the Patrick family's ranch. The Lincoln proceeded slowly down a gravel-covered road that meandered between several copses of trees both deciduous and coniferous. About twenty yards from the house, a paved driveway began. The black tarmac led them to a small parking lot underneath some maple trees that were beginning to bud with helicopter seeds.

"There's Addy's car," Kristen said, pointing at a compact. "And there's James' truck."

James was one of Teddy's friends from his high school football team. About four years ago, his friend had called Teddy out of the blue and asked him to be in his wedding. After reconnecting with his old school chum and his new husband, Jack, they had become good friends all over again.

Kristen had also taken to James and his beau. Contentedly childless, there were many nights where Teddy would kiss her goodbye and send her off to party with the two men, amazed at how he would still get a pang of jealousy despite knowing better. He would always just chalk it up to fragile male ego and move on, and never told his wife about his ridiculous insecurities. He was just happy she wasn't friends with any

Dustin Dreyling
Wendigo vs. Lizard Man: War of the Appetites
Duel of the Monsters Volume 2

raging sluts. Well... except for Addison Patrick, their host for the weekend.

Right on cue, Addison exited the front door of the huge house at the head of the driveway. The curly-haired woman was all smiles, waving like a little kid in a corny Japanese monster movie. Teddy used to laugh at them during *Super Scary Saturday,* hosted by Grandpa Munster, when he was a kid. She had a wide face with big eyes and the childhood memories flooding back caused her to remind him of one of the cheesiest kaiju ever, Godzilla's ugly ass son. When he was seven, he was plagued by nightmares for a week after first seeing the hideous bugger one rainy Saturday morning.

And now it was gaping like a jackass and waving at him from the front porch.

Kristen would kill me if she knew what I just thought.

His realization brought a smirk to his face, as Kristen got out of the car and ran up to Addison as she stood on the stairs. The two women embraced, and Addison said something to Kristen that caused her to half glance in his direction before she busted out in laughter. Addison joined her, both women snorting in the process, which caused them to laugh harder.

Oh joy, it's going to be one of those *weekends,* Teddy thought.

Addison had a tendency to bring out the worst in his wife, almost always at his expense. They would harass the hell out of him, and he and Kristen had gotten into fights on more than one occasion because of it. The tiffs were frequently exacerbated by Addison's presence, her mischievous grin always succeeding in stoking the flames of Teddy's rage from their excessive ribbing.

He got out of the vehicle, noticing the two other cars parked in the lot. One was obviously a farmer's truck, with its huge bed and enormous all-terrain tires. Mud flaps caked in drying muck mixed with grass told of the vehicle's recent excursion into the pasture just beyond the house. A single horse and rider galloped around the back acreage casually, getting in one last ride before nightfall. The helmeted woman riding the horse was likely Addison's mother, Anastasia.

Teddy had never met the woman, nor had Kristen, but Addison talked about her mother's love of horses quite often. Judging by the full

Dustin Dreyling
Wendigo vs. Lizard Man: War of the Appetites
Duel of the Monsters Volume 2

riding regalia the woman wore, their friend was clearly not joking about that love. Anastasia saw him looking in her direction and waved happily at him as she rounded the bend one last time and led the horse back down to the far end of the field. He involuntarily waved back, even though she was no longer looking at him.

Behind him, fresh fits of laughter erupted from Addison and Kristen. Teddy turned to see them looking at him again. His face reddened, and when Addison mocked him with a dramatic farce of the greeting gesture, he felt his blood pressure rise. His middle finger extended, and he thrust his retort towards the women. This, of course, only fueled their guffaws. For the briefest of seconds, he craved a cigarette, something he had not wanted since the last time they had hung out with Addison.

"Teddy!"

He looked up to see James and Jack standing on the porch, both holding bottles of beer.

Thank God. Teddy waved at them once and headed towards the house, ignoring both women as he passed. Kristen giggled.

"Aww, we hurted his feewings," she mocked.

Ignoring his wife, he ascended the steps and shook the hands of both men on the porch. Jack grabbed a beer off the table behind him, cracking the cap off before handing it to Teddy.

"Here ya go, pal, and ignore those two," Jack said reassuringly as Teddy took the sweating bottle of pilsner. "Addy is just jealous of you because she's in love with your wife."

Addison shot Jack an evil look full of hate, but quickly went back to listening to whatever hushed words Kristen was sharing with her. Jack chuckled softly.

"See?" he asked.

Teddy laughed. "Oh, I'm aware," he said. "She'd have already left me if she wasn't straight."

"You sure about that, Theodore?" Kristen's face was an angry scowl, as she reached her arm around Addison. "I'm sure I could get used to it." Addison beamed at him, pure mirth in her eyes.

"Would you all please chill out?" James' voice boomed in their ears, the stern tone in his voice silencing everyone. "We came here for a good time this weekend, did we not?"

Dustin Dreyling
Wendigo vs. Lizard Man: War of the Appetites
Duel of the Monsters Volume 2

The dark-haired man's eyes looked from person to person until all four of them met his gaze. Addison was the only one who kept it until he broke the eye contact. The look on her face was darker than it had been a second ago, and gooseflesh tore up James' arms. *God, she is creepy,* he thought. Then the woman's visage blossomed in a genuinely happy face before she replied.

"Of course, James. That *is* what we are here for, after all," Addison giggled. She looked at Teddy. "I'm sorry, Teddy. Friends?" She held up her fingers in a peace sign and batted her eyelashes in an obvious fashion at him.

"Yeah, sure, whatever," Teddy said before upending his bottle of beer and gulping down its remaining contents. He set the container down on the table by the door Jack had retrieved it from and walked into the house with his bags, adding one last thing before disappearing inside. "You can bring Kristen's bags in, okay, *friend?*"

Addison looked at Kristen, and both women turned to look at the three suitcases Teddy had pulled out of the back seat and placed on the ground when he had gotten out of the car.

"Really, Kristen? Three fucking suitcases for a weekend?"

"What? I never know what I'm going to need when I'm up North," Kristen said, playing innocent.

"Don't give me that bullshit," Addison replied. "You've lived in this state all of your life."

The wavy-haired young woman walked over to the suitcases and picked up two of them by their handles. As she passed Kristen on the way towards the house, she nodded her head back towards the remaining piece of luggage.

"You can get that last one, bitch."

***

Two hours later, after remembering and reliving the ghastly scene on the side of the road with everyone, Teddy made a useless phone call to some skeptical local police on the Addison family's phone. Then they all settled down to dinner at the huge dining room table.

Dustin Dreyling
Wendigo vs. Lizard Man: War of the Appetites
Duel of the Monsters Volume 2

The large furniture sat in the middle of everything on the first floor of the open air house. From where they were seated, they could all see the living room, the stairs to the second floor, and all the way into the kitchen. The smell of spaghetti sauce was thick in the air as they took turns passing around a plate piled with garlic bread, a huge bowl of noodles, and a two-handled pot of the tantalizing sauce.

Addison's mother, Anastasia, joined them, along with her grandmother, Eloise. Anastasia had pulled the old woman up to the table in her rocking chair. Her elderly mother's feet were swinging enthusiastically like an antsy child's. The frail old woman's eyes were alight with excitement at the ensuing meal, and she licked her lips with her tongue.

James regretted looking at it sliming her thin, wormlike lips for a second longer than he should have, a twinge of disgust hitting his gut like a stick poking him in the belly.

He looked at Jack next to him, his husband sporting a similar look of veiled repulsion. Teddy had a similar reaction, but kept his face emotionless, afraid of his wife's wrath, should she see him grimace.

A low chuckle caught the three men's ears, and they looked at Addison, who was very much noticing both James and Jack's discomforts with her grandmother's hungry display. Then she took the bowl of noodles from her mother and dropped a few slotted spoonfuls onto her plate before passing the bowl to Kristen. Once everyone's plates were full, Anastasia stood up again, a wine glass in her hand. She raised the transparent goblet of shiraz over her head.

"A toast! To my father, Mason Patrick, who has made all this possible, even if he's not with us," she said, turning to look at the painted portrait on the wall behind her.

The angry looking fellow in the picture had the kind of beard that would be home on *Game of Thrones*, with eyes that seemed to bore into everyone who looked at them. The two couples both felt their blood run cold at the sight, even Kristen, who had known the family for at least a decade.

"To Mason," Addison cheered, raising her own glass of wine.

Kristen followed, her glance prompting her husband to follow suit. James and Jack soon joined them, and they all toasted in unison.

Dustin Dreyling
Wendigo vs. Lizard Man: War of the Appetites
Duel of the Monsters Volume 2

"To Mason!"

"Now, so it will please my mother, Eloise," Anastasia said. "She will say Grace. Mom?"

She looked at the wrinkled woman, rocking away in her chair. Eloise realized she was being spoken to and looked up at her daughter, the creaking chair ceasing its repetitive movement. A look of confusion spread across her parchment-like visage before she suddenly seemed to understand. Eloise's face lit up before she spoke, yellowed teeth very visible in the incandescent lights of the dining room.

"Rub a dub dub, thanks fer the grub!"

They all cheered at the senile woman's prayer and dug in.

***

When dinner was ended, Anastasia took the empty plates to the kitchen and returned with after dinner mints. She placed one in front of each of them before unwrapping a final piece and giving it to her mother, who slurped it down quickly. Just as their host was about to sit back down, a pounding fist beat furiously on the front door, startling everyone but Eloise. The old woman had clearly heard it, however, for her face came alive with joy.

"He's here! He's here!" she chanted, wriggling in her chair, impatiently.

Anastasia got up and walked slowly to the door. Every one of her guests were wearing rictuses of uncertainty bordering on fear as she saw to the loud nighttime visitor. Addison's mom flung the door open once she saw who stood outside, backing up several steps and gasping at the same time. The musky smell of a furry mammal struck all their senses just as Anastasia stepped out of their view.

The form in the doorway entered the house hunched over, its immense form needing to stoop to get through the portal. Then it stood up fully. Long, shaggy white fur covered the thing's rippling muscles. Its body structure was disturbingly human yet stood a yard taller than the average male, the beast clearly being of that gender. The malevolent thing's hands and feet sported wicked talons – most decidedly *not* human-like. Neither was the drooling mouth full of sharp, protruding

Dustin Dreyling
Wendigo vs. Lizard Man: War of the Appetites
Duel of the Monsters Volume 2

canines. The beast gnashed his teeth together as he took another step into the house. The strong step shook the floor.

Teddy felt the vibrations through both of his feet. His bowels clenched up on him, threatening a very inopportune need to use the restroom.

"What... the... hell?" Jack stammered, grabbing James' hand on the table, and squeezing until he sucked in a lungful of air from the scared iron grip.

The hulking thing took another room-shaking step towards Anastasia, his blank stare fixed on the four dinner guests. With each step the wendigo took towards them, Kristen whimpered a little each time. Finally, the ivory-furred beast stood in front of Addison's mother. She shrieked a single word at the monstrous creature in front of her, and what she managed to utter made things instantly seem so much worse for the four guests.

"Daddy!" Anastasia screamed exuberantly.

Eloise began to cackle madly from her rocking chair, clapping her hands excitedly. "Mason's home!" she yelled.

Then with a bellowing roar, the monster charged.

The dinner party fled the table, all four guests running towards the kitchen and the back door. His thunderous steps closed the distance between him and the fleeing humans in three strides. The wendigo snatched Kristen by her hair, yanking the woman back and tossing her to the floor.

Teddy instantly spun around in fear for his wife's life. The monster's huge palm latched onto his face, its nails digging into his scalp and causing him to screech like a horror movie scream queen. Blood poured down the man's face from the puncture wounds created by the jagged talons, soaking his shirt in seconds. Teddy screamed obscenities at the thing as the wendigo dragged his victim close to his body in a wicked embrace.

The creature's maw opened wide right before he bit down into the man's exposed neck. A wet tearing sound was barely audible over Kristen's screams as she watched the monster rip her husband's neck apart with its teeth – both the carotid artery and jugular vein torn open in one bite. Crimson ichor gushed freely from the ragged hole in

Dustin Dreyling
Wendigo vs. Lizard Man: War of the Appetites
Duel of the Monsters Volume 2

Teddy's neck. His head threatened to fall off its body from the lack of connective tissues still holding it on. With a few pathetic gurgles, he went limp in the arms of the monster known as Mason.

"Teddy!" Kristen wailed, as Addison jumped up on the table.

As Eloise continued to cackle from her rocking chair, the youngest member of the Patrick family ran to the edge and dove off the far side, rocketing into her supposed friend of ten years. The bigger woman smashed into Kristen, taking them both to the ground.

Addison threw a flurry of punches at Kristen, pummeling the woman's face to a bloody, bruised lump of flesh in seconds. All the while, she screamed incoherently. Teddy lay motionless under the wendigo's prodigious mass. The white-furred monster continued taking bites out of the dead man's flesh, gulping it down loudly. His fur was stained red with Teddy's life fluid, and the wendigo smacked his lips together as he gobbled down bits of the man's left pectoral muscle.

All the while, Eloise cackled, her daughter Anastasia joining in as they both watched the carnage unfolding before them.

James picked up a plate from the island in the middle of the kitchen. He wound up and threw it like a frisbee at Addison with all his might. The ceramic dinnerware shot through the air like a Yeti Pro Aviar – James and Jack were both adept disc golfers – and hit Addison right in her nose. The crunch of the cartilage was sickening to the man who threw the improvised weapon. Addison screamed and fell off Kristen, holding her gushing nose with both hands, as she desperately tried to staunch the blood cascading down her face.

The wendigo got up from Teddy's corpse and charged at James and Jack in the kitchen. The men both began to throw plate after plate at the rushing beast, most of the projectiles shattering uselessly on the floor. Before he could get his jaws on them, a fetid smell hit them all, stopping the wendigo in his tracks and causing everyone else to retch. A sibilant hiss rose in volume from the still open front door, until it was almost a roar.

The wendigo spun around to see who had interrupted his gruesome feast, but a green blur slammed into him before he could tell what it was. Sharp talons raked across his ivory face and chest, as serrated teeth ripped a chunk of white-furred meat from the wendigo's shoulder. The

Dustin Dreyling
Wendigo vs. Lizard Man: War of the Appetites
Duel of the Monsters Volume 2

downed monster shook his stunned senses clear and looked up at the scaly thing on top of him.

"Holy shit!" Anastasia cried out. *"Daddy! No!"*

The creature atop the wendigo was some kind of lizard man. The abomination's head was a pair of big eyes positioned over a blunted snout, reminiscent of a monitor lizard or Komodo dragon, but partially human in appearance. Jack's half-shocked brain managed to get a memory flash of a magazine article he had read that discussed what a human that had evolved from dinosaurs instead of apes would have looked like. The bipedal monstrosity they were all looking at was the spitting image of the picture in the article.

"Thank God they're fighting," Jack mumbled to himself, but James heard and nodded, both men in a stupor from the impossible duel of the monsters occurring right before their eyes.

The wendigo tore the lizard man off with a wet ripping sound and blindly threw the snapping creature. The scaly monster sailed across the room before crashing into Eloise, silencing her cackles as it crushed both her and her rocking chair.

The wendigo roared in rage at what he had just done, as some part of the monster's mind that was still Mason Patrick was aware that he had just inadvertently murdered his elderly wife. The lizard man jumped to its feet, lowering itself into a crouch as it trained its eyes on the competition. Without breaking eye contact with the wendigo, the reptilian thing pulled Eloise's motionless form to its jaws… and bit off the woman's head. It shook clenched jaws back and forth like a dog until the head tore free in a gout of blood and tissue. Then it spat the head into its hands, holding it tauntingly, like some sick prize.

James and Jack made for the back door in the kitchen. They had no choice but to give up on rescuing Kristen with the two monstrous combatants duking it out between them. Addison was still laying prone on the floor, and her mother was cowering near her, sobbing over her murdered mother.

"Kill him, Daddy! He killed Momma!" Anastasia screamed at her inhuman father.

The wendigo rushed at the reptilian hominid, who was just standing there, waiting for him. Before he plowed into the lizard man, it threw

Dustin Dreyling
Wendigo vs. Lizard Man: War of the Appetites
Duel of the Monsters Volume 2

Eloise's head at the hirsute monster, so fast the wendigo could not react in time to prevent the dead woman's hard skull from striking him directly in the face. The agony of his smashed nose made the wendigo's legs seem to get pulled out from under him, and the creature fell hard to the floor, taking out a couple of chairs from the dinner table with him.

Addison stirred on the floor moaning and holding the quickly darkening welt on her forehead. She rose to her elbows and looked around, seeing the green thing that had killed her grandmother for the first time. Then she saw Eloise's severed head laying near her monstrous grandfather's feet. Addison screamed, sadness and rage both behind her shriek.

Her attention elsewhere, Addison failed to see Kristen get up and run at her. The recently widowed woman kicked her former friend in the face *hard* stockinged feet. Kristen's cries of agony accompanied the loud crunch of the bones in her foot breaking as it slammed into Addison's cheek, but the damage to *that bitch's* face made it worth it.

Her big toe had sunk into the evil woman's eye socket in the strike, rupturing her ocular organ. The ruined orb gushed blood and aqueous humor as Addison's screams hit a pitch that hurt everyone's ears. Kristen limped-ran towards James and Jack. The two men were screaming at her to follow them as they were running for the back door.

The lizard man jumped off the wendigo just he reached out for its scaled throat. Bounding away from his stronger but slower opponent, the humanoid reptile pounced on Addison, knocking the injured woman to the floor. Anastasia screamed out for her daughter as the serrated teeth of the reptilian horror tore out her daughter's screaming throat, silencing her permanently.

Anastasia's screams turned to cries of bloodlust, as she picked up one of the remaining kitchen chairs and smashed it over the scaley-skinned monster's back while it tore at Addison's corpse. The chair splintered into a thousand pieces, the hit sending the beast sprawling onto the floor next to the dead woman.

"You motherfucker!" the remaining Patrick woman screamed as she swung her arm back to strike the lizard man again with the remaining piece of chair still in her grasp.

Dustin Dreyling
Wendigo vs. Lizard Man: War of the Appetites
Duel of the Monsters Volume 2

She pummeled it again and again, each strike doing little else other than preventing the murderous thing from rising back to its feet. Its tail shot out and struck the back of her knees, dropping Anastasia to the floor. In one fluid motion, it jumped back to its feet, returning to the same crouching position it had held before.

The wendigo's fist careened into the lizard's head, and the reptile-man was sent flying through the air again. This time, it crashed into the painting of Mason Patrick hanging on the wall, both portrait and monster landing in a motionless pile. The sound of a vehicle starting up outside caught the wendigo's attention, and it hurried outside to stop the panicked guests from fleeing.

Kristen, Jack, and James had made it out the back door and ran around the house to where their cars were parked. James fired up his truck as the other two got in, locking the passenger side door. He put the truck in reverse and started to back up so he was facing the end of the driveway. Leaping from the top step, the wendigo dropped down onto the bed of the pickup, the impact destroying the rear axle in the process. The truck's back end dropped to the ground, the front tires revolving uselessly in the air for a second before the truck dropped down again, and the engine died.

"Shit!" Jack yelled and looked behind them.

The back window exploded as a white fist tore through the back window, obliterating Jack's face and showering James and Kristen with sharp shards of glass. James screamed at his husband's pulpy remains as they slumped against the door, with Kristen matching him note for note with her own cries of terror.

With a frenzied, bellowing roar, the lizard man jumped onto its foe's back. The reptilian humanoid's jaws latched onto the meaty flesh of the white monster's bicep. The wendigo roared in pain and teetered for a second before falling off the ruined back end of the truck. The beasts landed in a heap on the tarmac driveway, the girth of the wendigo loudly breaking several of the lizard man's bones as the greater mass fell atop the smaller monster.

As the two survivors got out of the truck and ran as fast as they could with a limping Kristen, the wendigo continued to roar as the panicked lizard man flailed at the bigger monster pinning it to the earth. The furry

Dustin Dreyling
Wendigo vs. Lizard Man: War of the Appetites
Duel of the Monsters Volume 2

man-eater stood up, ignoring the pain of so many claws tearing into his back, the lizard man hanging on with its nails like a cat on a window screen. The green monster then put its jaws to work, snapping and biting the wendigo's back repeatedly.

Roaring in pain for the umpteenth time, the wendigo suddenly jumped straight up into the air, rising a good ten feet off the ground, before falling back to the ground. Without warning, the bigger beast angled his back towards the ground at the last millisecond, the wendigo's mass meeting the driveway hard enough to crush the smaller lizard man latched onto his back. A spray of gore burst out from underneath the larger monster as his body flattened the reptilian enemy. The lizard man's claws twitched three times, then fell still.

The wendigo got up from atop his destroyed foe, which caused the lizard man's decimated corpse to slide off his ivory-haired body. It hit the ground with a meaty thump, blood splattering the wendigo's furry legs.

The winner of the battle turned around and roared victoriously at the dead monster by its feet. Satisfied that the scaly thing was indeed dead, the wendigo listened for the engine of James' truck as it sped down the road away from the ranch. His daughter picked up on what he was doing.

"Don't worry, Daddy, no one will believe them," Anastasia said behind her monster of a father. "Help me clean up Momma and Addison's bodies, please?"

The wendigo's daughter became choked up with a new round of sobbing, and the monster went to his daughter, embracing her in a fatherly hug. They stood that way for a minute, Anastasia's sobs finally lessening, and she pulled away from the blood-stained beast that was her father.

"C'mon, Daddy. We have leftovers to put away," she said in a voice like an eight-year-old girl.

Father and daughter walked back towards the blood-drenched house, holding hands.

Behind them, the lizard man's corpse started to move.

Dustin Dreyling
Wendigo vs. Lizard Man: War of the Appetites
Duel of the Monsters Volume 2
END

SEA SERPENT VS. KRAKEN: RAGING WATERS – Brion Halloway

Brion Halloway
Sea Serpent vs. Kraken: Raging Waters
Duel of the Monsters Volume 2

SEA SERPENT VS. KRAKEN
RAGING WATERS
Brion Halloway

The many-armed leviathan stirred in the inky abyss of the Atlantic Ocean. The multiple tentacles moved lordly through the twilight depths as if subtly demonstrating its dominance. The massive cephalopod's glowing eyes cut through the darkness like a samurai sword in search of enemies to kill. Combining the most terrifying traits of a giant squid and octopus, the beast's body glided through the water.

Looking like a malformed torpedo, the torso cut through the water with a vicious thrust. The beast's black and white hide was marked by intelligent, discerning eyes which swivelled throughout the darkness. Tentacles measured 140 meters long with sinuous grabbing arms poised to strike from the darkness. Within the centre of the tentacles was a bone-rending beak waiting for unwilling prey to be carried into the literal meat-grinder.

What made the beast all the more terrifying was that its body looked simultaneously muscular yet deformed, its sinews twisted in indescribable ways. Parts of the creature's body seemed to twist while thorny protrusions rose towards its mantle. Two larger protrusions at the mantle formed a horn-like crown, giving the marine beast a devilish appearance. If light shined onto its skin, patches of blood-red color mixed with the black and white would show. Its tentacles contrasted with the monochrome hide, showing off the crimson hue. It looked as one might imagine the Devil would if he was born in the cephalopod family. If said zoological group had an answer for the description, it would be *"a monstrous king"* to rule the abyss.

If it had the ability to remember back through antiquity, the monstrous cuttle would recall vividly that its ancestors have killed many sailors from various countries. That name rippled through centuries, spreading an epidemic of terror to those who live near the oceans. The one name to describe it that all would recognize and quake in fear: *kraken!*

It was the king of the North Atlantic, an insatiable monarch with a lust for carnage. Its ancestors were much older than the dinosaurs... and more frightening. While the surface produced its own terrors, none throughout the ages came close to the ancestors of the horror which patrolled the watery abyss. The lineage of such monsters survived the

K/T Extinction and the evolution of mammalian predators. And to this day, its pedigree still thrives in the abyssal depths as the hidden kings of the deep. The Scandinavian people were right to fear it. Its species' power was capable of crushing large ships and bringing down Navy submarines.

The giant cephalopod paused as it saw huge broken shapes protruding from the bottom of a deep sea chasm. One dark, smooth, and rounded object stuck out. The rest was revealed to be cylindrical in shape and sequestered deep into the floor of the ocean. The otherwise tough hull of the submarine was crumpled like a soda pop can. Edges revealed the handiwork of immense strength and pressure which had sculpted it into the decrepit wreck.

Deep, penetrating slashes bore into the already life-infested interior which had innumerable, smaller nightmares living within. Giant circular marks marred the thick ferrous hull like a katana sword had cut into the armour of a knight.

The giant cuttlefish knew what this was: a naval submarine that was crushed and destroyed by one of its kin. It did not know why. But being among creatures who do not like their territory trespassed, the sub was likely dispatched. What was guaranteed is that the giant's species would have brought a brutal end to the weaponized marine craft.

And out of the darkness, skeletal bodies of the tiny humans were contorted in terror, shock, and despair. If they still had eyes, they would have the faces of children seeing an army of boogeymen.

Before the many-armed creature continued, it stopped. Its large eyes swivelled as if something was near in the abyssal depths. *Something that was not supposed to be there.* The kraken changed its skin texture and made itself look more fearsome than usual. It proceeded in the direction where the presence had clearly gone. The monstrous cephalopod realized this presence was something equally powerful, yet different – and it was coming its way.

A low, moaning roar came over the abyss, ringing through the kraken's immense boneless body. Every nerve tingled in alarm and confusion. Every movement of the eye looked for anything in the darkness. The ocular organ pierced the inky gorge and looked further to see the mystery intruder. Its first visual revealed a massive, snake-like shape darting hundreds of feet up, about 300 feet away from the kraken.

Seeing an opportunity in front of its eyes, the monster squid blasted towards the new intruder, ready to tear into it with cold, savage intent. Its rule in the northern waters had never been challenged – *until now.* And it was not going to give up its rule so easily. This newcomer would have two options: either defeat the kraken and prove itself worthy *or become the vanquished.*

***

The creature suddenly raised its long-neck and began probing the area around it. Its long, coiled body stopped undulating as its senses became aware that it was not the only beast in the area. It was not the sub-Arctic waters causing it to cease its travels. The frigid temperatures barely registered on its thick layers of hide; it could stand this level of cold. The icy waters were its natural habitat – so, that was not the problem at hand.

Before it knew where it was, the great spinosaurid had wandered into the domain of an unrevealed predator that was equally as powerful, and as prodigiously large. However, it did not have the best of luck when it came to seeing through the black depths. The creature's reptilian head swivelled through the water, its feathery gills letting oxygen course through its veins. It needed this infusion, too.

The giant sea beast felt increasingly on edge, like a tiger instinctively aware of another predator being present in thick foliage. Its smallish eyes squinted as it continued to scrutinize the ever-surrounding darkness of the abyss, alert like a hunter in search of deer.

The more it moved into the inky darkness, the more its unease grew slowly like moss on a wet rock. It was not possible for the newcomer creature to ignore it now. Through the abyss, its eerie light blue eyes scrutinized the ink-black depths half expecting to see something approaching. In fact, there was something coming towards it – something with tremendous speed.

Before it could react, something huge and dark plunged into the creature's serpentine body. The snake-like giant howled in both shock and pain as it felt the brunt of the hit. The force knocked it into one of many seamounts on the bottom and the serpent hurtled through hundreds of tons of rock. Thousands of giant boulders exploded into the open water and silt blasted forth like a huge mushroom cloud. The massive dust cloud spread for quite a distance before it finally started to settle.

Eyes wide, the massive serpent turned towards the multi-tentacled beast which had unceremoniously gotten its attention and growled at the opponent. The cloud of silt still blocked most of its vision and it was unable to discern what was left or right. It heard a deep growl coming from the other side of the seemingly infinite cloud of dusty sediment. The serpentine leviathan squinted as it looked into the cloud, anticipating any attack that might come its way.

It did not have to wait very long.

Something long and sinuous shot out of the silt-masked water and wrapped around the massive serpent with lightning speed. This new thing had an elongated diamond shaped grabber at the front with multiple serrated, circular suckers that resembled miniature mouths with teeth ready to pierce thick skin.

On the underside of the winding appendages, the leviathan saw a row of other sharp-ended, rounded objects. The leviathan knew what these were! It had faced down similar things throughout its sub-oceanic travels.

The titanic serpent growled in irritation and fury. If it were human, it would have said, *"Not this again!"*

***

The kraken tightened its grip in satisfaction. The battle would not take long – it had battled sea serpents in the past; this would not be any different.

Suddenly, the colossal cephalopod felt a massive tug from the victim's end turned into a pull. Within seconds it was flying in the direction of its "prey," only to find itself in the grasp of the serpent's powerful clawed hands. Panic filled the kraken's boneless body for the first time as the rope-like neck of the sea serpent swiftly lunged towards the tentacled monstrosity. Shocked, the kraken could do nothing as the snake-like giant's teeth dug into the monster squid's hide and tore off one of its tentacles. The water filled with blood that clouded the surrounding depths, making it difficult for the tentacled titan to see.

The kraken roared in frustration and – determined not to lose to the leviathan – lashed out with its grabbing tentacles. Two arms shot into the dark abyss and grabbed the serpent's head, taking complete control. The giant cuttle spun around, its grip tight around its reptilian foe, and with a mighty swing it threw the snake-like goliath into lighter waters. The serpent let out a shocked grunt as it sped through the depths like a rocket. Finally, it managed to stop and reverse its course. The great sea dragon's body twisted as it gained slack from the slowdown mid-water.

The serpentine leviathan looked around, expecting to be in dark water, and its eyes widened. The creature instead found itself in clear, sunlit waters. Orange and red from the setting sun blanketed the waters in a coral-colored reflection. For a moment, bliss ruled – until the serpent felt something grab its tail in an iron grip! The leviathan looked down to see the titanic squid fully emerge into the sun-drenched waters, a bad vibe jolting its lithe body.

As the devilishly horned kraken rose out of the water, its eyes began glowing like fiery coals in hellish rage as it caught sight of its opponent. If it were a human looking at the kraken, the sea serpent would swear the beast resembled nothing less than the combined offspring of the mythical Cthulhu and Scylla. Its tentacles lifted ominously into the open water and shot with blinding speed at the serpent. The great aquatic reptile barely managed to dodge the attack, nearly overwhelmed at the speed of its attacker. This was the first fight that pressured the snake-like leviathan into such evasive maneuvers in a long-time. But it knew that would all change momentarily.

As it evaded its opponent's attack, the serpent turned and hurled itself towards the kraken at the speed of a torpedo. Now it was its turn to shock the goliath squid! The serpent slammed into the kraken, which was unable to react in time, and the ensuing blow was greater than the huge cephalopod had anticipated.

In a blur of motion, the kraken spiralled further outwards towards the surface. The massive tentacled terror broke the surface with water blasting outwards. Foam and spray spread out like a massive blanket as ungodly waves rippled through the water. Among them, veritable tidal waves raged through the water like hungry demons from Hell.

The calm ocean surface was now a 360-degree tsunami moving outwards from the kraken, which plummeted back into the water. Before the giant squid could react, it felt a biting sensation on one of its tentacles. It was then yanked back beneath the surface, creating a large downward splash in the process.

With the kraken back in the water, the serpent lunged forward and coiled its massive body around the titanic cuttlefish. It threw a barrage of stinging claw strikes at its adversary's grotesque, ruby red body with its forelimbs. Each brutal scrape ripped into the thick hide of the squid and caused more blood to seep into the water. The kraken bellowed in pain and fury, now turning its attention to killing its opponent once and for all.

The kraken swiftly reached for the serpent, its enormous tentacles encircling its snake-like opponent and preparing to crush the beast. Feeling the tightening appendages around its body, the serpent slashed one of the squid's massive eyes, causing the cephalopod to roar in agony and tighten the grip of its arms.

A sudden crack in the serpent's back sent an intense alarm to the elongated titan's brain and immediately the great Sea Orm [1]grabbed the kraken's hide in its taloned hands. The claws dug deeper into the skin of its opponent in a vicious attempt to make the squid release its grip. The kraken felt more pain and unconsciously let go, the agony further fuelling its anger.

The serpent immediately swam swiftly towards the wounded eye of the kraken and its powerful toothy jaws dug into the orb-like organ. The colossal cephalopod flailed in pain as its eye was torn out by the

---

[1] Yep, that is Sea *Orm,* not a typo for "sea worm," and that name for sea serpents has been in use for centuries. The Great Norway Serpent was alternately referred to as the Sea Orm by the 16th century historian and cartographer Olaus Magnus, who put the serpent – along with numerous other fantastic giant sea beasts – on his famous 1539 map of Norway, the *Carta Marina.* He depicted the Sea Orm as being truly daikaiju-sized. The section of the map featuring the Sea Orm is reproduced below.

serpentine behemoth, which dangled like a gleaming ball-shaped mass in the creature's alligator-like jaws.

The kraken had now had enough of this. It turned around with an almighty swing of its arm and slammed it into the giant writhing reptile. The snake-like behemoth spiralled upwards and breached the surface of the water. Its massive body churned up the water to such a degree that even naval ships were unable to stand the force of the resulting waves.

These massive currents rose like a collective army of liquid warriors and raged across the surface of the ocean, seeking a place where they could crest and crash onto. As the waves went farther out, everything was quiet.

The giant serpent coiled and undulated vigorously as it tried to locate the kraken.

It witnessed nothing more than the vestiges of the setting sun shining on the surface; only seeing the water morphing from calm to chaotic, an almost mesmerizing display of fluidity and power.

Without warning, a wall of tentacles exploded out of the water, nearly all of them surrounding the serpentine monstrosity. The great Sea Orm reeled in shock, not expecting such a terrifying shift to occur. Huge undulating tentacles formed a twisted, nightmarish version of flower petals with teeth-like suckers pointing towards it. Sunlight started to dim into a black nightmare as the serpent faced a wall of inward-pointing sucker blades. The elongated beast looked for any possible way out of this nightmarish situation.

Finally, the sea serpent saw a space where two smaller tentacles were trying to cover it and the writhing beast promptly sprang from the space towards the opening. Just as it did so, all the tentacles crashed down like a group of giant cobras lunging for their prey. They acted like living vines, all trying to find the creature attempting to escape their murderous intent. The kraken realized the serpent was escaping. Its strongest arms turned and blitzed towards the fleeing reptilian titan, seeking to ensnare their enemy. At the last moment, the Sea Orm leaped from the tentacled wall into the watery depths, all amidst a sunset.

Now it was the serpent's turn to get angry. *Very* angry.

The snake-like behemoth dive-bombed the kraken at astounding speed, murderous intent replacing intelligence for the time being. The impact blew the kraken hard into the water, causing a shockwave throughout the abyss. A massive wave resulted from the blow. Immediately the kraken retaliated, every tentacle shooting like a pit of vipers leaping at their prey. The serpent weaved through the attacking tentacles with remarkable ease and agility for a creature of its size.

The now single-eyed kraken noticed the charge and got out of the way of its snake-like attacker – and promptly *disappeared*. The giant Sea Orm suddenly looked around, shocked that its opponent seemingly vanished yet angered it would make such a cowardly move. The serpentine leviathan roared into the water, daring its opponent to continue their fight. The giant reptile looked to its right, then to its left. It looked up and down and every conceivable direction – but still no sign of its multi-armed adversary.

SLAM!

The serpent was knocked back from a vicious blow to the right side. The assault came out of nowhere but was harder than anything the titanic reptile had felt up to that point; so much so that the snake-like monster struggled to keep its composure. The leviathan was disoriented, and its eyes were blurred from the force of the attack.

WHAM!

Another blow came from behind the coiling colossus and this time the sheer viciousness of the attacks had definitely increased. It felt like a massive boulder slammed into its body at the speed of a rocket. The writhing behemoth was blown forward, again disoriented yet feeling angry at its predicament. Its eyes swivelled carefully for any sign of movement in its sight, remaining perfectly silent as it tried to focus.

The small feeling of movement heading towards its head prompted the serpent to dodge upwards – only for it to be hit over the head. The behemoth started to anticipate an attack from every direction, trying not to overreact. The sensation of movement from directly below prompted it to suddenly move to the right, only for it to sense an incoming blow from the left.

The sea serpent managed to dodge just as a sensation whizzed past its head. It heard grunting and hissing in the water, and *it was close*. The leviathan growled. Its opponent was toying with it and the great Orm of the Sea did not care for such manipulative behaviour. It bared its teeth in anger and looked closely at everything around it.

Suddenly, against the fading sunset light, it saw the bare outline of a sinuous something rushing towards it. The serpentine colossus instinctively dodged the incoming object and lunged to where the near-invisible tentacle was and grabbed hold of it. The extendible arm suddenly became apparent as the texture, color, and flesh transitioned from near-invisible to fully opaque.

As the serpent observed, tiny circle-like organs changed the colors from transparent to its natural dark reddish color. The snake-like monster tightened its jaw's grip on the tentacle and tore it from the squid's body, the severed extremity writhing spasmodically even after being ripped off. An angry, pained roar reverberated through the waters – *the Sea Orm was very close.* Another tentacle shot out, but the sunlight and angle made it stand out.

In a flash, the leviathan caught the next tentacle in its claws and bit hard into the flesh of the appendage, tearing out ample chunks and spilling blood into the water. Even more tentacles came towards the serpent, prompting the elongated beast to weave through them all – but the intensity of the attacks was increasing.

The sea serpent clawed and bit all the other tentacles before hurtling in the direction from which they came. Whichever of the multiple limbs were originally going towards the snake-like giant suddenly pulled back as if the kraken realized what its opponent was doing. Too late, however, as the serpent slammed into the kraken's face!

The camouflage wore off as the body of the kraken became fully visible, now reeling from the tremendous blow. The giant squid was sent careening towards a nearby seamount and crashed into its jagged peak. The impact could be heard from the surface and sounded as if a nuke had exploded underwater. A shockwave blew towards the leviathan which merely curled up to cover itself from debris.

Boulder-sized chunks hurtled outwards and smashed other nearby seamounts. A huge dust cloud formed and rippled across the ocean floor. It whipped up rubble, shipwrecks, and carcasses of god-forsaken beasts like a raging torrent.

Finally, the explosion-like collision and its effects subsided. The aquatic serpent could see much better as the silt and debris cleared. It saw the wounded kraken rising from the murky cloud of sediment. The shattered peak of the seamount and the impact crater created from the crash were showing clearly nearby. The serpentine leviathan bared its teeth as if to mock its wounded opponent, now slowly moving towards it in exhaustion.

The kraken threateningly approached the serpent. The sun began to go down behind the horizon for the night, its rays weakening into coral and orange colors, welcoming the end of the day.

The massive Sea Orm felt it in its enormous scaly gut: *the end was approaching.* And at the end of it, only *one* can be the survivor.

The kraken then struck, two longer tentacles snaking at missile speed, a blur against the weakening sunlight. The serpent acted on pure instinct and dodged the oncoming arms. The writhing behemoth then suddenly swung its long tail downwards and countered the undulating grabbers, just enough time for more counters. The leviathan slammed into the kraken, tearing off a portion of the multi-armed monstrosity's hide.

The kraken roared in pain but countered the serpent's attacks by coiling multiple tentacles around the Sea Orm's body, fully intent on crushing the life out of its foe. Before the coiling appendages could sufficiently tighten, however, the serpent weaved out of their grasp and threw multiple claw strikes and tail-whips at the giant squid. These attacks were only tidbits of the whirlwind of physical brutality which the snake-like titan brought to bear on its foe, and the squid's blood stained the water all around them. Then the kraken sped towards the serpent and a massive beak came projecting out of the center!

The razor-sharp parrot-like bill dug into the mid-section of the serpent's body and tore right into its scaly hide. The great Orm growled in agony, barely keeping itself from feeling the pain by focusing hard on the kraken. The monster squid's beak went to take another swift and vicious bite. For its part, the serpent jumped for a body part on the kraken it knew would cause serious damage.

The sea serpent's clawed hand reached for the remaining eye of the kraken. Just as it was about to grab and rip into it, the giant cephalopod's tentacles coiled tightly around the snake-like titan's body and threw it down towards a seamount. The serpent was stunned as it violently smashed into the underwater mountain, after which the kraken blasted towards the marine saurian.

The serpent was taken aback by the speed of the tentacled behemoth, only to realize the mistake it had made. Too late to react, the snake-like giant braced itself for impact from the giant squid. The kraken let out a near-Biblical bellow which rippled through the water. Up above, the water churned as tsunamis formed and created rogue waves on the surface.

The kraken smashed the serpent into the seamount. The blast fractured the mountainous rock formation into huge chunks of debris that fled into the open water. The sooty cloud ensuing from the impact rippled across the ocean floor like a nuclear shockwave, tearing up everything in its path. The remains of ancient shipwrecks were thrown into the briny depths and mega-boulders were blasted across the sea floor like underwater meteorites. As the shockwave rippled through the water, the mighty squid gave an unholy snarl at the serpent pinned under the tentacled terror's weight.

The kraken's beak shot in and out at intervals, trying to bite the dodging serpent it had pinned against the underwater mountain. The snake-like beast whipped its head left and right, trying to outdo the vicious, crazed biting of the beak. The colossal cuttlefish was tired of the fight and growled in annoyance and irritation. Besides, the serpent would not last much longer, and it wanted to end this creature's existence now.

In a blind fit of rage, the kraken floated upwards, pulling its beak backwards into its head for the final kill. But in the giant squid's rage it did not account for one critical thing. The sea serpent, which was pinned against the rocky seamount, retaliated.

The giant reptile swiftly coiled its lower body and tail where the head portion of its torpedo-shaped opponent was – effectively creating a death-trap. An enraged roar issued from the reptilian titan; its snake-like face contorted with thirst for more of its opponent's blood. The kraken realized how helpless it was as the goliath serpent delivered the final blow.

In one swift motion, the mighty Sea Orm lunged right into the kraken's siphon located just above and between its eyes. The monster cephalopod shrieked in pain as its opponent tore into its brain, ripping myriad pieces of the delicate organ out of the giant cephalopod's torpedo-shaped body A cloud of blood filled the surrounding depths as the deadly scarlet colossus tried its best to continue fighting.

Then the kraken went limp as its massive body started to sink towards the ocean bottom, only to be grabbed by the gaping maw of the serpent. The great Sea Orm dragged the fallen squid upwards and in one spectacular display, threw it over the ocean surface.

The tentacled corpse created almighty crashes in the water before it came to a dead stop. The enormous carcass lay still in the water as the sea serpent's crocodilian head watched from the surface. Before it could be seen, the serpent slipped back into the depths where it could reign as the ruling monster king of the sea.

***

The sea serpent was victorious, and it was happy to receive its reward: an expanded territory. The beast undulated gracefully through the water in search of a place to convalesce while the multiple wounds it had taken in the battle healed. The snake-like goliath moved out of the sunlit waters and into the inky depths, the light casting a warm glow onto its scaly skin. The leviathan gurgled in pleasure and relief as something akin to a small smile formed on its face. It was good to see that life was not always about fighting to the death or trying to survive. Sometimes it was the little moments that counted.

However, as it wriggled into the deep blue sea it felt as if it was being watched by an unknown presence. The sea serpent thus made its way further into the depths where it could not be seen. The last thing the beast needed was to get into another fight when the wounds on its body indicated it had to take the time to heal.

As it did so, the creature stopped and cocked its head. It heard a whirring sound in the distance indicating the presence of something keeping a hawk-eye watch. The leviathan turned towards the direction where the sound emanated and squinted in the hope of catching sight of its source.

In the darkness, faint lights creeped closer, the whirring sound now more mechanical in nature. Then a group of gargantuan silhouettes appeared. They were shaped like manta rays, but more mechanized in appearance. From their wings, signs of bubbles in a vortex could be seen and the distinct whirring had grown louder. The front portion of each construct had a transparent, smooth surface with what appeared to be figures looking out into the darkness of the lower depths. The sea serpent did not see any weapons, but it would not be surprised if the manta-shaped vessels were armed.

And besides, it was not about to find out whether they had weapons or not. The great Sea Orm did a very uncharacteristic thing: it turned away from the manta-things and swam away into the darkness of the abyss.

The fighting could wait until another day.

THE END – FOR NOW!

The Sea Orm, a.k.a., Great Norway Serpent, on Olaus Magnus's *Carta Marina* circa 153

Robert E. Wronski, Jr.
Man-Beast vs. Swamp Monster: A Battle in the Green
Duel of the Monsters Volume 2

MAN-BEAST VS. SWAMP MONSTER: A BATTLE IN THE GREEN – Robert E.
Wronski, Jr.

Robert E. Wronski, Jr.
Man-Beast vs. Swamp Monster: A Battle in the Green
Duel of the Monsters Volume 2

Robert E. Wronski, Jr.
Man-Beast vs. Swamp Monster: A Battle in the Green
Duel of the Monsters Volume 2

Within the swamp, goes the local legend, there is a Heap… a man-monster who protects the swamp. But behind every legend is a kernel of truth…

The Heap watches from afar. The men come. The men who work for Doctor Arcanus Cabal. Cabal is an enemy of the Heap. His creator. His murderer.

Today, the usual men of arcane science and the men with guns are accompanied in their boats by someone new. A scientist? They call him Bradford. He is not like them. He is nervous. Naive, but curious.

The Heap watches, but he does nothing. They are not harming the swamp for now, but Cabal must always be watched.

***

Daylight has faded into darkness. The Heap of the swamp rests, until a noise is heard. Running through his waters. It is the man… Bradford. His clothes are torn. The men with guns give chase. The Heap concentrates, and around those angry men the greenery grows and entangles them, enough to allow Bradford to escape. The men know how this happened. They know when they are being warned. They will go back for now. But Cabal will not let this rest.

***

Daybreak. The men return. This time, Cabal accompanies them. He warns, in his Australian accent, that Bradford is more than he seems.

***

Afternoon. A local guide and another stranger. He is a reporter. He calls himself Jack. The other calls him profanities under his breath.

"So, this newspaper, what was it? *The Chronicle? The INS? The Weekly World News?*"

"*The Register…?*"

"Yeah, that's it! You say they'll pay me if we catch this thing?"

Robert E. Wronski, Jr.
Man-Beast vs. Swamp Monster: A Battle in the Green
Duel of the Monsters Volume 2

"Yes… well… please tell me again. You say this… swamp Heap of yours… he's been spotted quite a bit as of late?"

"Yeah, that's right. Usually, men come out of here all bruised up, saying they've seen him. He likes to smash, that one."

"So, you say he's big and angry… a sort of a man-monster…?"

"That's right, Mister Magoo. A big ol' man-monster just like you talk about in your stories."

"That's McG… look, just call me Jack. That's fine."

The two men head off undisturbed. They are of no threat to the swamp.

***

Night falls. The Heap rests, dreaming of another life. Memories are faded. His name was Emelman? No… that's not right. But he remembers his biplane. And his lovely Baroness. The quiet chirping of the swamp is disrupted by gunfire. Alerted, the Heap runs to the chaos that has ruined his dreams and has invaded his swamp.

Cabal stands behind men with guns. He sees the Heap and has a mixed look of relief and fear. On the ground is the guide from before, bleeding and unconscious. The reporter called Jack is sitting, looking at a broken camera.

The reporter spots the Heap of the swamp, but despite his surprise, Jack's attention moves back towards what the guns are pointed at. There, in the waters, is another Heap. He is some sort of hulking man-brute. In the night it's difficult to determine his color… blue perhaps? But whatever his hue may be, it's clear he is rage incarnate. He screams like an angry child throwing a tantrum.

The Heap does not like Cabal, but he will not tolerate murder in his swamp. He concentrates, and as before, the flora grows around the incredible man-brute, his legs becoming entangled. To the astonishment of the Swamp Heap, the brutish brute breaks free.

The Heap of the Swamp recognizes that a battle of direct brute strength may be called for here. The bog beast comes running out from the trees to tackle the Brute. He barely nudges him when they clash. As the two grapple with nearly equal strength and power, the Heap

Robert E. Wronski, Jr.
Man-Beast vs. Swamp Monster: A Battle in the Green
Duel of the Monsters Volume 2

spawned of murky waters realizes that they are both being shot at. The bullets easily pass through the swamp monster, as he is more plant than human; however, they do strike the Brute, though to little effect. The man-monster bleeds, and he flinches, but is not slowed down.

Knowing that this one-on-one combat is futile, and that these men are a distraction, the Heap of the Swamp, who once was a man of strategy, quickly analyzes the situation. With little thought, he summons a swarm of mosquitos in unheard of numbers. This is not for the Brute, to whom the insects would have little effect.

The mosquitos attack the men with guns, and they flee – along with Cabal, the reporter, and the awakened guide. Now, with those mortal beings out of the way, the Heap of the Swamp is free to use all that he has in battle.

The Heap is not only of the Swamp. He *is* the Swamp.

The man-brute encounters pain, as thorny branches come from the surrounding trees and wrap around his form, holding him tight. The Swamp Heap breaks free of the man-monster's embrace. Astonishingly, the Brute breaks free of the branches merely by flexing. Is he growing larger, the Swamp Heap wonders? Is he even growing stronger? Is such a thing possible?

The man-brute picks up the Swamp Heap and holds him above his head. *This is new*, thinks the Heap who has mastered his domain.

Beneath the Brute, the ground begins to soften and swallow him within the muck and mire. The man-monster cannot break free while holding the Heap. Hence, he throws his anthro-botanical foe, and the bog beast smashes against the trees of his swamp.

Ironic, he thinks.

The Heap thinks that he must use all his powers as he watches the brute struggle to pull himself from the ground. The Thing from the Swamp realizes that any child throwing a tantrum needs a nap; a time out. So, he calculates, using the mind of Emelman – flowers bloom with unnatural quickness around the Brute, who is now enveloped by the ground up to his chest.

The florets open and out flows a smokey mist. The Swamp Heap creates a breeze, and the billowy vapors are inhaled by the raging Brute, an easy task with the heavy breaths this blue goliath takes when

Robert E. Wronski, Jr.
Man-Beast vs. Swamp Monster: A Battle in the Green
Duel of the Monsters Volume 2

rampaging. The monster man begins to slow, his pounding against the ground weakened, and soon he is asleep.

As the legendary Heap of the Swamp approaches the slumbering man-brute, wondering what to do with this thing that he believes to be another of Cabal's creations. Suddenly he is witness to another astonishment for the night: the transformation begins, and the hulking Brute becomes a man – Bradford.

The Heap pulls the man from the ground, an easy task as the hole the Brute filled is much larger than the size of the person the latter has become. The swamp creature now senses the unnatural radiation within him and understands. The man is brought to a cave to rest.

***

Morning. Bradford awakens. He finds himself in a strange place, unaware of the complete circumstances that brought him there, as usual. He hears a familiar reporter in the distance. He knows what to do: find some clothes, hitch a ride, move on to a new town. In the distance, the Heap of the Swamp watches.

END

**INVISIBLE WOMAN VS. INSECTOID ALIEN: WHEN KILLERS CROSS PATHS –
Patrick Rahall**

Patrick Rahall
Invisible Woman vs. Insectoid Alien: When Killers Cross Paths
Duel of the Monsters Volume 2

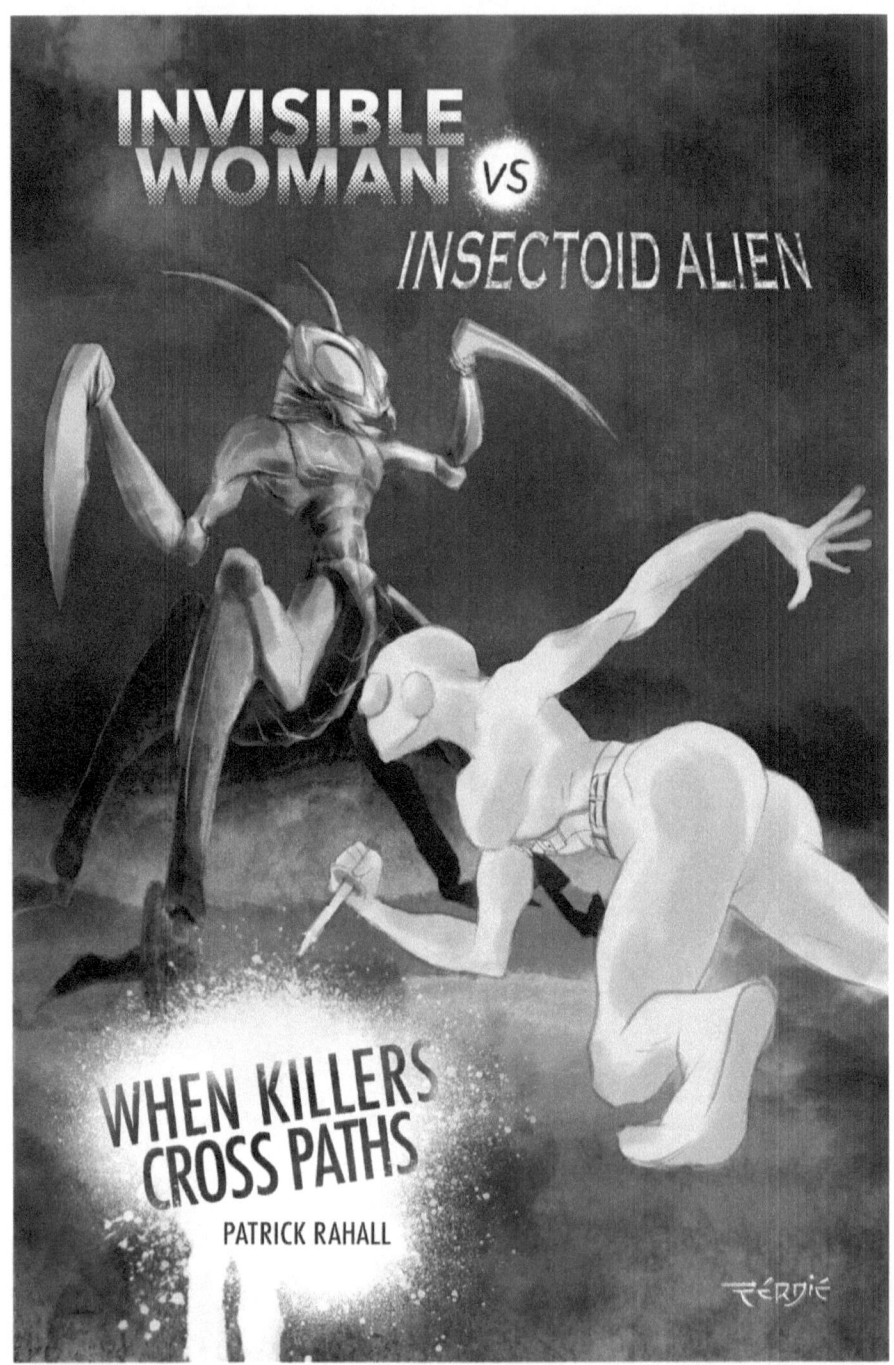

Alyssa Griffin watched as the green hatchback that was blasting '90s pop music pulled off the main road and onto the side thoroughfare that led to a secluded cabin. She opened her eyes wide and then blinked, using them like the shutter of a camera as she burned the image into her mind. Her photographic memory was always reliable when she performed this little ritual. She supposed that the blink was not necessary, especially since she could not remember when she began doing it; it was more like a psychological trigger that eased her mind and assured her that it *would* work. At any rate, it had never failed her, and if she needed to blink her eyes like a camera to take her mental pictures, so be it.

Alyssa would drive about five miles above the speed limit at all times; not fast enough to draw attention to herself, but not slow enough to make someone angry that they had to pass her and get a good look at her face. To that end, she always wore sunglasses while driving and kept her surgical mask on. In all honesty, the pandemic had made things much easier for her, and she was someone who had become an expert in concealing her identity.

She drove her white sedan another couple of miles down the main road, counting the number of dirt trails split off from the only paved street she had seen since arriving in this rural town. Everything she did was designed to allow her to blend in and remain inconspicuous – from her clothing to her car and the way she drove it. The secretive killer wore outfits that were neither plain nor flashy; her music was not playing at a high volume. She avoided wearing extravagant jewelry that would be so ostentatious that it would stick out in someone's memory and make her easily identifiable. She was tattooed extensively, but through the skilled manipulation of her family's secret scientific breakthrough, even that was not a problem.

Her attempts to blend in were a deliberate decision because of how unique and extraordinary she was. Alyssa was descended from the pioneering scientist Dr. John H. Griffin, a misunderstood genius who could not cope with what he created, and the weight of it crushed the fragile shell of his sanity. He killed a great many people, and his descendants were no better. Of course, *they* hadn't had much of a choice; for so long the various iterations of the formula needed to be tweaked and enhanced and improved upon as science progressed.

However, no one was able to remove the unfortunate side effect of madness. There was something about the treatments that altered the chemical balance of the subject's brain, and as advancements were made to the formula and its applications the effects became more diverse.

The first formula had the distinct disadvantage of being permanent and easily detectable by animals with heightened senses; dogs would be keenly alerted to the presence of individuals under the original chemical's influence. As technology became more advanced, so too did the requirements of the formula. Invisibility meant nothing if the subject's body heat could be easily tracked, or movements picked up. Improvements had to be made.

Skin-tight bio-memetic clothing with the ability to absorb the newly improved formula and render the wearer invisible was now available (albeit not easy to obtain) and was lightweight enough to be effortlessly concealed under regular clothing. Eventually, more improvements would be made – it could now be applied to any clothing treated to be bio-memetic; and it would render the subject unobservable by either the heightened senses of animals, or even thermal and motion detection technology.

Alyssa was different, however. She was precise, calculating, patient. She relished the hunt, stalking her prey from a distance and slowly wearing on their sanity as she would disrupt their environment in a variety of ways: from calling out to them as a disembodied voice, or making objects appear to hover and move about, to inflicting small but increasingly noticeable injuries upon them, finally revealing herself before striking the final blow.

Her quarry in this instance was a group of five college girls away for a "Ladies' Weekend." She had followed them for three hours since she crossed paths with them standing in line for coffee. Alyssa was not overly picky when she chose her victims but was more of an opportunistic hunter.

When the obnoxious young women came into the coffee shop, they were loud and seemingly unaware that there was anyone else in the entire world aside from themselves. They had walked side by side, taking up the entire path from the door to the counter. One of them, a blonde named Alyxx, had even bumped into Alyssa because she was so oblivious to her surroundings. Alyssa managed to save her drink from spilling and stared daggers at the girl.

"Watch where you're going!" Alyxx said, annoyed that anyone else *dared* to occupy any space remotely close to her. However, Alyxx was in the wrong because she was walking in, for lack of a better term, the oncoming traffic lane. Her friends immediately surrounded her, ready to come to blows in her defense should the need arise.

"Oh, I'm sorry sweetie, that was entirely *my* fault," Alyssa said as pleasantly as possible to mask the homicidal rage that made her want to drown Alyxx in her own scalding pumpkin spice latte.

"Whatever," Alyxx replied, rolling her eyes and walking away.

That was when Alyssa knew that *this* was her next target. She would take them out one by one, leaving Alyxx for last. She decided in that instant that she would destroy her target's mind and drive her to the brink of insanity before butchering her.

Alyssa watched all five of the women, and to her, they were nothing special. Two blondes and three brunettes, they were bland facsimiles of average, dime-a-dozen women with nothing unique about them aside from the way they spelled their names.

Alyssa made sure to listen to them order predictable beverages so she would be sure to know exactly who she was killing. She was meticulous in her methods and paid attention to every detail available to her. It certainly did not hurt that she had an eidetic memory.

That's *Sheighlah!"* the tallest blonde hollered at the barista. "Ugh, why are you so dumb?"

"I thought that was what I put," the confused bartender replied, looking at what was written on the cup.

"No! You put S-H-A-Y-L-A. That is *not* how to spell my name!"

"Sorry, you didn't specify. Is the drink right, though?" she asked, thinking that was the important part.

"That's not the point!" Alyxx shrieked. "S! H! E! I! G! H! L! A! H!" She screamed each letter, along with accentuating them, by pounding on the counter.

The barista could not believe what she was seeing. The manager came over and tried to intervene.

"What is the problem over here?" the boss asked, confused but looking to resolve the issue as quickly as possible.

"*She* intentionally spelled my name wrong!"

"That's not true! I spelled it how I thought it sounded! I even apologized!"

"Lying *bitch!*" Sheighlah screeched and threw the scalding drink at the barista, who managed to move enough so that only the bottom of the cup hit her on the shoulder. That sent the cup tumbling into the sink behind her, where the cover popped off. As a result, scalding-hot pumpkin spice splashed all over the laminated food preparation poster above the sink.

"Leave! Now! All five of you, before I call the cops!" the manager yelled to the applause of everyone else in the coffee shop, except for Alyssa, who was above such things.

"Ugh, let's go," said Karyl, another blonde in the group. "This place smells like shit and poor people."

"Haha, you're right, Karyl! It *does!*" Alyxx said with a grating laugh.

The quintet of ladies – comprised of Alyxx, Sheighlah, Karyl, Hanna, and Ellynn then departed the shop. Alyssa made a note of that. She casually followed the quartet out the door and watched them get into the car. It was driven by the fourth friend, and the vehicle remained several car lengths behind them until they turned onto the dirt road.

The two short brunettes do not seem like part of the group. Hmm. Too bad for them for keeping the company that they do. Now I get to kill them too!

Alyssa found a cozy little motel off the main road about two miles from where her prey had left it and gone up to the isolated cabin. It was there that she decided would become their tomb.

As it turned out, there were many more people than she expected in such a small town. There was also a heavy news presence because of reports of an explosion and missing hunters who had decided to investigate it; as well as those who had gone into the woods to search for them. The entire town was on edge, and Alyssa was glad for the distraction because it would make her work that much easier. She checked into the motel under a false name, went to her room, and began her preparation ritual.

The room was small but clean and comfortably furnished. There was a queen bed, a small table with two chairs, a nightstand with a lamp on either side of the bed, a television mounted to the wall above the dresser, and a small bathroom with no tub but a standup shower. The dresser was short but wide, which worked in her favor. She placed her suitcase on the left side of the dresser and opened it in a way that would have looked dramatic had anyone been watching her, but it was part of her ritual.

Alyssa lovingly removed what looked like a rolled-up wetsuit from the left side of the suitcase and unfurled it on the bed. She smoothed out the wrinkles and ran her fingers over the material. It was soft, almost ethereal; wearing it was like being dressed in a shadow. It was composed of Nightblack, a material so dark that it did not reflect light and was a design of her innovation.

She smiled at the garment as she would a lover – a knowing look of the intimate moments she had shared with it that was deeper than any connection she had ever had with other people, except for those she had killed. To her, there was no greater intimacy than taking life slowly and with great care.

Next, Alyssa took a rolled-up nylon bag with many compartments in which she had stored all manner of syringes and blades. Under that was a black bandolier in which she placed these implements. It crossed from her shoulder to her hip, and also wrapped around her waist.

Alyssa slid her tools of death into their proper places in the bandolier, and each one moved into place with almost sexual satisfaction. She placed the bandolier on the bed next to her bodysuit and turned her attention back to her suitcase.

It appeared empty, but as Alyssa knew, looks can often be deceiving. She pressed a small panel at the back of the case, directly under the hinge on the right side. The door of the panel swung open to reveal two buttons, one green and one red. She pressed the red one and pulled her hand back. The suitcase emitted a hissing sound as coolant was expelled in small puffs and the false bottom lifted on a pneumatic hinge. A cold storage compartment with multiple containers and delivery systems for her version of her family's formula stood revealed. Several of these went into the utility belt. Smartly, each of the containers was also coated in Nightblack to hide the brightly colored fluid contained within.

Alyssa Griffin stripped her clothes off, rubbed herself down with one of the clean towels from the bathroom and began the process. First, she took one of the glass jars and a paintbrush from the suitcase. Next, she unscrewed the cover and dipped the brush into the metallic-looking liquid. Alyssa then began applying a generous amount on herself.

It had the viscosity of paint and stuck to her skin in the same fashion, except that instead of flaking off when it dried, it behaved more like latex and flexed with her skin. It was removed by peeling it much in the same way. She had developed this contingency after her last suit got torn in a struggle with a particularly frisky target, exposing her flesh underneath and creating an unnecessary risk.

Alyssa had a specific process for covering herself.: First she stood and applied it to the front of her body, then the sides, and then to her back. The last portion of her body for application was more difficult, but she used an extension attached to the brush to reach everywhere. From there, she covered her face; and when it came to her hair, she simply put it into a ponytail as it was dyed with Nightblack.

Alyssa checked herself to see if she had missed a spot. This was simple enough, as it was only a matter of looking to see if any part of herself was visible to her eyes. The bathroom mirror enabled her to see if her backside was fully invisible. She had to be careful not to completely envelop herself with it because it would cut off her air, which she had learned when experimenting during the development stage. Once she was satisfied, she slipped into her bodysuit.

Much like donning a wetsuit, Alyssa simply stepped into it, pulled it over her arms, zipped it up, and pulled the hood and mask over her head and face. It had built-in gloves and sound-dampening boots, so it was all a single piece that fit her as if it were painted on. After donning her bandolier and belt she was almost ready to go. One last step was now required: she went back to her suitcase and closed the cold-storage section, then opened up the compartment next to it. Within that slot were her goggles, which she removed. Finally, she returned the suitcase to its unobtrusive-looking state.

The goggles fit perfectly into the opening between the mask and hood and did what was required of them: shielding her eyes. This is because there was no way that she was putting the formula into a contact lens or any other type of liquid that would potentially compromise her vision, and she refused to even attempt it. Alyssa was very cautious about her vision and did whatever she could to protect it. Hence, the reason she had constructed the goggles.

The lenses were composed of shatterproof plexiglass, but the side of each rim contained technology that the most advanced military agents would have given their firstborn to possess.

Not only did they reveal multiple light spectrums, but they were also advanced enough that they could not be overwhelmed by a sudden influx of light. This was the most difficult part for her, and the longest and most frustrating of the adaptations she had to learn. She had gotten the real-time GPS and targeting HUD installed but needed the final part of the puzzle to be the most efficient hunter possible. Once she had it, however, she knew there was not a force on Earth that could stop her.

She opened her motel room window and slipped out silently into the night.

***

Deep in the forest, roughly a mile beyond where the five women were drinking Long Island Iced teas and Midori Sours, there was a highly intelligent hunter in its own right. It was easily the rival of Alyssa Griffin, except that it had evolved over millennia to be an apex predator instead of merely creating the necessary technology to become one. The Visitor possessed a name, but it would be impossible to express in any human language, either written or spoken; the human speech system was simply incapable of creating the necessary sounds. As such, there were also no characters in any dialect that represented those resonances.

It had come to find itself stuck on this backwater world dominated by psychotic apes purely by accident. But as it was what humans would refer to as a member of its species scientific community, it took advantage of the situation as best as it could. It had been on a refueling mission to the moon of the planet on which it had currently found itself.

The moon was rich in what humans referred to as "Helium-3," which was invaluable as a starship fuel. Landing on the far side of the tidally locked satellite meant that it would have access to the tunnels and mining facility its species had put there decades ago.

That was also about the time the uneasy alliance had been brokered with the humans as well. In exchange for technology and weaponry – which by the time the humans got it, was already obsolete and had been for some time – many of the visitors to the lunar surface were able to abduct and experiment on humans. Their governments thought it was a fair trade, only thinking of internal conflict between the planet's many nation-states, and never understanding that they were providing the blueprint for their own extinction.

The Visitor had intended to stay hidden as much as it could be, staying in its ship while it attempted to repair the vessel. The craft had been temporarily disabled by a solar flare, so it was simply a matter of rewiring a few of the systems and rerouting power to the propulsion and life support. This was a simple matter but one that consumed a significant amount of time. In fact, it would take longer to repair the ship than it would to pilot it back to the base of operations on Europa.

That was a fairly mundane task as well, but the fact that humans kept wandering around its ship complicated the matter, although they provided a much-needed diversion. The Visitor to our world easily dispatched the hunters that had crossed its path. They were no match for its superior hunting skills. For the Visitor was a *true* predator, and it did not require artificial weapons or blinds, or the other tactics humans employed against species compared to which they were evolutionarily outmatched. Humans had no claws, their teeth were not sharp, their night vision was a joke, their flesh was soft and weak, their olfactory sense could only detect the most powerful of scents; they were not predators without their inventions and weaponry.

They were merely prey.

The Visitor was opportunistic and refused to allow quarry that had willingly wandered into its lair to escape so easily. For one thing, it did not wish to attract any further attention to itself; and for another, it was hungry. Like so many of the decisions that drive human behavior, the Visitor also pursued an evolutionary directive – survival not only of itself, but of the species as a whole. The unwary humans it had in its possession were a means to that end, as well as a way to satiate its hunger.

The Visitor's ship was small, as it was an interplanetary vehicle, only used to travel back and forth in the relatively small arena of a specific solar system. With its species' technology, the matter of hundreds of millions of miles was no different from the human's cross-country trips of a few thousand miles and took roughly the same amount of time. Hence, a large vehicle was not necessary, just a well-stocked one.

The alien's craft was similar to that of a tour bus. It was saucer-shaped, gyroscopically stable, and capable of traveling at speeds only dreamed of by humans. Moreover, this was accomplished with minimal propulsion thanks to the nature of the alloys from which it was built – far more advanced than anything on Earth.

The way the ship was laid out would make little sense to a human, but that is because the Visitor was not humanoid. Rather, it looked more like an Earth-evolved insect than anything else. That made sense, as the oxygen level of its home planet was incredibly high and had been for eons. As a result, life there took a very different evolutionary path.

The abundance of oxygen on the Visitor's home planet allowed its species to achieve great size. As a result, insects became the dominant species on that world, and very specific subspecies were able to gain intelligence on par with early man and continue along a similar path. They did so, however, with a much greater speed due to the cooperative nature of hives and the strict hierarchy of said hives.

All the members of the hive know and adhere to their place in it, but as time went on, there were more and more subclasses involved. Instead of drones and workers and warriors, there soon came smiths and builders and eventually, scientists. They were able to evolve beyond the hive mind and became individuals, but the deeply ingrained instincts to serve the colony at their core continued to be their driving factor.

The Visitor resembled a praying mantis with a sextet of tridactyl appendages that were all capable of using tools. Six tool-wielding appendages compared to two on humans was another evolutionary advantage that helped speed the advancement of its species. Its means of locomotion varied depending on its needs – sometimes on two legs, sometimes on four, sometimes on all six. Its compound eyes were another evolutionary advantage, coupled with its segmented, multi-jointed appendages because it could focus on two tasks simultaneously due to the independent hemispheres of its brain.

The Visitor made its way to a chamber in the rear of the ship (although given the shape of the outside of the vehicle, a human observer would be unable to determine front or rear orientation). This was the second-largest area of the craft, as it was used to house collected specimens from various planets the Visitor had explored. As such, it required ample space for specimen jars, vats, and other containment vessels, including those for larger samplings.

There were six of these larger vessels and they were large enough to accommodate a full-grown grizzly bear, albeit not comfortably. To be honest, though, comfort was not the aim of the Visitor once a specimen was collected. It was not capable of empathy or other emotions humans liked to ascribe to anything even vaguely humanoid. Love, anger, compassion... these were as alien to the Visitor as the latter was to the worlds it visited. It had only the primal drives of hunger, reproduction, and curiosity. In some ways, this was another evolutionary advantage.

Two of the containment units currently held a different life form. One contained an exceptionally dangerous life form that was of great interest to the Visitor; it was a parasitic organism capable of replicating its host's cells to form an exact duplicate and blend in perfectly with the surrounding life forms. The Visitor believed that there was much to learn about this alien, but also made sure to keep it at sub-freezing temperatures to ensure that it remained inert.

In the second, there was one of the humans that it had caught. Several of Earth's dominant species had crossed the Visitor's path, and most of them were now liquified to be fed intravenously to other life forms. Humans, it had learned, were exceptionally nutritious to it and its kind. Did it prefer to consume its prey in solid form, and had it not evolved to do just that? Between its terrifying mandibles and the incredibly strong grip of its forelimbs, the Visitor was particularly adept at catching and restraining prey that it preserved to eventually consume it alive in most cases.

The human in the containment vessel was no longer living, but that mattered little to the Visitor. It preferred prey that was still breathing, of course, but that was not a requirement. Dead flesh – if properly preserved – would provide as much sustenance as was necessary. And the Visitor required more nourishment than usual as it was nearing the point in its life cycle that required it to deposit its eggs into a host.

The host would remain living until the eggs hatched and would then be devoured from within by the newborns. After that, all but the two or three strongest of the progeny would subsequently be devoured by their siblings.

There was no room for weakness among the Visitor's kind.

The insectoid alien opened the containment vessel holding the dead but preserved human. It then picked up a cutting tool that looked like and was, for all practical purposes, a bone saw. With this implement the Visitor opened the transparent tube and removed a large chunk of flesh from the unfortunate victim. Its powerful jaws tore through bone like butter, crunching through to the tasty marrow. Once it was finished, the Visitor cleaned itself of any remaining detritus from its meal and returned to the control section of the ship to monitor its surroundings and digest in solitude.

***

Alyxx and her four cohorts were back at their cabin venting frustrations over their experience at the coffee shop, completely unaware that they were being watched. Alyssa was able to make her way into the cabin through an unlocked window and was completely undetected. Of course, that would have most likely been the case even if she had not been so heavily camouflaged because the quintet were so preoccupied with their perceived slights and their beverages.

Alyssa crouched in the corner, waiting patiently for an opportunity to cause chaos. She had already slashed two of the tires on the green hatchback that had transported the five girls to this cabin. She had originally considered only slashing one, but if by some miracle these women knew how to change a tire, they would have a chance to get away. Alyssa did not think this would be an issue, but better to err on the side of caution.

The invisible woman made her way to the kitchen and waited for the first of her five targets to venture in there before beginning her manipulation. As luck would have it, it was Sheighlah. An unseen smile crossed Alyssa's face and she flexed her fingers in anticipation. Alyssa's prey unknowingly walked directly towards her like a blind fly approaching a spider's web.

Sheighlah opened the fridge to find ingredients for more drinks. Alyssa tapped her on the left shoulder, and her quarry looked in that direction immediately, then to the right, and decided that since she did not see anything; that it was probably nothing. So, she went back to her mission in the fridge.

Alyssa waited until Sheighlah had her hands full with bottles and stuck her foot out. It was juvenile, she knew, as was tapping her on the shoulder, but that was partly the point – start small and build to something devastating.

It happened a little quicker than the invisible woman had anticipated. Sheighlah stumbled over Alyssa's outstretched foot. Instinctively she reached out to break her fall but did not relinquish her grip on the bottles. The young woman fell hard, and the glasses shattered under both her momentum and her weight. Sheighlah screamed as shards of glass exploded from the bottles and, having nowhere else to go, embedded themselves in the soft flesh of her face and neck. A particularly jagged piece lodged itself snugly in her left eye, getting cozy there and refusing to move.

With her one good eye, the injured coed was able to survey the carnage, seeing the blood oozing and pouring from *dozens* of wounds all up and down her arms and chest.

The other four ladies came charging into the kitchen, temporarily alleviating their lack of sobriety by replacing it with abject terror. Sheighlah was on her knees, shrieking like a banshee and covered with blood. It was pouring not only from her punctured eye and the wounds on her arms, but also from various spots on her forehead, cheeks, neck, chest, and stomach. The girls nearly retched in tandem when Sheighlah pulled the thin shard of glass out of her eye just before collapsing on the floor screaming.

Alyssa nearly laughed at the looks of astonishment and horror on the faces of Sheighlah's friends. It was almost comical, and the invisible woman was someone who found comedy in tragedy.

"What the fuck happened?" Karyl hollered over the cacophony of pain and fear coming from Sheighlah.

Alyssa was frankly impressed that her voice had not given out yet, considering the force and volume of the screams she was producing.

Ellynn, ordinarily the quietest of the quintet, was now stamping her feet and yelling, "Oh my god oh my god oh my god...!"

"There's blood everywhere! We have to help her!" Karyl yelled.

"I'm not touching her! This is a new shirt!" Hanna snapped back.

So much for her not belonging in this group, Alyssa thought to herself.

"Or, can't you just throw a blanket or something over her so we don't have to look at this?" Ellynn queried.

Or her, Alyssa thought.

"Wrap Sheighlah in a towel or something before we take her to the car," Hanna continued. "And I am *not* cleaning all this up. She can do it. She made this mess."

Hanna sipped her drink and watched Alyxx and Karyl gingerly wrap dishtowels around Sheighlah's wounds as best as they could, while Ellynn quietly looked on with a revolted expression.

"I'll get my keys and wait for you in the car," Hanna said.

"Are you okay to drive?" Karyl asked.

"Shut up, I'm *fine*," came Hanna's slurred reply.

That seemed to be good enough for the three of them and they went back to trying to help Sheighlah, who had already bled through the towels. Hanna retrieved her keys from her purse, dropped them twice, and stumbled out to the car without bothering to help her grievously injured friend.

Karyl and Alyxx were trying their best to get Sheighlah to her feet. Or, at the very least, get her to stop screaming long enough for them to be able to give her some kind of instruction that would allow them to get her the help she desperately needed. Ellynn simply followed them from behind while trying not to barf.

Hanna fumbled with her keys, trying in vain to find the right fob to unlock her doors. She managed to set off the panic alarm, but that was about it. The young woman swore, pressing every button at once. Finally, she managed to shut off the alarm and get the doors unlocked. She entered the car, started the engine, and music began blasting from the speakers. Hanna then leaned back and closed her eyes, frustrated and angry over waiting for her friends.

She was completely unaware of the predator in her midst. Karyl and Alyxx were slowly managing to walk Sheighlah towards the car – with Ellynn trailing slowly behind them – when Alyxx noticed that both back tires were flat. She looked and saw that all four tires were likewise deflated. The girls were not going anywhere.

Karyl started to panic. "Sheighlah's gonna *die* if we can't get her to a hospital!"

"Calm down, she's not gonna die!" Alyxx said unconvincingly.

"Hurry the fuck up!" Hanna yelled.

"Oh, god," Ellynn remarked quietly.

Sheighlah was no longer screaming. She was not, in fact, doing anything at all. The tall blonde was no longer trying to walk or struggle but was simply slumped in her friends' arms and being dragged along. Alyssa knew she was dead, but it took the others a moment to come to that realization.

"Come *on*, Sheighlah! Work with us a little!" Karyl complained.

"I don't think she's breathing!" Alyxx shrieked.

Karyl instinctively let Sheighlah go, and she crumpled to the ground in a heap. They looked at her there for a few seconds before checking her pulse. She was cold, gray, and unresponsive. Her wounds oozed thick blood, starved of oxygen and useless. The two of them began hysterically crying, while Hanna rolled her eyes and turned the music up higher to drown them out. Ellynn simply sat staring ahead glumly with her head on her knees.

Watching from the doorway, Alyssa was disgusted. She decided to finish things off.

The invisible woman sauntered out after them, taking her time and keeping her distance. She had already slashed the tires, so she was assured that they would not be leaving. The unseen killer was getting ready to make her next move when something caught her attention.

The four remaining coeds did not notice it, but this was unsurprising. Alyssa did not think they were all that observant even without alcohol. The invisible assailant was not sure what she was seeing, but she knew that whatever it was, it was most certainly nothing good.

The Visitor she saw could only be described as a giant insect. Alyssa was not sure if it could see *her*, but she was ready to fight if it could. She had completely lost interest in the five women... well, four now. Hanna was in her world of shitty pop music, Ellynn merely sat there lost in unknown thoughts, and the other two were sobbing uncontrollably over their friend's body. This Visitor seemed to be a predator, as it had the head of a mantis, and Alyssa knew what they were capable of. Needless to say, she wanted no part of that.

The invisible woman watched as the insectoid interloper crawled low on the ground and made its way towards the open door. Hanna was drunkenly singing along to a tune that Alyssa recognized from her time listening to the radio in high school. She hated that song.

The Visitor reached into the car towards Hanna just as Alyxx and Ellynn were coming over to tell her what had happened to Sheighlah. Alyxx saw the Visitor before Hanna did and screamed.

Hanna did not break from her reverie until the deadly mantis-like alien had pulled her from the vehicle. She barely registered Alyxx's screams over her own. The often-quiet Ellynn simply dropped her jaw to the ground and began twitching in terror. Hanna managed to piss herself just before the Visitor tore her head off to silence her.

It dropped Hanna's decapitated corpse and moved in on Ellynn, who was frozen in place with fear while Alyxx fled. In the meantime, Hanna's severed head continued its grotesque display of screaming as the last remaining impulses were sent out by her brain in a vain, hopeless attempt to survive.

On all six legs, the alien scurried with terrifying speed towards the immobile Ellynn, who could do nothing but stare in silent horror as the thing elevated itself on its back four feet and raised its two scythe-like forelimbs. The alien was about to show the hapless young woman exactly how much it appreciated being discovered and having to chase down some of her friends, and how much it wanted to remain hidden.

Ellynn gave no resistance as the alien pulled her right arm to its mouth and began devouring her fingers much as a guinea pig would rapidly consume a leaf of lettuce. Before she could cry out, it grabbed her windpipe with its final appendage, allowing enough air for her to gasp but not enough to scream. It crunched the girl's fingers like someone indulging in some particularly tasty breadsticks and ultimately ate her entire hand to the wrist.

It took several minutes for Ellynn to finally die, and the agony she experienced was beyond description. Nothing she could ever have imagined could have prepared her for the suffering she endured. Not even the most elaborate torture Alyssa had ever before concocted came anywhere close to Ellynn's pain and psychological torment in the moments leading up to her death. If the hapless coed had lost her sanity, it would have been a blessing. However, it appeared that Ellynn was not so fortunate and maintained her rationality throughout the ordeal, giving it up only when she also gave up her life.

Alyssa was no stranger to carnage, but the speed and ferocity with which this alien creature attacked were enough to make her stomach churn. Watching the insect feed was concurrently repulsive and hypnotic, and she could not turn away despite her revulsion. The sound of desperate cries and snapping sticks attracted her attention and she turned in the direction of the sound to see Karyl running away.

The mantid alien turned its attention to the fleeing woman, dropping its kill and charging on all six legs after her. It moved much differently now than it had before. Perhaps the sudden sense of urgency was due to a fear of being discovered? Or, perhaps it was something else? Either way, Alyssa's curiosity was piqued, and she was almost helpless against the pull of her need to know where they were headed, so she started after them.

The alien was able to keep up easily, as Karyl was not that fast. But she was smaller and more agile, able to run through the thick brush and low branches that impeded the mantis. It was able to crash through or over everything in its way, but it took time its and allowed Karyl to maintain a slight lead. The Visitor seemed to be getting angry, frustrated, and almost as desperate as Karyl. This frightened Alyssa because an alien like this with emotional drive and intelligence instead of blind, primal instinct meant that it was more dangerous than she had originally thought. Hence, the invisible woman began second-guessing her decision to pursue it.

Karyl was the first to reach the clearing in which the ship had crashed, and she skidded to a halt in front of it, understanding what she was seeing, but still not fully comprehending it. The Visitor, not overwhelmed by the enormity of the realization that life could exist outside of Earth, caught up to Karyl and lashed out at her.

First, it sliced her Achilles tendon and she dropped to the ground with a shriek. It grabbed her left leg and snapped it like a dead stick to further immobilize her, and she screamed louder. The alien stood up on its two rear legs and used three of its remaining four limbs to hold her other leg and both arms.

Despite her injuries, Karyl tried to struggle. This was in vain, however, as the Visitor forced its mouth over hers. Its strange mandibles felt almost pleasant because of how soft the flesh of its maw was. She expected teeth, but there was just flesh and some kind of secretion. Karyl then experienced an acute gagging sensation as something was forced down her throat. Feeling as if she was being choked and asphyxiated, the young woman's eyes rolled into the back of her head and she suddenly ceased moving.

Alyssa made up her mind then and there to destroy this Visitor. Not for any altruistic reasons, of course; but because if there were any more of them it could spell disaster for all life on Earth – including her own, which was the one about which she cared the most. First, however, there was a previous matter to attend to: Alyxx. She was determined to get to the blonde college girl before the mantis did, as she refused to let this alien beast deprive her of the pleasure she had been planning for much of the day.

The invisible woman could hear Alyxx huffing and puffing as she pushed her non-athletic body beyond its limits to escape. She was trying to force herself to run through a clearing where she believed safety awaited. Alyssa felt pleased to prove the girl wrong as she ran diagonally to cut the blonde off. Of course, her target could not see her, and the unseen killer ran quietly through the combo of her padded footwear and experience with stealth.

The invisible woman spotted the alien moving towards Alyxx as well, but it quite obviously did not see Alyssa. Hence, she knew that her Nightblack made her invisible to the mantis's perceptions. Thus, she again resolved to deal with the monster following her interception of their mutual target.

Alyxx disappeared into a grove of tightly placed trees, hoping she would manage to evade the pursuing alien. She succeeded, but that did not save her life. She realized that when an unseen sharp object suddenly sliced open her right cheek. She screamed in agony and placed her hand over the wound to staunch the flowing blood.

The invisible Alyssa then struck again, pulling her victim's head back by her hair and shearing off her left ear with another swipe of the blade. Alyxx screamed again, and her invisible assailant lamented the fact that she would have to make this quicker than she had hoped for since the girl's screams would invariably alert the mantis to her position.

Hence, Alyssa jumped in front of the shrieking Alyxx as she fell back against a tree, blood spurting out between the fingers she had clenched tightly over her torn face and the gaping hole where her left ear used to be. The invisible killer than swiped both knives in an X-shaped arc, cutting open Alyxx's abdomen and causing her bowels to splatter down onto the grass. The college girl managed to release a final throaty yelp as she slid to the ground and moved no longer. Alyssa smiled at the sight of her fallen victim's blood flowing like a scarlet river and her gastro-intestinal organs glistening in the moonlight like wet hoses.

It was a moment later that the invisible murderess heard a loud scampering that signaled the mantis arriving in the clearing, having been attracted there by Alyxx's screams. Alyssa simply stood her ground unseen while the alien's multi-faceted eyes glared at the mutilated body of its intended target. The creature tilted its head, as if quite confused as to what had cut the human girl to pieces before it could do the job itself.

Clutching a blade in each hand, Alyssa crept silently up behind the Visitor. Not sure where to cut first, she decided to take out two of its six limbs. Accordingly, the invisible woman drove her blades into the segmented joint halfway down the Visitor's front and middle appendages on its left side, what Alyssa could only think of as its elbows.

The alien made a high-pitched sound of surprise and anger as the blades pierced its limbs and ripped them off with a quick swipe of both embedded blades. The mantis spun around to fight, lowering its head like a battering ram. It connected with Alyssa directly in her stomach and knocked her rearward. She flew back several feet and landed hard on the ground, her goggles slipping off her head from the impact.

The Visitor then looked around, scanning everywhere for its assailant. Alyssa's grunts of pain alerted it to her presence, and it gingerly made its way over to her, almost cautious in its movements – partly due to its pain and recently acquired handicap but also because it had just been taken by surprise and gravely injured.

The mantis was confused by the fact that it could not locate whatever had just attacked it. The voracious alien assumed that it was a member of the clan of women that had just been slaughtered, because what other reason would a human have for aggressively harming a Visitor such as itself? It had previously observed that behavior in humans, but never before had one managed to injure it so severely. It had to find its attacker and finish it off so that it could attempt to heal… or, at least acquire retribution before it died.

Alyssa kept her eyes closed, as she knew that without her goggles her eyes would be exposed. She also tried her best not to gasp for breath or grunt any more than she already had. Like the Visitor, Alyssa was unaccustomed to being hurt during a hunt.

The invisible woman opened her eyes just enough to see where the Visitor was located and shut them again quickly as soon as she ascertained that information. She had settled her breathing down as quietly as she could so that she could listen to the footfalls of the alien. It was getting closer and moving very cautiously, but it was headed right for the invisible woman and would end up stepping on her if she weren't careful.

Once it was nearly on top of her, Alyssa allowed herself to open her eyes and contorted her body in a way that kept her from getting stepped on while simultaneously pulling another blade from her belt. Once the Visitor's exposed underbelly was directly over her, she struck again.

Alyssa drove the knife into the Visitor with all her strength, plunging it so deeply that her elbow ended up inside of it, eliciting more high-pitched sounds of anguish from the alien. Before the invisible woman could pull her arm free, the Visitor grabbed hold of her with its left forelimb and pulled its unseen opponent off the ground.

Alyssa did not relinquish the grip on her knife, though, and managed to tear a massive hole in the Visitor's thorax. Again, it screamed, but this time it was in pain and confusion because it was unable to see what it had in its grasp – aside from a human arm covered in green-black ichor from the wound she had inflicted.

The alien was now holding Alyssa by her left arm a few feet off the ground. It used the two legs on its right side along with its remaining leg on the left to maintain balance.

The invisible woman was trying in vain to break the alien's powerful grip when it suddenly and quickly slammed her to the ground. The unseen killer gasped as she struck the earth and the air was forced from her body.

The Visitor attempted to take advantage of this by leaping upon the invisible woman and doing the same to her that it had done to Karyl.

Alyssa, however, had already seen that move performed this night and was not inclined to endure it herself. She swiftly placed her left arm over her mouth and yelped in pain as the alien mantis sunk its mandibles into her limb. The invisible woman angrily pushed past the pain to take advantage of the Visitor latching onto her appendage.

She began by jamming her knife into its head over and over and over. The extraterrestrial monstrosity was unable to pull away, as its serrated mandibles were apparently stuck in her flesh. Eventually it could take no more damage. and the creature then simply collapsed on top of Alyssa with a forceful exhalation.

The invisible woman wormed her way out from under the dead thing's carapace with some effort. She yelped in stifled agony while prying the mantis's serrated mandibles out of the flesh of her arm with the help of one of her blades.

Alyssa was rather impressed with herself. This thing was massive, at least three times her height and hundreds of pounds heavier. She looked at the trail of the carnage she had left in her wake and was pleased. The killer had expected to be disappointed that she had failed to get most of the prey she had initially stalked, but this was a grander trophy in her opinion.

She did, however, begin to feel a strange pull from her scientific and intellectual curiosity. She finished what she had started with her knife and removed the severely damaged head of the Visitor at its shoulders and carried it with her. It was more than a mere trophy, as she believed she could learn many things from it.

The battle had taken its toll, however, and Alyssa felt terrible. She was certain that several of her ribs were broken, or at least cracked; not to mention the damage to her arm. Nevertheless, she was hardy enough to walk the half mile to where her vehicle was hidden, her precious and bizarre trophy in tow. She could hardly wait to plan her next kill as soon as an opportunity presented itself. To Alyssa, that was truly living the life.

***

Karyl woke up to find that she was alone, the alien monster that attacked her having disappeared. The young woman was not okay, however, as she was feeling quite nauseated. At first, she felt that the trauma she had experienced was doing a number on her stomach, but it quickly turned out to be more than that. She was in so much pain that it was difficult to figure out where it was coming from. It was like she was experiencing kidney stones, extreme menstrual pain, and back spasms all at once.

Suddenly there was an intense flare-up of agony, and it was so bad that she began gagging incessantly and beating at the ground with her fist. She was unable to get up since the alien had disabled both her legs, and they had now gone completely numb, this being why she failed to notice any pain upon regaining consciousness.

The crippled college girl was in blinding pain, to the point that all she could do was curl up in a fetal position, then writhe on the forest floor. She rolled back onto her hands and knees and began vomiting. It was the most violent expulsion she had ever experienced, and even felt something inside herself being torn, but she was unable to cry out. Bright red, well-oxygenated blood and blackish bile spewed forth from her mouth.

She heaved one more time, and a mass of unrecognizable, thick greenish-black fluid passed from her, tearing open her throat and breaking her jaw from the force with which it was expurgated from her body. As life slowly drained from her and the light faded from her eyes, the ill-fated Karyl saw what she thought was three sets of compound eyes staring back at her from the mass she had just regurgitated.

***

In their black fatigues and with the various weaponry adorning their outfits, the Sweeps would not have looked out of place as the opposing force of a single-player first-person shooter video game. Overseeing the carnage that had been caused by the rampage of the Visitor was the woman known as Crystal Pierrot. She wore a mask over the lower portion of her face, showing only her eyes. The cover was decorated in the style of a terrifying clown with a large, shark-like grin surrounded by bright grease paint.

The commanding woman stood with her hands on her hips surveying her crew as they eradicated every trace of the alien, as well as the human victims it had claimed… along with two that appeared to have been massacred by a human killer using conventional knives (along with shards of broken beer bottles) that was no less brutal than the mantis from beyond.

Her interest was piqued as her most trusted and loyal soldier, Jeremy Lane, approached her. He was carrying something, but she was unable to tell what it was.

"This is bigger than we thought," he said excitedly.

"What've you got?"

"The Griffin Formula!" he cried, holding up a vial of shimmering liquid. "It must have been accidentally dropped here by whoever it was that killed the alien during the fight. Probably the same killer who cut up those other two girls."

"Impossible! That formula was all destroyed!" Crystal said as Jeremy handed it to her.

"Seems that was erroneously reported," he replied. "We found a lot of human blood at the scene that didn't belong to one of those college girls that were slaughtered. Along with human tracks likewise not belonging to them that indicated someone wearing some type of boot whose style we didn't recognize.

"That same unidentified person's blood was smeared on the alien's mandibles and some of its ichor was found on the unknown person's tracks. The alien obviously fought with that person, and if they were rendered invisible by the Griffin Formula and armed with blades at the time, that could go a long way towards explaining how the human opponent actually managed to win that confrontation."

Crystal had been searching for the formula for years, and now they had found it.

"Have you pieced together what happened? And who the user of the Griffin Formula may have been?"

"Looks like the work of a female serial killer who has been stalking and slaughtering people across the country. We figured it out after seeing the two victims killed by conventional weapons and cross-referencing the database on unsolved murders. At first, we thought our 'out-of-town' friend here was responsible for some of them, but the psych profile matched some of the other Griffin killings. We think it may be a particularly dangerous and demented member of that clan named Alyssa Griffin. We'll do what we can to track her down.

"As for the Arcturan, we have it in cold storage. Griffin actually killed the fuckin' thing!"

"Jesus," Crystal muttered. "Arcturans were incredibly difficult to injure, let alone kill."

"We have another serious issue, though," Jeremy hastened to point out. "Ovipositor tests conducted on one of the girls killed by the alien showed signs of use and sure enough, the woman was torn apart on the inside. Throat and jaw ripped wide open too." He cut Crystal off before she could voice her concern. "We rounded up the three offspring that hatched and survived. We're hanging on to them in case we need something to exchange. Arcturan young are very popular."

"Good. I don't like to think about what kinds of chaos *three* Arcturans could cause together. One at a time is bad enough. It's already difficult enough keeping this shit from the public. You have the ship?"

"Yeah. Sending along through the Bell Gate to Base 6."

"Excellent. I'll head there as soon as I'm done with my business at the Tower. You go ahead and oversee preparations at Base 6, but don't start until I get there."

"Of course," Jeremy said before turning on his heel and walking away.

"Jeremy!" Crystal called to him. He stopped and turned towards her. "Great work."

He nodded and continued on his way. Crystal looked at the communicator on her wrist, scrolled through the displays, and nodded at the information exhibited thereupon. It was time to return to the off-world base. The Arcturans were going to be curious about their explorer, and she was going to have to deliver the news about the treaty violation. They would not be happy about it, but it was what it was. Things happened and could not be undone, and the only thing to be done would be to move forward.

Crystal strolled back to the Quonset hut that had been erected to house the main communications equipment. She went to the tech officer and gave her the coordinates for the upcoming journey. Next, she stepped on the pad and the tech officer punched in the alphanumeric code, followed by the transmission parameters. There was a flash, a burst of heat followed by a blast of cold air and a popping sound, and Crystal was gone.

Things were now set in motion that could not be undone.

END

Zach Cole
Werewolf vs. Gargoyle: Guardian of the Church
Duel of the Monsters Volume 2

WEREWOLF VS. GARGOYLE: GUARDIAN OF THE CHURCH – Zach Cole

Zach Cole
Werewolf vs. Gargoyle: Guardian of the Church
Duel of the Monsters Volume 2

Do you remember when you were a kid, lying in bed, scared of the thing under there or in your closet? Do you remember when you'd cry for your parents, and they'd come soothe you and reassure you that there was no such thing as monsters? Then they'd tuck you back into bed, pat you on the head, or kiss you on the forehead and you'd go to bed not fearing the thing that might or might not have been there?

I remember.

I also now know it's all a fucking lie.

Monsters are real.

I know because I was attacked by one. Turned into one.

Who am I?

The name's Arthur Osmond. I live in England. I had my first encounter with the supernatural a year ago while on a camping trip with some buddies. I... was the only one to make it back. The Lancashire Forest, which was where we decided to camp, is known for wolves, but we knew that. Took the necessary precautions. Stayed away from known areas with wolves. Though nothing prepared us for what we encountered...

And the doctors who treated me didn't believe me, either. I'm sure I sounded like a sodding loon, spouting off about a big bad wolf that walks on its hind legs. I stopped before they decided to lock me in a psych ward. Said my shocked mind must've exaggerated what I saw. That it was probably just a regular wolf.

I, of course, knew better.

The year that followed was hell.

I couldn't control the beast I turned into on those nights of the full moon. I've watched it kill. Watched it feast. I... remember every victim's face.

But it's been a year.

I've had a year to try and gain control of the beast.

Not complete control, sadly, but I've managed to be able to influence where the beast goes. And tonight, that will be to an abandoned church I heard about in the town I'm currently passing through. I didn't catch the name. I guess it's more of a rural village, actually.

Zach Cole
Werewolf vs. Gargoyle: Guardian of the Church
Duel of the Monsters Volume 2

Anyway, as we reach the church, I look it over. It's a bloody mess, let me tell you. Its brick façade is missing sections. The windows are broken and boarded up with planks of wood. The only real pristine piece of the thing is its doorway and the gargoyle that guards it. The demonic creature has a few scuffs and cracks, like it's been in a few fights. But… that's just bloody mad, right?

I heard the stories about the place from villagers. That the church was abandoned because it was haunted. Not haunted by a spirit, though. Haunted by that damn gargoyle. I didn't believe it at first… but now that I get a look at the demonic statue, I'm having second thoughts.

It has a skull-like head with horns twisting out the back of it. Its eyes, sunk deep in their sockets, are closed; the creature slacking on its duties. Its arms are long and boney, its fingers equally so, tipped with sharp talons and gripping the doorway's roof. Its back legs are double jointed, like an animal's; its toes also tipped with talons. Bat-like wings are folded against its muscled back. The tip of a long devil-like tail hangs over the edge of the roof.

If the body I currently inhabited was my own, I'm sure the sight of the thing would've sent chills down my spine.

The wolf's eyes narrow as its fur stands on end, the creature detecting danger. At the same time, the gargoyle's eyes snap open, glowing a ghostly white. The winged monster rises slowly on its hind legs, sizing up the beast before it. A low growl reverberates from the wolf's throat, growing in intensity.

Bloody great, I think, doing my best to pull the beast away from the church to no avail. *I guess we're fighting this thing, then…*

The wolf snorts as if in reply before howling into the night sky and the bright moon that hangs above us. The gargoyle answers with a spine-chilling wail that even the wolf feels.

Our leathery-winged adversary makes the first move, leaping from the roof and into the night sky, beating those bat-like wings that are definitely not stone. Pretty sure its skin has just adapted to look like granite as a sort of camouflage.

The gargoyle dives at us, slashing with those long talons. We roll out of the way, but not unscathed. One of those long nails found our shoulder, tearing a deep gash in the hairy flesh. The wolf howls in pain.

Zach Cole
Werewolf vs. Gargoyle: Guardian of the Church
Duel of the Monsters Volume 2

I can feel it too. Damn does it hurt, but I have no voice to express the pain.

Like an attack plane, the gargoyle comes around for another dive-bomb assault, this time with his front claws, fingers hooked. I'm no fighter. I was just a college student studying to become a doctor before I was turned into a werewolf. But I do have an idea on a counterattack. I relay it to the beast I inhabit but can only hope that the animal in me understands.

I'm surprised when it does exactly what I thought.

The wolf drops to his belly, avoiding the gargoyle's swinging claws without a scratch this time. As the stone-like creature sails overhead, the wolf jumps to his four limbs, reaches up and bites down on the gargoyle's tail. The flying monster is jerked to a stop in midflight, losing all airflow underneath his wings. He falls face-first onto the ground with a loud *thud*.

The wolf shakes his head, teeth tearing through surprisingly soft flesh. The gargoyle screeches in pain, trying in vain to get away from the wolf.

Rrrrriiiiiipppppp!

The gargoyle's tail is ripped away, leaving behind a stump gushing red blood. Our winged assailant thrashes about, losing a lot more blood, coating the dirt around us a dark crimson before falling still. The wolf walks over to it, looking it in the eyes as the white light within slowly dimmed.

The wolf howls into the night sky. I can sense its feeling of victory. Then I cringe as it begins to feed on its fallen foe.

The next day, as I walked through the village, I hear about how they found the gargoyle they were all afraid of dead. How relieved they were.

Maybe I can turn this curse into something good? I wonder as I unlock my cell phone and look for reports of other creatures terrorizing people.

I select my next target and start on my way.

END

MAN-MADE MONSTER VS. GREAT APE: THE MASTERPIECE CREATION – D.G. Valdron

She was perfect.

The Monster and I agreed on that. She was the Master's Masterpiece.

Her skin was milky white, the exquisite pallor of grubs found under a rock; the stitching that wound around her every joint was delicate and fine, the metal staples and bolts that held her frame together shone as if polished silver. That hair, somehow stiff as wire yet supple, raven black with its white streaks, entranced us. What joy when the Master allowed me to comb it. What jealousy when the Master allowed the Monster to caress it.

Even her bandages and wrappings – the linens that covered her – were pristine. Everything about her, from her graceful form, to her artfully manufactured hands and feet, to her exquisite face, was perfect.

Sometimes, working in the lab, I could not help but stop and stare, transfixed by her beauty.

All she lacked was a brain.

How different she was from the Monster – that crude lumbering frame, stitched and bolted together from decaying corpses, pallid and leprous, burnt and battered, and yet somehow unyielding, that the Master had breathed into life those many years ago.

The Monster moaned to signify thirst and rattled his chains. Hurriedly, after glancing at the Master, still occupied by his tasks, I filled a bucket of water and carried it over as quickly as a two-legged gait would manage.

The Monster occupied a corner of the Master's lab, behind iron bars and bound by heavy chains. Only occasionally did the Master allow him even limited freedom.

I supposed I was luckier. The Master found me useful and reliable, so I was seldom chained. But then, where was there that I could go? And what could I do? At least the Monster was not treated as a mindless slave, not assigned endless vile and menial tasks. At least the Monster had the Master's respect. Or perhaps it was fear, for the Master respected nothing but his own genius.

As I passed the Master's polished autoclave, I caught sight of my own reflection: the beetled brow, the heavy jaw and polished fangs, the leathery chest, dark brown fur, and squat build of a Great Ape – I looked away. I was another of the Master's experiments, an effort to grant an Ape human intelligence. Human intelligence… and human desires.

I grunted as I approached, signing with my free hand.

"Sorry, forgot, many jobs."

The Monster moaned, signing back, "Not mad. Finished book. Return?"

I placed the bucket close to the bars, where the Monster could dip a cup into it. I glanced around. The Master occupied a castle, maintained a great lab; by any standard, his wealth must be immense. But he allowed the Monster no more possessions than a battered cup, some worn blankets, and a few trinkets. As for myself? Scarcely more.

I signed, "Later. After Master sleep, put back. New book. Wine and chess tonight?"

The Monster moaned extra loud, nodding. It was a shame that the Master had never repaired his vocal cords. But then, the Master had little interest in his failures – not the Monster, not I.

Then we heard the Master's call, loud and hectoring. The whip cracked, and I cringed automatically, though it was nowhere near me. I grunted and scampered off, leaving the Monster with nothing to do but gaze at her perfection as she lay inert on the table.

I envied him.

***

I have positioned the chess board so that we both have a clear view of her. The game is not going well. I think I will be forced into a desperate winning strategy that has saved me once or twice. When the Monster looks away, I'm going to eat his bishop.

"Gorilla," the Monster mutters, staring at the chess board.

It's one of the few words he can speak, after long painstaking practice. It's a joke, of course. I'm not a Gorilla, or a Chimpanzee, or an Orangutan, though I've been mistaken for each. I'm actually a Great Ape, closer to human than any other primate.

Perhaps that is why I desire her too. The Master says that unlike Gorillas, the Great Apes often lust for human women. Perhaps that is why I hunger for her body, why she fills my mind with lust. I have no interest in my own kind.

It is *her* I want.

The frame that she lays upon, a slab of wood and metal, is rotated so that her body is almost upright, facing us. A subtle torture for the Monster, I am sure, devised deliberately by the Master. The frame is mounted on a platform at the center of the lab. It's built to be elevated up to the roof, to the lightning rods.

The Master insists on its practicality. But I rather think it's an altar to his own divinity; or, more accurately, his vanity.

We have both been chained to that frame at different times, the Monster and I, though I was never raised up to the heavens to be given life, as he was. For me, it was simply the needle.

That's all I remember of my old life. Being chained to the frame, screeching with fear and terror as the needle came closer. The way it plunged into my breast, the glowing green liquid oozing.

What was I before? Was I happy? Was I raised in the jungle? Or was I a product of some zoo or circus? Did I have a mother? I must have. The old life is swept away. In its place is a new life, a new existence, thoughts coming so rapidly they tumbled over me.

This is a thing that the Monster and I have in common. Whatever we were before, it was swept away when the Master breathed his life into us. All we have is now. When finally she comes to life, will she too be a blank slate? Will the Master's face be the first sight of her new life?

The Monster's relationship with the Master is more complex than mine.

With me, at first, the Master was elated by his success, took pride and delight in my rapid learning. But as it tapered off, as his miraculous alchemy's limits became apparent, he lost interest just as rapidly. I moved from prize to disappointment; and then to slave, servant with a thousand chores, a creature whose usefulness barely outweighed his disappointment, never more than a whim away from destruction at his hands.

In contrast, the Monster's fate was neither elation nor enslavement, but abandonment. The Monster was driven out, cast off, forced to roam the mountains and hills. He was free.

Free! I have thrilled to his clumsy descriptions of those outdoor vastnesses. The rolling hills, the streams, the artfulness of homemade cabins, the exquisite complexity of towns nestled in valleys, the artless beauty of sunsets.

The Monster's soul is full of poetry. How ironic, as the Monster is a creature of mechanics, a clockwork of flesh and bone. I, in contrast, am considered a creature of primordial passions.

The books he loves the most are romances, whereas I am entranced to technical works of physics and mechanics. I have actually assisted the Master in his experiments, been permitted to stitch together his homunculi, working to his directions as he solves the problems of anatomy by examining my results.

He is my only friend, and I am his. I sign this to him, and when he looks away in embarrassment, I pluck his bishop from the chessboard, pop it into my mouth, and swallow straight away. When he looks back to the board, his brows furrow in puzzlement. I look completely innocent, something I've practised often.

She exists because of the Monster. It was his loneliness and pain, his wanderings with every hand turned against him – except for a handful of literary journals and the occasional poetry slam – which drove him back to the Master.

The Monster's story is different in every telling. Sometimes, he accosts the Master and demands a bride. Other times, he bursts in bent on revenge, and the Master fearfully offers to build him a companion. But whatever the path, the result is the same. The Master wearily sets about building a bride, the Monster acquiesces to chains and captivity, his own body the road map for the Master's construction, watching as his bride takes shape.

His bride.

When I think those words, that's when I know hatred for my only friend as my heart burns with jealousy and resentment. He stands in the way of my beloved, of my desire. I could tear him apart with my fury.

But then I think of the Master – his pride and selfishness, his complexity, his labyrinth of emotions and rationalisations. He will never allow his Masterpiece to couple with the Monster. Or with a "goddamned dirty Ape." He plans betrayal, I can tell. He will keep her for himself.

"Is it wrong to hate your creator?" I sign this question to the Monster, and while he ponders the morality of it, I eat his knight.

He still manages to checkmate me.

***

Afterwards, as the Monster slumbers, as moonlight shines down through the skylight, I climb into my hammock up near the rafters. The laboratory is quiet. The Tesla coils are dark, the autoclave silent. The patchworks of gears and tubes no longer pulse. Even the glassworks, filled flasks, and pipettes synthesizing chemicals do not bubble; the burners and mixers are turned off. The tables of polished instruments, surgical tools, clamps, scalpels, magnifiers, all sitting in wait.

There are books everywhere – manuals, many written by the Master himself along with copious notes, diagrams on blackboards, ancient treatises, letters from learned scholars, and of course, experiments everywhere, on every form and format, half begun, half abandoned.

Such wondrous, erratic brilliance, tucked away in behind medieval stone walls, sheltered by ancient timbers.

And in the center of it all, she waits. My dream, my vision, my perfection, my goddess, my empty vessel, *my* bride.

An exquisite manufacture of flesh and bone, rivets, and wires. An empty house, awaiting animation.

Sometimes, I wonder about that. About my fascination for this empty vessel. Is it wrong? Is it foolish? Sometimes I wonder if we are fools and worse. Do I worship her, or the absence of her?

What will happen when she is brought to life? Will she look upon the Monster and scream with horror? Will she look upon me with disgust? Will she resent us, and our base desires, for having brought her into existence, with no other intent than applying her to those desires? Will she yearn to be free of us, as we yearn to be free of the Master? Wouldn't she have the right to do so?

Perhaps, then, she shouldn't be brought to life? Perhaps she should remain inanimate perfection, an empty house, a breathing doll? I ponder the morality of that. Having come so far in her creation, do we have the right to deny the final stage of existence for our own pleasures?

I keep these speculations to myself. There was a time when I discussed it with the Monster, in our careful sign language. I could see that the morality of it disturbed him, and even more, the despair of rejection. He ventured that should his bride reject him as monstrous, then he saw no other choice, for her or himself, but to destroy themselves with explosives. He whispered painfully, "We belong dead."

It troubles me. Where did our conscience come from? The Master has none to bestow.

***

Disaster!

The Master, upon coming into the lab, tripped upon a homunculus on the stone stairs. With a cry he pitched headfirst, his skull impacting upon a step with a nauseating crunch as his cranium dented, and then a pop as his neck snapped. But that wasn't the conclusion... like a rag doll the Master tumbled and flopped end over end, down the staircase as it wound along the circular outer wall of the laboratory, bones snapping, blood smearing all the way, until finally coming to rest with his brains splashing across the floor.

We gazed at the sight in horror. The body, a mangled carnival wreck? That did not disturb us, for were we not monsters? It could be repaired, remade, or at least constitute useful spare parts.

But the Master's exquisite, terrifying mind? That mind was now gone, its wreckage scattered in lumps of gray strewn about the foot of the stairs.

How could this happen? How many times had the Monster and I shared fantasies and plots of revenge against the Master, never acting upon them?

Now this? We shared a look of appalled incomprehension. She is not finished!

With the Master gone, all comes crashing down. The outside world will come closing in. First grocers and deliverymen, bill collectors with unpaid invoices; then bankers, policemen, angry villagers with torches.

The laboratory is finished. All is undone. What is left but to flee, flee to alien forests so far from the jungles of my ancestors, flee to an unyielding blue sky and harsh and implacable rocks; to hide in caves, to subsist on roots and scraps, and to endure a furtive existence of danger and deprivation, always hunted.

She is not finished! And now she never will be.

However, the Master's journals, his diagrams and drawings, his instructions, remain. Perhaps I might have the skill, from my own work under his supervision.

But where would we find a brain?

All ruined, all undone. I fling the Master's instruments around wildly, hooting and bellowing. I overturn the autoclave, taking satisfaction in its great clash. I throw wrenches at the Tesla Coils, sending streaks of lighting flying every which way, setting small fires. All is lost. Nothing but misery lies ahead. The Monster howls and moans, shaking the bars of his cell.

And in my despair, there is her. What reason to wait? Why deny myself any longer?

Hooting, I leap up onto the platform, onto the framework that holds my beauty, my bride, in place. The gears swivel to ninety degrees, until we are level. I touch her cold alien flesh, pull away the linen cover.

The Monster roars, sensing my intention. But I am heedless. What matters but this fleeting moment of pleasure before a lifetime of misery? My rough simian hands grapple with the bandages, positioning her limbs.

The Monster cries out, and suddenly there is a mighty crash. Startled, I turn to look. The Monster has torn the door from his cell, flinging it away. His chains have snapped, and he strides out, his face contorted with anger and fury. He marches rapidly and clumsily towards the platform on which I stand astride our bride. His howl is hoarse, but there is no mistaking his meaning.

"Mine!" he cries out.

I snarl, my great brow furrowing, the fur rising all above my back. For the first time ever, instinct takes over, as I stand and beat my breast with my fists, my black lips pulled back, my eyes bright with rage.

I roar, "Mine!"

As the Monster staggers towards me, I crouch and spring leaping to the attack like the Great Ape that I am. Our bodies crash together. My prehensile feet brace against his hips, as my hairy arms rain blows down upon him. It's all he can do to keep my fangs from sinking into his neck.

But then the Monster braces himself, balances, and I feel his meaty misshapen hands clasping me. And suddenly, despite my fury, I find myself lifted over his head.

As I thrash wildly at this indignity, he grunts. Suddenly I am flying through the air, tumbling head over heels, to smash into the tall air compressor. My head collides with its steel casing and my eyes cross momentarily. Once again, my simian instincts save me from falling as I instinctively grab the regulator's gauge and swing myself around.

I shriek with fury and leap, bounding down and past the Monster. He is stronger, it is clear, but I am faster and more savage. As he pursues me, I climb up the central platform, tearing her loose from the buckles and braces. I hold her in my arms, striving to remember this moment, to crystallize it forever, to keep it as an eternal jewel. How long have I dreamt of this? And now the moment is so fleeting.

The Monster is almost upon me. I leap off the frame, cowering as he tears it bodily from its mountings, ripping heavy bolts from raw wood as he flings it aside.

But I am already moving. Carrying my bride in one arm, careful to ensure no harm comes to her limp body, I bound in a series of apelike hops to the transformer tower assembly -- a web work of steel frames and capacitors, built to channel the raw electricity of lightning bolts.

Hand over hand, as the Monster moans and shakes the steel base, I climb swiftly and dexterously with hands and feet. There I carry my inert bride to the metal cup at its apex, my improvised marital nest atop a metal tree.

In triumph I slap the sides of the steel frame, hooting and bellowing. Before we consummate, I pause to beat my breast, and utter the cry of the bull Great Ape.

And then the whip curls around my neck. I am abruptly pulled away and down, falling half the length of the transformer before the whip loosens away and I can grab the steel frame to save myself.

But salvation is only temporary, as once again, the whip strikes my back. I howl with pain and anguish. The Master is back with his whip and his pain, the lash against upon which I was so cruelly broken, the stinging snap that fills my nightmares. In blind panic I try to flee, but the lash follows me again and again, until I find safety under an overturned table.

Only then does it come to me that it is not the Master, but the Monster, wielding the whip.

This ultimate betrayal, the instrument of my torture in the hand of my only friend, fills me with fury. I hurl the table at him, which he casually brushes aside. No matter, though, as I am quickly hurling piece after piece of laboratory equipment, and beakers of acid and caustic liquid are smashing against his flesh. He tries to bat them away, but many get through.

The Monster drops the whip to raise his arms to protect himself, and then I am upon him. I sink my fangs into his arm, biting again and again, from wrist to elbow, tearing at the bolts and wires. In turn, he hammers against me with shattering blows.

We are both bleeding and bruised. Broken wires and torn bolts protrude from the Monster's flesh. I try to limp away, but my ankle shoots pain with each step and refuses to bear my weight. As we break hold of each other he advances on me.

I promptly dart out of his reach, flinging whatever comes to hand at him. But the Monster is implacable.

I look around wildly for a path of escape, and ultimately retreat to the stairs. The Monster follows, and so, we battle along the spiral staircase that winds around the walls of the laboratory, rising higher and higher. I tear a rail loose from the side of the staircase and batter him with it but he catches it, tears it from my grasp, and hurls it away.

The patchwork monstrosity is upon me now, just below the support beams of the roof. The Monster looms above me. I squirm to avoid his blows as his fists come crashing down. As he tries to push me over, I see my chance. Below us is a hanging lit torch. Desperately clinging to the edge of the stair with one arm, struggling to fend him off with the other, my prehensile feet swing blindly below, searching.

An agonizing burn across the tender sole of my foot tells me that I have found it. I reach down with both prehensile feet now, ignoring the pain and the burns as I yank the torch from its mounting and pass it foot-to-foot-to-arm. As the Monster comes in for the final fatal blow, intending to hurl me thirty feet to my death, I thrust the torch into his face.

The Monster's shriek is pure misery and horror, and were there room in my bestial, blood-crazed heart, it would have gone out to him in pity. No one should have to endure such pain, such fear. But the Monster stumbles back, and now it is my turn. There is no mercy, only animalistic triumph as I thrust the torch at him again and again, at his face, his hands, the legs of his pants, his chest. I smell burning flesh and see flames licking at his clothes as he desperately slaps at them.

He howls forlornly, his voice dripping with terror and torment as he stumbles ever upward along the steps, too frightened now to attack, to even defend himself. I pursue my friend-turned-foe avidly while snarling, baring my fangs and barking at him, beating my chest with my free hand, and thrusting the torch. Every step is an agony, but I do not care.

She will be mine!

The Monster, my friend, my enemy, my rival, will die!

He reaches the top of the steps, and the heavy wooden door is no obstacle to him. In his desperation to escape the fire, the Monster tears it from its frame, backing away along the rooftop. His heavy boots scuff against the skylight, cracking windowpanes.

All around us is a vista I have never been allowed to see: the open sky, the forests, the mountains; the valley nestled below, including the village. Some tiny remote part of me, almost drowned in bloody fury, nevertheless registers the beauty.

This was where the Monster was raised up and first brought to life. So, I find it fitting that this is where he will be ended.

Barking and grunting, I advance, thrusting the torch into his face. I have in mind to push him from the ledge, to let the fall to the rocks below break him. And if there is anything left, then I can climb down and dismember it.

But the Monster perhaps senses my plan. That, or in his panic, he understands that there is no place left to retreat to. As I thrust my torch for the final push, he stumbles forward and wraps his hand around the burning brand. I can hear wires and tendons snap as he does so, along with the sound and smell of his flesh sizzling

The torch is torn from my paw and hurled below.

The Monster steps forward, embracing me in a bear hug. His strength is immense, and he pays no attention as I punch and kick and bite at him. Instead, his grip around me inexorably tightens, pushing the air from my lungs. My vision grows dark, my ribs crack, my spine is bent.

Desperately, I have only one chance. With the bestial strength of the Great Apes, I grab his head, feeling the bolts of his neck between my fingers. As I feel the blackness take me, feel my spine begin to crack and ribs splinter, I give one mighty heave, pushing upwards.

As I do so, I tear the Monster's head and neck from his shoulders, lifting it high into the air. The misshapen face has only a moment to register surprise and shock, and then his eyes roll up white and his features go slack.

The mighty arms that were crushing me go limp and fall away. My feet find the roof and grip it, then I stumble back.

For a second, the Monster's body sways, standing on its own as if possessed of its own will and intention.

Then it topples forward, crashing through the glass of the skylight and tumbling down end over end, to the remains of the platform far below, irretrievably broken.

I am left alone on top of the laboratory roof, holding the Monster's head in my hands. The Great Ape is triumphant.

The fury suddenly drains out of me as I look into the Monster's face. My victory goes hollow. What have I done? What have I won?

A future of loneliness and exile. A lifeless bride. My existence was wretched, but at least it was bearable, at least there were pleasures, stolen wine and pilfered books, a secret language of hand signs, a friend.

A friend.

I have killed my best and only friend.

A wave of shame and remorse sweeps over me, and for a second I have an impulse to destroy it all, to burn the laboratory, to expiate my shame by leaping from the roof with the Monster's head in my arms to the rocks below. To end the sorry, shabby story of the Master and all his experiments once and for all.

But somehow, in the wash of shame and guilt that consumes me, that rational part that managed to appreciate the beauty of the rooftop finds a voice, a suggestion, a way to save my friend and myself.

***

The Monster's eyes open.

I stare into them pensively. Is there anything of my friend in there? Is there anything of the memories we shared?

The eyes narrow, the brow furrows, and I can see in the Monster's gaze: first the shimmer of recognition, the beginnings of a smile. But then equally comes confusion, recollections of our battle, a shadow of anger in a frown, a sadness that we should have come to blows; the final instants, blackness, and now puzzlement at being alive.

I watch carefully, studying each muscular twitch and tick, the movement of tissue and wire under the skin, the slight pulls against careful stitching. The Monster blinks and breathes, savouring the sweet air filling its lungs. The eyes move side to side, the gaze seems to turn inward as musculature tense and relaxes, exploring its body for damage and finding only perfection.

Perhaps the Master made me better than he knew. Perhaps he taught and trained me better than he realized. Perhaps he'd learned from his experiments after all. His notes and diagrams and drawings were certainly detailed and copious, and I made my best use of them. The Monster's body had been smashed beyond repair, and yet, I was proud of my handiwork.

"Wait," I signed.

The Monster's eyes tracked my fingers, understanding communicated with the slightest nod. The last memory would have been having his head torn off, so I suspected that a small nod was all the Monster was prepared to risk.

I held up the mirror for the Monster to gaze into. I was a little afraid at this moment, broodingly so. There was no way the Monster could anticipate what it would see, and so no way that I could predict the reaction. I had been desperate to save my friend, more desperate than I had ever known. I had done my best, had improvised, adapted.

But now...

The Monster gazed at the milk white skin, the pallor of grubs found beneath a rock... the delicate porcelain features, the wiry black hair with its white streaks. The black eyes opened wider, perfect lips parted in shock.

The Monster raised a feminine hand to its cheek in wonderment, then peered at the hand, so exquisitely crafted. Beneath the sheet, I could feel the Monster's other hand moves as it felt across its new body.

The Monster's body had been wrecked beyond any hope of repair. All that had been left was a head, and all that mattered of the head was the brain within.

And there had been a perfect body in want of a brain.

"What...? What have you done?" the Monster asked in wonderment at the sound of her own voice.

The Master had done a better job of the vocal cords this time around. I grunted.

"I saved my only friend," I signed back.

But she barely heard me. Instead, the Masterpiece Creation-stared at her fingers, her hands, at the exquisite artistry of her new body, her new life. Finally, she looked at me.

She reached out, pulling me closer, her hands closing around the sides of my head in the same maneuver which I had decapitated my friend.

"My friend," she repeated. "My friend..."

Her head tilted birdie, her eyes bright and shining.

"I love you," she said, and drew me closer, into a kiss.

It seems that Monsters may have happy endings too.

END

VAMPIRE VS. VELOCIRAPTOR: BLOODTHIRSTY – Tyler Shepard

Matsuda Research Facility Number 86, Oregon, somewhere within the Willamette National Forest

"And Auburn has the ball again – that's a third turnover from the Alabama offense this game!" the commentator proclaimed on the small TV screen "This Iron Bowl game has been full of surprises!"

Harold Benson cheered at the sight of his favorite college football team knocking their old school rival down a peg. Though he wished he was back home watching the game with his wife at his side on their forty-inch TV screen, the fifty-three-year-old security guard was at least thankful that the control room had a small TV for those who would be working the nightshift. It still bothered Harold that he had to come in to work regardless of the schedule saying that he was off tonight, but he could thank Mike's poor choice of eating raw oysters the night before for putting him in this spot now.

It wasn't that he hated this job; far from it. It was slower pace than his previous place of work, but he did not care much for how whenever someone either called in sick or caught a bad case of "no fucks given" that he was the first person they would contact as back-up.

Maggie would often tell Harold that they called him specifically because they liked his work ethic, though honestly, he figured that they only called him first because they never bothered to call anyone else to do the fill-in shifts, and he was dumb enough to say "yes" every time. It was not that he needed the money, as the pension from his retirement fund at the police force was more than enough to take care of him and Maggie until the day he died. His reason for heeding those calls was more along the lines of trying to avoid boredom. Too often he had seen his friends let their retirement be the death of them, a fate that Harold himself was afraid of sharing during the final months before he left the police force.

Luckily, dying from boredom was something he would not have to dread, for shortly after retiring, he found a job as a security guard at a science lab that was owned by the Matsuda Corporation. Admittedly, his wife was not exactly thrilled at the idea of her husband, who spent so much of his time away from her during his career as a cop as it was, to go and find *another* job that would keep him away from her. However, Maggie finally relented and let her husband pursue his new occupation, knowing that he would be miserable if he lacked something to keep his mind off the boredom.

Thankfully, he was in a much lower risk profession compared to his last job. Here he only had to work four night shifts a week – though that was excluding the days he would have to cover for others, such as the one he was doing tonight. As Harold stared intently at the small TV screen watching the two rival college teams war it out on the football field, a small tap on the doorway nearly made him jump out of his skin as he snapped back to reality.

"Hey, Harold," Joey, a fellow security guard, said after the former answered the door. "I'm going to the lower levels real quick. Hank and Raymond haven't checked in yet."

"Eh, it's probably the radios again," Harold brushed off. "You know how those things don't get great reception down there."

Joey only rolled his eyes at Harold's comment before heading off toward the elevator that led to the lab's lower levels. While the former cop did not have access to that section of the facility, he was aware that the walls in those parts of the lab had been reinforced with stronger material, though what those said materials were, he was unsure of. Harold could only assume that the stronger built walls were meant as a form of defense for whatever manner of secret work that went on down there.

Despite working here for nearly two years now, there was very little in terms of the inner workings of the international company employing him that he was privy to. Granted, he knew the basics of the company like everyone else did, which in his book was more than enough for him.

Originally based in Kyoto, Japan, the Matsuda Corporation had their hands in several fields of science, all of which they were masters of. Whether they are medical, environmental, or even genetic, the Matsuda Corporation had their hands in all forms of scientific research. Under the watchful eye of their founder, Hiroshi Matsuda, the company had gone global in the near-forty years since its formation. Recently, the company had announced that they had begun a new endeavor: genetic engineering. As one would expect, there was a public outcry against this newest enterprise of Matsuda Corp. True, the new venture had its supporters, though that was mostly from the company's investors and other major companies that the corporation did business with.

However, the vast majority of the general public, most stemming from major religious groups, were appalled by the very idea of creating life from a test tube. Amidst the rallies and protests, Hiroshi himself assured the masses that this experiment was not meant to play God, but to help humans in medical need by manufacturing organs that were genetically identical to those who needed a replacement. This also included a new type of synthetic plasma that could be compatible with any blood type.

Matsuda swore that these new advances in medical science would be affordable for the common working man, but personally, Harold had his doubts, for he had heard that same song and dance before from other people throughout his life. The facility that the former cop was working security for was one such site where the Matsuda Corporation's scientists were researching and designing the genetically engineered organs that would soon be used. From what he understood, those who sought an organ transplant would give the corporation a sample of their DNA and the scientists would grow a perfect replica of the patient's required organ that would then be surgically inserted into that person. This could normally be done at any hospital across the globe.

However, in recent weeks Harold had taken note of a sudden change around the building. It began with a surprise delivery of unknown material from an armored truck. Harold did not see much of what was inside of the vehicle as the lab's staff and the truck's delivery crew moved the items down into the lower levels. He did, however, notice some of the hardware the adjoining security team that had accompanied the delivery group had brought with them. Instead of carrying the standard Glock 19 and batons that Harold and the rest of the lab's security team were issued, this new team was armed with MP5 assault rifles, cattle prods, and high-powered tranquilizer guns meant for large animals such as rhinos and elephants.

The head of the research team, Dr. Glenda Callan, informed the staff that the genetically grown organs project would first need animal testing before they could start human trials, hence the need for the prods and tranquilizers should one of the animal test subjects get loose. As for the extra security, Dr. Callan explained that with this new venture came the threat of corporate espionage, which was to be met with zero-tolerance according to Mr. Matsuda himself.

So, the once fifteen-member security team was now increased to a thirty-five on-site team, but Harold had not seen the new guys since their arrival because they stayed solely on the lower levels. Though the former cop had not met any of the new security team members one on one, he had a strong feeling that they all had some manner of military training – perhaps even Special Forces, for that matter.

Just then, out of the corner of his eye, Harold spotted something that took his attention away from the football game that he invested so much time in. The distraction in question was on one of the many monitors in the security control room. On this screen Harold caught a brief glimpse of something winged moving at a break-neck speed across the grounds. At first, he assumed that it was either a small bird or a bat that was flying past the camera, but the ex-cop's instincts told him otherwise. The shape was moving too fast for any kind of winged organism he knew of, and it was also too big to be either type of animal.

Luckily, the corporation's hi-tech surveillance equipment was described as "exotically advanced," otherwise Harold would likely have missed the airborne anomaly.

But he was certain that the object had wings. An owl, maybe? He had seen some large owls in his time; however, something deep in the pit of his stomach was telling him that this was not some animal that wandered onto the facility's grounds. Acting on his uneasy feeling, Harold took out his walkie-talkie to radio in one of the four guards who patrolled the grounds.

"Mendez, come in," he said into the radio "You there?"

Silence was the only answer Harold received.

"Mendez, come in." Harold repeated in a firmer voice, "Pick up, Carl!"

Again, no answer came. Thinking, or better put, hoping, that it was a simple malefaction with Carlson's radio, Harold switched over to one of the other guards.

"Besly, you there?" he asked into his device.

Silence again. Fighting through the fear that was slowly rising in his chest, Harold again switched over to another fellow guard.

"Mayfield, come in!" the former cop practically shouted into his radio.

"Jesus Christ, Harold!" a female voice shouted back on the other end of the radio. "You don't have to shout into the fucking thing!"

"Laura... oh, thank God!" Harold sighed in relief. "I thought something happened to you. Listen, can you get a hold of anyone else out there?"

"I tried to reach Besly and Mendez, but I can't get through to them. Kurtzman isn't picking up either. I was just about to radio in to see if you had heard from them recently. But I guess that's not the case, is it?"

"I couldn't reach either of them as well, Laura," Harold admitted, "and if you can't reach Kurtzman, then something is seriously wrong."

"Can you see them on any of the monitors?"

Harold quickly looked back at the advanced displays that were connected to the outside of the lab. He began to frantically cycle through each screen to find the missing guards. It made no sense to him – how could three well-armed men just up and vanish without a trace? Mendez was a former cop like Harold, only he worked the hard streets of Los Angeles before moving to Oregon after his retirement. Kurtzman was an ex-marine with three tours in Iraq under his belt, so sneaking up on him was all but impossible.

As he came upon one empty screen after another, Harold thought about what he had seen earlier and began to wonder if that winged creature may have had a hand in all this. However, the retired officer quickly shook off that notion, refusing to believe that some animal, no matter the size, could make three security guards just up and disappear.

"I'm getting nothing on my end, Laura," Harold finally said. "Come back inside. I'll radio in for some back-up and we'll go look for them as a group."

"Wait a sec, Harold..." Laura replied. "I think I see someone."

"Is it one of the guys?"

"I can't tell, it's too dark," Laura answered before calling out to the newcomer. "Who's there? Show yourself!"

Once again, Harold was met by that dreadful silence. Suddenly, a scream of horror erupted over the radio, making the ex-cop nearly fall out of his seat from fright at the high-pitched sound. He then heard the brief eruption of gunfire as the screams continued before they then became more choked and gargled as the sound of flesh being torn soon overtook the audio coming through the radio. Without giving it a second thought, Harold jumped to his feet and sent out an immediate distress call to the other guards.

"All units, we have personnel down – I repeat, we have guards down! I need all available units to meet me outside the lab with med-kits now!"

As Harold drew his sidearm and dashed out of the control room, he tried to reach Joey, who was no doubt still on the lower levels. However, while the former cop was preparing himself to face an unknown threat on the outside, he had no idea that another danger was brewing right beneath him...

***

As the chaos began to unfold topside, Joey Cranston had already stepped inside the elevator that led downward into the lab's lower levels. That was where the staff's major research and development took place, well away from the prying eyes of visiting business partners who may attempt to steal any secrets and the press who could potentially leak any top secret information to the public at large. Due to the depths and the thickness of the walls that surrounded this part of the research facility, it was all but impossible for any and all radio contact to reach anyone down here. Because of this, it was ordered that of the fifteen original security staff members, only three would be given access to this part of the facility.

It wasn't that they needed the extra help, as the new security team took care of that; it was that they needed messengers between here and topside due to the inability to make radio or cellular contact to the upper parts of the building. In other words, they were nothing more than messenger boys, something that Joey tried not to think about and instead focused on the ten-percent upgrade in his paycheck that his new duties gave him. It was a bonus he could keep so long as he kept his mouth shut about the inner workings of whatever he saw down there... which most of the time wasn't much. Like Joey, the only other topside guards who were granted access to the lower labs were the two men whom he was in search of at the moment, Hank and Raymond.

They were called down to the lower levels for unspecified reasons, but they were assured that they would return within the hour. An hour came and went and neither of the guards had returned from their unknown task. Now normally, Joey would not be too concerned about it, merely chalking it up to something mundane such as the two being caught up with some simple task, such as moving equipment that the scientists could not move themselves.

He had the nagging feeling that something was wrong, however. So, acting on the uneasy feeling in his gut, Joey headed down to see what had become of his comrades, hoping that the holdup was only Hank trying to keep Raymond from starting another fight with the other guards.

He never said it out loud, but Joey really hated this new batch of guards that had been stationed at the facility. Whenever he, Hank, or Raymond were down there, they would always be given condescending looks by them, or mocked behind their backs on the sole ground that they had no military training like the new batch possessed. Joey had attempted to address these issues to Dr. Callan since she was the head of the research facility, but she brushed off his words, saying that if he liked his job than it would be in his best interest to allow the lower-level guards to do their tasks in peace.

Dr. Callan, or as the guys called her in their group text, "the Cunt Queen," was a cold, 38-year-old biochemist who had only one love in her life: her work. From what Joey heard from Dr. Callan's staff whenever he had lunch with them, she had fought tooth and nail for her current position and was obsessed with proving herself to Mr. Matsuda so she could move higher in the corporate ladder.

Dr. Callan was more than willing to step on someone if it meant that her work was not only completely to her liking, but if it also meant that it would make her look better in the eyes of the corporation's CEO. What Joey would not give to see that bitch get what was coming to her one of these days.

The "ding!" from the elevator reaching the lower levels brought Joey back to reality, allowing him to focus on his task of finding out what had happened to his fellow guards. As the doors slid open, the guard was subjected to a sight that nearly made him jump out of his skin. Alarms blared while the once bright lights that lit the windowless laboratory had become a dark shade of red to reveal the sight that horrified Joey in the first place: a corpse. It was one of the low-level security guards, lying face down in a pool of blood with his small intestines strewn out across the floor. His assault rifle laid beside him broken in half.

As Joey stepped out of the elevator to better inspect the corpse, he noticed a series of deep cuts across the guard's back. Whatever had slashed the now dead security officer was able to cut through his body armor like a knife going through butter, something only a weapon like a sword could do. Upon a closer inspection, Joey saw that the cuts were not random, but were an even set of three, like those left by an animal.

The upper-level guard was aware that Callan and her research team conducted animal testing down here to help with the cloned organs experiment. However, he had only seen rats, rabbits, and monkeys; whatever had done this was vastly larger than the animals that were being kept down here.

Joey wanted nothing more than to run back into the elevator and rally the other topside guards to help him, but another part of him told him to stay and find Hank and Raymond first – assuming that they were still alive, of course. Ignoring his fears, Joey drew his sidearm, switched on his flashlight, and preceded to head deeper into the lab, all the while praying that his friends were still among the living.

***

The cold autumn air hit Harold's face as he and the other security guards ran outside the complex to find the others. Aside from the lab's outside lights, the surrounding forest that engulfed the building was completely pitch black, only visible when clouds that hung over the nights sky parted for a few seconds to reveal the moonlight before vanishing back into the darkness. Harold had given up on reaching Joey and the others who were on the lower levels, thinking that either they could not pick up on the radio or that something else had distracted them. Either way, he would have to make do with what men he had with him right now. With his police training taking over, the ex-cop had his team fan out and secure the area.

Harold's mind was still reeling with questions. Who would attack this facility? How could they slip by the security systems and cameras without being detected? And who could take down several guards without tripping any alarms in the process? He knew that Matsuda had made some powerful enemies over the years, enemies who had some very deep pockets. Could it be possible that one of Matsuda's corporate rivals had hired some professional team of specialists to break in and steal the lab's research on the genetics program?

The ex-policeman and his team fanned out in the hopes of finding at least one member of the outside squad that was still alive. With guns drawn, they began their search, all the while calling out the names of those who had gone missing. Silence was the only answer the guards received for their calls; and not just that of their missing comrades, but their surroundings as well. Even at night, the forest that the research facility had been built on was alive with the calls of owls, insects, and various other nocturnal animals that inhabited the surrounding woods. But tonight, the forest was unnaturally silent, like a shroud of death had swept over the woods and had consumed every living thing in its wake.

Harold was not much of an outdoorsman, but when he was younger his uncle would take him hunting on the weekends. During those hunts, his uncle taught him to pick up on certain signs the forest would give him for when a predator was around. One of these was the way the woods themselves became as deathly quiet as they were now. Contemplating what could silence an entire forest with its presence put him greatly on edge.

He then thought back to the image of the winged creature he saw briefly on the camera moments before the disappearances began. Could it be possible that the unknown animal that he caught a brief glimpse of had a hand in what happened to Laura and the others? While the thought of a single animal being the reason behind something like that sounded utterly preposterous, Harold could not help but entertain the possibility regardless.

Not many knew this about the former law enforcement officer aside from his wife and some of his closest friends, but he was a firm believer in the paranormal. Now, that was not to say he thought such things as ghosts or demonic possession were real, due to his atheist background, but he did hold a belief that there some things in this world that could not be so easily explained by known science. Living here in Oregon, one always did hear stories of unknown creatures, whether they are tales of a Sasquatch sighting, or someone seeing a Thunderbird flying over their home.

While Harold had never had a monster tale himself, deep down he wanted to at least see one cryptid before he died. However, between the image of the winged beast and mysterious vanishing of Laura and the other guards, it began to make Harold dread the idea that he had finally gotten his wish.

"Over here, quick!" one of the other security guards, Royce Meyers, called out to the others.

The rest of the team rushed over to where Royce was located. As the former cop and his co-workers ran toward him, Harold noticed that Royce was standing over something, but due to the darkness he could not make out what it was. It was not until he and the others got close that they could make out what the guard had found. It was the body of Laura Mayfield, and the very sight of her corpse made at least one or two of the security guards vomit at the sight before them.

Harold had seen enough bodies during his time on the police force, but this corpse lying at his feet was vastly different than the shooting or stabbing victims he had come across as a cop. Laura's throat had been torn open, as if a bear or a wolf had attacked her. Yet aside from the fatal neck wound, there appeared to be no signs of assault on her person. The appearance of the cadaver itself confused Harold. It looked as though her entire body had been drained of blood, leaving what was left as nothing more than a withered husk.

Normally, the rate of decomposition took weeks to rot a dead body to the extent of Laura's corpse. However, it had been less than fifteen minutes between the time that Harold lost contact with her and the discovery of the body.

"This doesn't make any sense..." he muttered in confusion as he kneeled to get a closer look at the corpse.

"Don't touch it!" another guard, Gary Matthews, suddenly spoke up. "We can't contaminate the body before we call the police!"

"Did you forget that I'm a former cop, Matthews?" Harold reminded his fellow guard. "I know protocol."

"Then you know that protocol says that we need to call the cops!" the fellow guard shot back. "Seriously, I didn't sign on for this shit!"

"Matthews is right, Harold," Royce agreed. "This is way over our heads. I mean, what the fuck could do that to Laura? And where the hell are the others?"

"I don't know, but I doubt we'll find them alive," Harold said. "I also know that we can't lose our cool right now. Let's get back inside and tell the others what's going on. Then once we get the lab on lockdown. we'll call this in."

As the group spoke among themselves, none of them noticed the strange mist that seemed to seep in around them. Harold had to resist from reaching out to take a closer look at the fatal wound on Laura's throat. The former cop had seen enough injuries inflicted to the neck by the blade of a knife to know that this incision was too jagged and messy to have been done by such a weapon, let alone with the steady hand of a professional to guide it. The mist that the group of security guards had given no mind to had grown in size and density, becoming thick and heavy around them in a matter of seconds.

However, despite this sudden change in his surroundings that his co-workers finally began noticing, Harold was still trying to decipher what could have taken Laura's life, unaware of what was now encircling him and the others. Suddenly, a quick, shrill shriek snapped Harold back into reality and the realization of something that his fellow guards already knew: the shriek came from a now missing Gary Matthews. Harold and the other guards began to frantically search around the now heavily clouded area for their missing coworker.

It boggled his mind that Gary could just vanish without anyone seeing who or what had taken him. Harold shot up and drew his sidearm;

all the while his eyes darted around, trying in vain to peer through the dense mist that engulfed the security team. Just then, another shriek rang out. Harold and the others looked to see that now Royce was missing from the group.

At this point, the other guards were in a state of panic. Many of them lacked Harold's steadiness in a hostile situation. However, despite holding himself steady, the former cop began to feel his own fear creep into his mind. He had been in at least three gunfights during his time in the force, and he was as afraid then as he was now.

The images of the winged beast that he saw on the advanced digital camera flashed through his mind as he and his comrades tried to get their bearings in this accursed mist. Harold suddenly jumped when he heard the surprise sound of a gunshot ring out from one of the other guard's weapons. He turned to see that the person who had fired the shot was the rookie, Ritchie Peirce, who had a look of pure terror on his face as he looked out into the surrounding mist.

"I saw something!" Ritchie proclaimed. "It's in the mist!"

"You fucking moron! What if you shot at one of our own?" Harold shouted at the rookie.

"They're dead and you know it, Harold!" Ritchie shot back. "There's something out there and it's gonna kill us all!"

Before Harold could continue the argument, Ritchie was suddenly yanked backwards into the depths of the dense mist by some unseen force. The ex-officer was shocked by what he had just witnessed, but his state of terror was far from over. Harold was not the only one who was now in fear of his life, for the remaining guards had begun to fire blindly into the mist, not knowing if they were hitting whatever was killing their coworkers or not. All they could do was pray that they were at least scaring their mysterious assailant away.

Suddenly, another guard was dragged off into the mist before another was taken shortly thereafter. All around Harold his comrades were being killed left and right by something he could not see. Was it a hitman hired by another company? A wild animal? At this point the ex-lawman did not care; all he wanted to do was survive the night.

As the last of his comrades vanished into the mist, the former cop realized that he hadn't fired off a single shot from his gun – though he imagined that he would have no success in hitting whoever or whatever was attacking the lab due to the mist covering their tracks. Knowing that he had no chance against the unknown attacker, Harold made a break for the lab. If he could reach it, he could finally reach Joey and the others in the lower levels and put the lab in lockdown to keep their unseen enemy from reaching them.

There was, however, a major obstacle in his path: the mist was so dense he was unable to make out what direction the lab was in at this point. Still unaware which was the safe route, Harold took off into the soupy fog, hoping that he could reach the lab. As he ran blindly through the billowy substance, he could hear the screams of the other guards being slaughtered all around him. He kept his sidearm close, only wanting to fire when he had a target in his sights like he was trained to do.

At one point, Harold spotted for the briefest of moments what appeared to be a pair of bright red eyes glaring at him through the cloudy vapors before disappearing. Harold was so focused on the eyes that he was not paying attention to where he was running and tripped over his own two feet. As the former cop fell to the ground, he accidently discharged his firearm, sending a bullet through his leg in the process. Harold let out a cry of pain as he clutched his fresh gunshot wound and desperately tried to drag himself in the direction that he hoped was the way back to the facility. As he did so, the mist began to recede around him at a fast pace.

While this was occurring, the security guard noticed that as the mist was pulling away, it seemed to be taking on a new, almost human-like form. Harold's eyes widened in stunned horror as the billowing haze took the shape of a man, though it was not any man the security guard had ever seen before.

The stranger was tall with a slender build, making him look more like a scarecrow than a man. His skin was sickly pale, like a person suffering from a disease. He was bald with an aquiline nose as well as pointed, bat-like ears. The strange man's ghoulish appearance was punctuated by long, clawed hands and the possession of a pair of fangs protruding from underneath the upper part of his bloodstained lips.

The stranger's attire was equally as odd as his physical appearance. He wore a dark blue overcoat with a sharp, upturned collar to it. Beneath his coat was a white dress shirt with a black vest over it, all of which was covered with spatters of blood. The strangely archaic raiment was completed by a pair of black dress pants and dark pointy-toed shoes.

But the one feature that drew Harold's attention the most was the man's eyes. They were deep and sunken in with dark red irises that seemed to pierce right into the security guard's very soul. Those eyes remained locked on him as the bloodstained humanoid creature approached. Harold wanted to scream, to call out for help from anyone left inside the building; but no words could escape his throat, for the fear he felt had rendered him unable to so much as move.

Harold did not want to use the word "vampire" to describe this strange man, but what other word could he use for what was standing before him? There was no rational explanation to properly explain the sight he now beheld other than stating the obvious. In just a few gore-filled seconds, everything the onetime lawman thought he knew had flipped upside down. As the former cop's mind raced with panic and terror, the vampire bent down so he could look the frightened guard directly in the eye.

"Good evening, sir," the creature greeted in a tone that fringed genuine politeness as he snatched the guard's gun and casually tossed it away. "Allow me to introduce myself. I am Anton Herzog and, as I am sure you have already surmised from my little performance, I am, in fact, a vampire."

"W-what… how?" Harold was at a total loss for words.

"Ah, yes, the typical shocked response," Anton dryly remarked with an added eye roll. "Well, permit me to keep things simple for you: There is something in that lab you are guarding that I want, and you, my friend, are going to help me acquire it."

"N-No!"

The vampire merely scoffed at the guard's refusal, acting like he had heard a bad joke. He then jammed one of his sharpened fingernails into the bullet wound before twisting it, making Harold scream in pain.

"I was not asking," the undead creature stated firmly just before twisting his claw in the wound again, which earned him another scream of agony.

Anton then took Harold by the collar of his shirt before hoisting his newly made hostage to his feet with the ease of picking up a penny from the ground.

"Now then, lead the way," the vampire commanded. "And please, do not try to anger me. I have only just begun to hurt you."

***

"Hank? Raymond?" Joey called out as he cautiously walked through the lab's corridors. "Anybody?"

The young security guard carefully rounded the corner with his sidearm drawn. The lab's emergency lights blanketed the hallways in a dark shade of red that matched the puddles of blood covering the floor. Every path taken by Joey seemed to lead him down another death-filled corridor. All he had been able to find in terms of people were the dead bodies of said individuals. Everywhere he turned he found the slashed up remains of the security guards of this level, as well as the scientists who worked here. He still had no idea as to who or what could have done this and found nothing that could show him what was capable of butchering these men and women. The only evidence he had were the deep slashing wounds the bodies were covered in.

It just made no sense to him. How could someone manage to sneak past the guards and security team topside, get down to the lower levels without proper access, and kill everyone there with only the use of knives? It was then that the guard had another theory form in his head: What if the attacker did not come from the outside, but *inside* the lab?

It was a crazy thought, but it was not totally out of the question. Dr. Callan's team was in charge of top-secret research, some of which was rumored to be used for military purposes. Could one of those projects be the reason for this carnage?

No, that was impossible, as this was a lab that was meant to research and design things that would be used for the betterment of humankind, not some sort of sci-fi experiment. Still, it was becoming harder and harder to rationalize what Joey was seeing all around him. A part of him wanted to return to the elevator and tell Harold and the other topside guards what he had discovered, but he had to find Hank and Raymond first. But the young guard was grimly aware that the deeper he traversed into the lab and found only more death, the less likely he was to find his missing friends alive.

As Joey traveled down the hallway, he noticed that one of the doors to the many labs was open. With a mix of curiosity and a resolve to find his comrades, the guard slowly entered the room. As he took a few steps into the open chamber, the first thing he took note of the inside was that it appeared more like a pen to hold an animal than it did a lab. The pen itself appeared to have been busted outward, a clear sign that whatever was being held here had broken free.

It was then that Joey heard the low groan of a person from behind him. He spun around to find none other than Dr. Callan lying face down on the floor in a pool of her own blood. On her back were a set of three deep cuts down across it, similar to the horrendous gashes he had seen on the rest of the now dead personal he had come across.

Joey quickly put his gun away before rushing over to the chief-scientist's side before gently lifting her so she could sit up. The young guard then took off his jacket and put it against Dr. Callan's back to apply pressure to her wound. The scientist's eyes slowly opened and closed, a clear sign that she was drifting in and out of consciousness. If Joey was going to get any answers, then he had to keep her alive to figure out what had happened here.

"Dr. Callan, can you hear me?" he asked. "Can you speak?"

"Y-Yes…" the woman answered weakly. "Who… are you?"

"My name's Joey. I'm from the topside security team. Can you tell me what happened here?"

In a sudden burst of energy, Dr. Callan reached out and grabbed Joey by the shirt before pulling him forward to look the young man directly in the eye.

"It was because of them!" she exclaimed. "They kept teasing Seventeen – they wouldn't leave him alone!"

"What are you talking about?" Joey asked, pulling himself out of her grip as he did so. "Who was teasing what?"

"It was them!" she continued as she pointed off to the corner of the room. "Every time those two idiots came down here, they would harass Seventeen! Always poking him with the cattle prods when we weren't looking and taking his food away when he wasn't finished eating – all of this was because of *them!*"

Joey looked over to the darkened corner Dr. Callan was pointing toward. It was there that he saw a pair of bodies, or better put, the remains of two bodies scattered about the floor. Joey's eyes widened in horror when he realized what he was looking at.

There, torn into chunks of flesh and entrails, were what was left of the bodies of Hank and Raymond, though the only way Joey was certain that it was them was from the bloodstained named tags he could see that were attached to what was left of the two men's torsos. A cold fusion of rage and terror took hold of the young guard's whole body as he turned back to where Callan had been sitting and yanked her to her feet.

"You're going to tell me what the fuck is going on right now, or so help me God, I'll—" he attempted to threaten.

"You have to get me out of here right now!" Dr. Callan cut him off in a panic. "It's going to come back now that it knows that you're here!"

"*What's* coming back? I want answers – now!"

A loud, animalistic screech suddenly echoed throughout the halls of the lab. Joey let go of the chief-scientist as he drew his pistol yet again. With his weapon drawn, the security officer slowly crept out toward the doorway of the room before leaning out and peering down both sides of the connecting hallway to see what had made the sound. However, he saw nothing but the bodies that littered the corridor.

Not wanting to let whatever was down here with him to just walk into the room; Joey quickly closed the metal door and locked it. He then turned his attention back to Dr. Callan, who was currently trying to limp over to one of her computers.

"Hey! Hey!" he shouted as he stormed over to her. "What the hell do you think you're doing?"

"I have to save my research," Dr. Callan replied as she logged into her computer. "Even if we have to terminate Subject: Seventeen, I'll still have something to show to Mr. Matsuda when all of this is over."

"When all of this is – do you even hear yourself right now, lady?" Joey harshly scolded the injured woman before him. "Whatever you cooked up in this lab is still out there and it's probably trying to find a way in here as we speak! So, you're going to tell me what exactly you created that killed my friends right now!"

"You wouldn't understand." Dr. Callan answered simply and coldly, keeping her attention on the screen in front of her

Before Joey had a chance to either shout at the woman or smack her, a loud bang against the door made the unlikely duo jump in unified fright. Whatever had hit the door had struck it with such a great force that it had dented the metal. The beast on the other side let out a deep, crocodile-like hiss in anger before banging on the door again, leaving several deeper dents as it began to snarl and roar at the humans on the other side of the barrier.

Joey opened fire in response to the attack, putting three holes through the door in the hope of killing, or at the very least scaring, the creature. This action earned him a deep yowl in response. There was then an ominous silence on the other side of the door. The quiet did not give either human any comfort, however, for they feared that the beast at the door had not been slain. Sure enough, their terrors were confirmed when a large, yellow reptilian eye peered through one of the bullet holes as the creature let out another hiss, anticipating the kill to come.

Joey's gun shook in his hand as he stared at the eye that hungrily looked back at him. The fear he was feeling had made him unable to do or say anything in response to the current situation. The creature known only as Subject: Seventeen screeched again before backing away from the door before starting another onslaught on the obstacle before it. The attack snapped the security guard back into reality and he fired several rounds through the door to try to ward the animal off.

"That won't do any good!" Dr. Callan shouted at him. "His hide is too thick for small arms fire to pierce!"

"Then tell me what we're fighting so I can stop it!" Joey shot back.

"It's the perfect killing machine," the scientist explained in fear. "When Mr. Matsuda's team sent us the genome to reconstruct, we had to fill in the gaps with DNA strands of some of the most aggressive species on the planet. Subject: Seventeen was the most dangerous of his litter – he even killed the rest of his siblings when they were just two months old. But he didn't eat them; it was almost as if he seemed to enjoy killing them. That's all he did when he broke out of his pen – just kill!"

"What is it?"

"I-I-I knew that Seventeen's brain patterns were off, but I just thought it a minor side-effect of his rapid growth into adolescence – I never once thought that he would be psychotic!" Dr. Callan continued in a fit of hysterics, "Oh, God, forgive me, I created a monster!"

"Goddammit, tell me what it is!" Joey shouted in her face.

A horrendous mixed screech of Seventeen and a chuck of metal being pulled back made the two trapped humans look back at the door as three long, clawed fingers that were connected to a scaled hand peeled open a much larger hole. This allowed the beast the opening it needed to strike down the one thing that was keeping it away from its prey. With the door down, Joey could now finally see in total disbelief and horror the monster that had been created in this very lab. He quickly reloaded his pistol.

With a cry of both fear and false bravado, the security guard raised his revolver again and began to fire bullet after bullet into Seventeen's thick, scaly hide, dealing not even so much as a scratch on its reptilian skin in the futile attack. Shrieking in rage, the monster swung its tail at Joey, knocking him across the room. With the guard out of the way, Seventeen turned its elongated head back toward Dr. Callan, who had since began backing up from the beast she had created. Seventeen tapped the sickle-shaped claws on the floor as it slowly crept closer to her, as if it were savoring every second of drinking in her fear before the inevitable kill.

Dr. Callan suddenly tripped over a piece of fallen equipment, causing her to tumble onto her back. Callen cried out in pain as the fall had caused her to land on her still fresh wounds, which in turn sent a blaze of agony throughout her body. Seventeen placed his foot down on the scientist's abdomen, holding her down while putting more agonizing pressure on her injury that forced her to scream even louder.

The giant reptile then leaned down to look his creator in the eye as he bared his rows of blade-like teeth to her in a sneer. Saliva dripped down from its open jaws and onto Callan's face. Then, in an instant, the beast's head darted forward and engulfed the woman's head in his gaping maw. Callan screamed as her creation violently shook her head like a dog with a toy while his sickle-claw stabbed into her torso, effortlessly splitting it open to allow her organs to spill out onto the floor. Blood sprayed out as the monster dug its fearsome talons into whatever artery they could cut into.

Dr. Callan's screams took on a gurgling sound as she began to choke on the blood that was spewing from her mouth while her creation continued to mutilate her. As the creature mauled its creator, Joey had been locked in a state of total fear. There was no saving the scientist now. The guard's only rational option was to escape back to the elevator. He had no idea what to do after he had made it back to the upper levels of the building, but right now he did not care. All that concerned him right now was getting out of there.

Staying low to the ground, Joey slowly inched toward the door, keeping his eyes on the monster as he did so. Seventeen paid Joey no mind, for the raptor-like beast's full attention was on the prey that was beneath his claws. Once the guard was close enough to the doorway, Joey sprang to his feet and bolted out of the opening.

His escape attempt did not go unnoticed, for the beast instantly stopped his slaughter and let out a roar at the fleeing security officer before giving chase. Subject: Seventeen lunged forward at a breakneck speed, but in his haste, the genetically engineered monster lost his footing for a moment, causing the reptile to stumble forward and bang into the wall, thereby giving Joey a head-start to the elevator.

Subject: Seventeen quickly righted himself before giving chase once more, letting out a furious screech as he resumed the pursuit. There was no thought in Joey's mind other than to run. As the guard rounded another corner, he could hear the creature's snarls as it continued to give chase. The only advantage he had over the monster in terms of evasion was that the hallways were too narrow, and the corners were too sharp for the beast to properly maneuver in, forcing the engineered dinosaur to trip whenever he tried to round one.

Joey fired his last four bullets blindly behind him as he continued to run, hoping that at least one might hit the creature somewhere vital and deter his pursuer from continuing the chase. Sadly, the bullets not only missed their intended target, but also only infuriated the monster even further.

Thankfully, however, Joey had managed to reach the elevator, which he quickly opened with a swipe of his keycard. The only thing the security guard could hear at this point was his pulse racing through his skull as fast as his heart pumped blood through his veins as the elevator doors began to slide closed.

For the briefest of moments, Joey felt a small wave of relief wash over him as he watched the image of the monster begin to vanish behind the closing doors in front of him. But just before the elevator doors could fully shut, the monster reached out with his claws and forced the doors apart, thus allowing the raptor access inside the elevator. The beast's eyes narrowed down at the frightened young man before lunging forward with his claws and fangs ready to cut deep into the guard's flesh. All the way back up toward the upper levels, the elevator shaft echoed with the dying screams of Joey Cranston.

***

As Anton carried, or rather, dragged, Harold through the topside of the building, the former cop was still shellshocked by the fact that his bizarre captor was a real member of the Undead. If this weren't a truly horrifying experience, he would almost be amazed by all of this. Long had he wanted to peer into the world of the paranormal, but he failed to anticipate that not only would it find him first, but it would also literally have his life in its hands. Harold had to wonder if he was losing his mind or if this was all just a dream.

However, the pain in his leg gave him a grim reminder that this was all too real. The vampire still did not tell him what exactly he was after, though if the security guard had to guess it may have something to do with the organs project that the facility was researching. As Anton continued to drag his captive across the floor, the bloodsucker continued to look through the windows of each lab they passed by, another clear sign that Harold's theory could be right.

"You're... you're after the organs, aren't you?" he asked.

Anton turned away from the window he was looking through and stared down at his human hostage with annoyance in his reddish eyes, as if he had been asked a stupid question.

"Have you ever known a vampire to consume organs?" Anton chastised.

"Then why—?"

"Because it isn't *just* organs the Matsuda Corporation is growing. They are developing synthetic blood as well."

Harold had heard rumors of the company's development of artificial hemoglobin that could be used for all types without the requirement of a donor. It would make sense that a creature that feasted solely on blood would want something that would quench its thirst without needing the effort of hunting for its next victim. Suddenly, a red-hot wave of pain seized Harold's body, making him let out a shout in agony. Anton had once again jammed his claw into the human's gunshot wound so that he could grab his attention.

"Where is the lab that holds the blood?" he demanded coldly, twisting his fingers in the bullet hole again as he did so.

"I don't know!" Harold cried out as another surge of pain struck him.

"You're lying," the vampire sneered as he applied more pressure to the wound. "Where is the blood?"

"I swear I don't know!"

Anton let out a low, inhuman growl as he reached down and grabbed the security guard by his shirt before effortlessly heaving him off the ground and pinning him up against the wall. The undead monster's eyes flared bright red as he bared his fangs to him. Harold's whole body went rigid as the fear overtook him once more. He knew that if he angered the vampire any further, the creature would easily tear him to shreds without giving it a second thought.

"Listen to me very carefully," Anton began in a low yet sharp tone of voice. "You will take me to the facility that contains the synthetic blood this instant, or I will inflict pain upon you that you never thought possible before!"

Thinking quickly, Harold thought of the one place that could possibly hold what the vampire had sought after.

"I-it's probably somewhere in the lower levels. That's where they were doing the major research for the organs."

"Then take me there," Anton commanded.

"I can't," Harold admitted, knowing that this response could mean the end of him. "Those labs require a special access card, and I don't have one."

Anton let out a snarl at his captive's answer, obviously enraged that his prize continued to elude him. Saying nothing, the vampire raised his claws in the air, ready to plunge them right through Harold's torso. Facing death, all the security guard could think of was leaving his wife alone. Would she even know what had happened to him? Would the company even tell her or the rest of the slain guards' families about what took place tonight? All Harold could do was close his eyes and pray that his end would be quick and painless.

However, just before the vampire could gut his captive, the two heard a strange sound coming from down the hallway. They both slowly turned their heads to see a sight that shocked Harold. Crawling on the floor and covered in blood, was Joey. The fellow security guard's body was covered in deep slashes and lacerations. His left eye dangled from what was left of his face which had three deep lacerations across it while the inside of his mouth was exposed from the massive gash where his right cheek once was.

Chunks of flesh hung from Joey's throat as he gagged and wheezed on the blood that poured from his open wound. Several of his fingers had been roughly severed from his right hand, some of which still had broken shards of bone sticking out from where the digits once were, as if they had been roughly bitten off.

Before Joey could fully crawl round the corner, something from behind him suddenly reached out and took him by the legs. The younger security guard let out a gargled, blood-choked scream as he began to desperately grab at the corner of the hall with his left hand in an attempt to hold onto something. But his last-ditch effort to save himself was futile as he was dragged out of view, screaming as he did. Harold could not see who or what was ripping his co-worker to shreds, but he could see the massive spray of blood and organs hit the adjacent wall like a wave of gore.

At first, Harold thought that it was another vampire who was assisting Anton but judging by the vampire's confused expression at the violence unfurling in front of him that he was equally unaware as to exactly what was going on. It was then that Joey's unknown killer stepped out from behind the corner to reveal itself to the vampire and his human captive. What now stood before them made Harold question his sanity even more than he had already done that day.

What he and Anton beheld was a dinosaur. The resurrected reptile in question was a Utahraptor, the largest of its species, and often mistaken by the layperson for its cousin, the Velociraptor. Though this one was young, it still stood an imposing six-and-a- half-feet-tall, putting it several inches above Anton's height. The coloring of the raptor's body parts that were not covered in the blood and gore of his victims was a dull greenish-brown hue, like that of a crocodile's skin.

If this had been a true Utahraptor, then it would have had bright feathers and a more avian appearance, but Dr. Callan and her team used the DNA coding of various modern reptiles to fill the gaps in the raptor's genome, thereby giving this genetically altered beast a resemblance to that of the raptors seen in films or novels. Its massive eyes were bright yellow with black irises that were narrowed directed at the two confused onlookers. Seventeen snarled at them as he began to crotch down with its claws at the ready, a clear sign that the beast was preparing for an attack. Sneering back at the dinosaur, Anton dropped Harold on the floor before turning to face the cloned monster, ready for the fight that was to come.

"What is this beast?" Anton questioned as he faced off with the raptor.

"It's a dinosaur – a prehistoric animal that—" Harold attempted to explain.

"I *know* what a dinosaur is, you idiot," the vampire scolded. "I meant what is one doing here?"

"I-I don't know!" his captive admitted.

"Well, in any case, I will deal with you after I have taken care of this," the bloodsucker informed him. "And just to make sure that you do not try to flee…"

Anton suddenly stomped on Harold's kneecap, snapping the bones in his leg like a twig. As Harold rolled around on the floor screaming in pain, the vampire refocused his sights on the raptor, who roared at his undead challenger. The vampire hissed back at the dinosaur as a way of showing his reptilian opponent that he was not backing down. The cloned creation let out a screech as he bolted forward toward the undead creature who likewise darted forward towards him was well.

The raptor and the vampire collided into each other in mass of violence, the dinosaur claiming the first strike with a quick slash of his claws across Anton's chest. The bloodsucker snarled in pain before retaliating with a strong punch to the raptor's snout that made the raptor stumble backwards a bit. Acting on his attack, Anton lunged at Subject: Seventeen in an attempt to tackle the other monster, only for the dinosaur to do a quick spin around and strike the vampire with a whip of its tail. The vampire flew into the wall from the blow before slumping onto the floor.

But before Anton had a chance to pick himself back up, the raptor shot forward and bit into his arm. The vampire let out a snarl in pain as the dinosaur's blade-like teeth dug into his cold, undead flesh. The reptilian beast began to shake his adversary across the ground like a ragdoll before finally flinging him several feet down the hallway.

Anton let out a growl as he picked himself up off the floor. He clutched the bite wound the young raptor had inflicted on him tightly as his body surged with pain. It was a little-known fact that among the few ways to successfully kill this particular type of vampire was to inflict enough damage on their person to the point where they would bleed out all the human blood they had consumed; making it the closest way for a vampire to die like a normal human being.

Fortunately, Anton had consumed enough blood during his long trip from between here and Germany to allow him to keep fighting, but the more injuries he took during the battle meant that he would eventually succumb to the blood loss. He had to finish this fight as fast as possible before he met a slow, painful fate.

Anton watched as the raptor darted toward him again, only this time he was ready. As the carnivore's jaws snapped at his throat, the undead monster swiftly evaded the oncoming attack and slashed the prehistoric

191

predator's side, earning him a screech of agony from the beast. The dinosaur reached out with his jaws and snapped at the vampire again, only to be punched in the eye by its opponent. With the raptor stunned, Anton grabbed the beast by its tail and with all his strength, lifted the reptile into the air before slamming it back into the concrete floor.

The vampire lifted the dinosaur into the air again, but just as the Anton was bringing him back down for a second drop, the cloned creation's foot shot forward and sliced a deep gash across his opponent's pallid face with its sickled claw. The kick made the blood drinker let out an agonized cry as he released his grip on the raptor in mid-swing.

The dinosaur quickly corrected himself by landing on his feet before touching the ground. Anton clutched his face as he reeled from the pain, giving Seventeen an opening to unleash his next attack on the raptor's undead rival. With a screech, the raptor leapt forward with sickle-claws at the ready and pounced onto the vampire. The resulting impact knocked both combatants through a window and into a lab.

Now pinning Anton against the floor, the genetically engineered monster's jaws shot down at the bloodsucker's head, only for the vampire to reach out and stop the onslaught of teeth from reaching his face. Though the vampire's strength was great, the raw power of the raptor's muscles allowed him to push back against his opponent. It was not before long the bloodsucker's arms began to give way against the force of the dinosaur's oncoming fangs, which now inched closer towards him. With one more great push, the raptor managed to snap his jaws forward and engulf the vampire's head in his fang-loaded mouth.

However, rather than taste the rotten flesh of the undead creature, Seventeen instead only tasted air. Instead of a vampire at his clawed feet, there was a cloud of mist covering the floor that expanded outward and away from under the dinosaur. The raptor cocked his head to the side in puzzlement at the sight of the sudden surging substance as it moved across the floor. The mist then began to pull itself together and take on a new shape as it became solid.

The billowing fog reformed into that of a large black wolf with blazing red eyes. The lupine creature snarled at the raptor as it snapped its jaws as the dinosaur. Still perplexed by what had just happened,

Subject: Seventeen shrieked back as he readied himself for another fight before charging at the cursed canine. With almost blinding speed, the wolf suddenly leapt over the raptor's gaping maw and landed on its back. The cloned dinosaur screeched in anger as the wolf bit and clawed at its opponent's back while the reptilian monster tried desperately to buck the animal off its body.

The raptor snapped at the wolf but was only able to reach the demon dog just as it dug its fangs into the back of the dinosaur's neck, eliciting another cry of rage from his rival as it did so. Seeing no other option, Seventeen used one last ditch effort to stop this assault.

With all the might he possessed, the raptor flung itself backwards and landed on the floor, smashing the wolf between his scaly body and the concrete. Now with the vampire off his body, Seventeen clutched onto one of the shapeshifter's legs and flung it across the room. After hitting the ground once more, Anton transformed back to his original form as he slowly pulled himself back to his feet – only to be tackled by the raptor before he could get his bearings again.

The cloned beast sliced into the vampire's chest as he bit into Anton's side, only to be swatted back by another punch. The nosferatu then reached out, grabbed a nearby table, and cracked it across the dinosaur's face, knocking Seventeen to the ground from the force of the blow. The undead creature stood over his enemy; waiting for the reptilian beast to suddenly spring up again for another attack, but the raptor remained lying still at the vampire's feet.

Anton could see that Seventeen was still alive from his scaly chest rising and falling, meaning that the vampire had only stunned the reptile. Wanting to end this now, the bloodsucker kneeled down with his fangs at the ready to drain the life out of the cloned creature.

Suddenly, when he was only inches away from the dinosaur's throat, the giant reptile's head shot up and bit off a chunk of one of Anton's pointed ears. The vampire let out a high-pitched screech as he stumbled backwards from the raptor as the reptile jumped back to his feet. The cloned monster charged at Anton again, who was still reeling from the sudden loss of his ear.

But just before the raptor could bite into his enemy again, Anton turned back into his mist form, causing the prehistoric monster to run headfirst into the wall. The vampire reformed behind the raptor and seized this chance to attack by slashing his claws down the reptile's side, who in turn smacked his undead foe onto his back with a swing of his whip-like tail. The cloned creation then pounced on Anton in an attempt to pin him down once more.

Only this time proved to be different. Just before Seventeen could lay a claw on the bloodsucker's person, the vampire reached out and took hold of the dinosaur by the ankle and flung the reptile out of the window the two monsters had broken through. The raptor landed right next to Harold, who at the time was trying to crawl away from the battle. The dinosaur, so enraged by the fight with his undead adversary, ignored an easy victim and kept his attention solely on the vampire as he climbed through the broken window.

If Harold had any sanity left, it was slowly leaving him. Here he was, lying on the floor with a broken and perforated leg as he watched two creatures that should not exist fight one another to the death right before his very eyes. One thing was certain: whoever won this battle would surely be the end of him.

"Enough!" Anton proclaimed. "I am Anton Herzog! I have walked this Earth for over seven hundred years – and I will not be defeated by some mindless beast!"

The raptor shrieked back in defiance at the words that were being spoken to him, as if he actually understood them. Before the dinosaur could strike again, however, Anton raised his claws in front of him as his eyes began to glow a dark shade of red. The cloned beast stopped dead in his tracks as his expression changed from one of rage to a look of dazed calm. It was almost as if Anton had some sort of mental hold on the raptor.

"Come," Anton ordered the dinosaur.

The raptor began to slowly step forward, still entranced by whatever sort of psychic power the vampire had wielded against him. Harold was stunned by what he was witnessing. With but a simple gesture, the vampire had seemingly quelled the reptile's savage nature and had made the reptile as tame as a trained dog. As the raptor approached his new master, Anton began to bare his fangs once more. It was at that moment that Harold figured out what the vampire's plan was.

Once the raptor was close enough, the vampire was going to land a killing blow with a swift and fatal bit to the dinosaur's neck. Within seconds the cloned creation was near enough that Anton prepared to sink his fangs into the creature's neck.

Before he could do so, however, the raptor's head suddenly shot forward and engulfed the vampire's outstretched hand in his mouth. With a quick yet powerful twist of his head, the reptilian marauder tore Anton's hand off before quickly spitting out the foul-tasting appendage and keeping up the attack.

As the bloodsucker screeched and cried at the loss of his hand, the raptor tackled him once more and pinned him against the wall. Kicking upward with one strong blow, the cloned reptile's sickle claw impaled itself into Anton's stomach, tearing it open with a downward motion. As the undead monster's fetid organs began to spill out of his body, the vampire made a final attempt to slay his enemy. With everything he had left, the bloodsucker bit into the raptor's neck and sank his fangs deep into the scale-coated throat. The raptor screeched in agony as the vampire held his grip on the powerfully muscled neck.

The dinosaur plunged his clawed hands into its adversary's chest and began to slash wildly in an attempt to make Anton let go. The two monsters struggled against one another until finally they collapsed to the ground in unison in a massive blood-soaked heap. Harold was silent, waiting for either of the creatures to rise back to their feet and kill him. But despite his fears, neither of the monsters got back up.

Harold breathed out his first sigh of relief before wincing at the pain in his leg, reminding him that everything he had just witnessed was all a reality. The injured security guard began to crawl back toward the control room, hoping that he could out a message for help.

He knew that there would be questions from the higher-ups about everything that had transpired here tonight, but he did not care about that. All that mattered was seeing his wife again. Suddenly, Harold felt a sharp pain dig into the center of his back. As he grunted from the surprise stab, he heard the sound of an all too familiar hiss right above his head. Harold closed his eyes, silently praying that this would be over quickly. It would not.

Before she had met her grisly demise, Dr. Callan did manage to get a distress call out to the company about Subject: Seventeen's escape. In response, Mr. Matsuda sent a squad of the finest soldiers for hire money can buy. He sent them in with a former colleague of Callan's, Dr. Miles Walton, who had been in touch with the scientist and her team's attempt to create life for military purposes. However, when the team arrived at the lab, they found that the strangest of massacres had seemingly occurred there.

Several of the topside guards were found with their throats torn out and completely drained of blood – save for two of the guards, who were found brutally mauled like Callan and everyone else in the lower levels were. There was also claw marks and Seventeen's blood all over the hall and one of the now destroyed research labs, a clear indication of a struggle between the raptor and some unknown assailant.

But the biggest mystery was that of a large pile of ash that had been strewn about the hallway where the fight had taken place. Currently, Walton was relaying his team's finding to the company's CEO over the phone.

"No, sir, we haven't found any trace of Subject: Seventeen yet. Or, where he might've gone, either," he informed his boss. "What do you want to do about the bodies?"

"Dispose of them," Mr. Matsuda's voice ordered over the phone. "We'll say that they all were exposed to carbon dioxide from an unforeseen leak. We'll write a check for the families tomorrow."

"Understood, sir," Walton acknowledged. "And what should we do about Subject: Seventeen if we find it?"

"Capture it if you can, but if it tries to escape the facility, or has already done so, terminate it," Matsuda answered. "We can't afford letting it escape and ruin the company. Regardless, if you get it dead or alive, I want you to bring it back here to the labs in Japan. We may be able to salvage this project if we can get the subject; or, at the very least, learn what we can from its body, so we do not repeat the same mistakes as the late Dr. Callan did."

"Of course, sir," Walton replied. "I'll call you when we have more information."

With that, Walton hung up. As he did, he noticed that one of his armed escorts, Decker, was looking past him with an expression of sheer terror on his now pale face. Confused as to what exactly was scaring the mercenary, Walton turned around to see that Decker's fears were very much warranted.

There, standing only inches away from his face, was Subject: Seventeen. However, the raptor looked vastly different than what Dr. Callan had grown in the labs. His scales had changed from brownish green to a dull, dusty gray hue. The dinosaur's yellow eyes were now replaced with a dark crimson coloration that seemed to stare into Walton's very soul. Small leathery, bat-like wings now adorned each of the dinosaur's arms while black spines ran down from the back of the raptor's head all the way down to the tip of his tail.

Among the scars that riddled the raptor's body, Walton only noticed two very prominent puncture wounds on the reptilian beast's neck. But the biggest change that the scientist took note of were the pair of long, serrated fangs that jutted out of the top half of the dinosaur's mouth. The monstrous hybrid of dinosaur and vampire roared in Walton's face as a sign that he was to be his next victim.

Consumed by panic, Decker ran off screaming in hysterics down the hall, leaving Walton to face his end alone. "Oh, God..." was all his fear ridden mind could allow him to say.

The scientist did not have a chance to even scream before the hybrid monstrosity sank its fangs into his throat and consumed his life fluids.

END

CACTUS CAT VS. HIDEBEHIND: THE DROP – Cody Bratsch

Vasquez Rocks, Los Angeles California

Bill Chan, wearing his usual denim vest and shorts with a tye-dye Grateful Dead shirt, took a deep breath as he sat and waited patiently for whoever he was supposed to meet. He waited... and he waited... and he waited; and then he waited some more.

The stoner dude did not know exactly how long he waited, but it felt too damn long to him, and he was beginning to lose his cool. Part of it might have stemmed from a sense of paranoia, for as he waited, Bill slowly started to develop a suspicion that he was not alone out there in the middle of the Vasquez Rocks Natural Park. He felt like he was being watched by something stalking around out there in the area.

However, every time he felt the presence nearby or heard even the tiniest scraping when he turned to look, there was nothing. There would only be thin air and the desert-like terrain of the valley where the rock formations he sat atop stood. Sometimes, Bill felt it really was just his paranoia; while other times he felt if he had been just a split second faster, he would have seen whoever or *whatever* might have been stalking him.

He wasn't sure whether it was a human presence he felt... or if it was something else entirely. All he did know was that the feeling of being watched in such a wide-open space in the middle of the night was putting him on edge.

It finally got to be too much for Bill. All that built up anticipation, paranoia, and fear manifested in a scream of agitation and partial terror from the hapless stoner.

"Fuck this! Fuck Roland! Fuck this guy who ain't showing up! Fuck these rocks! Fuck the night! And fuck whatever the fuck is out there watching me! I shouldn't even be in the middle of this park so late at night. It's against the fucking law!"

Bill scoffed in irritation after all his yelling as he reached into his bag. "I'm gonna be needing some weed to be dealing with all this illegal shit."

The stoner dude pulled out his stash, his wraps, and his cell phone. He looked to see how long he had been sitting out there waiting for whoever he was supposed to meet with and give the stuff to.

"Forty minutes? It's only been *forty fucking minutes?* You've gotta be *fucking kidding me!* It feels like forty fucking *days!* How much longer have I got to wait? Man, I really need to get stoned."

As Bill wrapped himself a doobie, he considered possibly getting on his phone and giving Roland a piece of his mind. Before he could come to a decision, though, Bill's ears picked up a sort of scraping sound, the kind made by footsteps. The burnout of a man completely froze as he listened more intently and heard more steps.

Oh, shit. Please don't tell me there's really something out here trying to eat my head.

Bill looked to his nameless horse (something Roland required him to get for this drop for some reason) standing at the bottom of the rock formation where he had left it. A bone-chilling tingle ran down the stoner's back as he worried about what could be out there. If it was not his horse making that noise, then what was it?

It could be the guy I'm supposed to meet. Yeah, that's it, just the guy. Good thing, too. Now I can make this drop, get paid, and forget I was ever out here.

But another scraping sound nearby gave Bill the impression that it was not his contact. He tried to stand up, but except for his fearful trembling the freaked-out burnout could not get himself to move. Every time he heard noises from one direction, he would hear a similar sound from another a second later. It was getting to the point where Bill feared that whatever it was, it could not be just one person.

Finally, Bill Chan was unable to take it anymore. "Fuck this shit! I'm out!"

Despite his proclamation, Bill could not force himself to move from his spot. That is, until he felt several instances of sharp pain poking into his leg, which was quite intense despite being barred by his denim shorts.

"*Ouch!*" Bill shouted as he sprung up on his feet, his pain giving him the will to do so. "What the fuck is—?"

Before Bill could finish his rant, he was cut off by his own shrill scream – not to mention his terror at the sight beside his leg. The creature that had painfully wrapped itself around his limb was prickly... and *feline!* There was actually five and a half feet of cat on his leg, which seemed to be made of... cactus matter!

As hard as it was to believe, there was a cactus cat on Bill Chan's leg. However, he knew it was real for two reasons:

One: He had not gotten stoned yet.

Two: The points of its thorn-covered body had pierced his leg in a few places, and they hurt like fucking bee stings.

"Get off me, get off me, get off me!" Bill yelled as he shook his leg around violently.

Despite causing himself more pain by doing this, the tactic proved to be fruitful, for the cactus cat was sent flying off his leg and onto its feet. Bill instantly took several sprinting steps back before bending down to check on his perforated limb. Every spot where he had been pricked by the prickly feline's spines still felt like multiple bee stings. The hapless stoner dude rubbed the bleeding spots tenderly as he looked at the cactus cat, which had rolled itself onto the ground.

"Oh, fuck, not this shit again," Bill said, having remembered a previous encounter with such odd critters of the wilderness[2]. He tilted his head to the side as he tried to reckon how this was even possible. "Where did you come from?"

He got no answer from the cactus cat, although he was not really expecting any because it was, well, a cat.

As Bill stared at the loafing greenish feline, he noticed it did not seem to be in a hurry to chase or maul him in any way. No, the cat was actually purring and seemed to even have a look of satisfaction on its face. This greatly confused the stoner even more than he usually was. He watched as the cactus cat rolled onto its back and started pawing at the air and stretching its legs out.

There was something very familiar about this cat's behavior and mannerisms to Bill Chan. Not that he had ever done these exact things

---

[2] See *Duel of the Monsters* Vol. 1 for Bill Chan's first encounter with a pair of "fearsome critters" in Cody Bratsch's tall tale "Goofus Bird vs. Hoop Snake: How High Am I?"

before, but the mood of the spiny feline that enticed these actions seemed to ring a bell. It took Bill a moment to think, a bit longer than it would most other people, but he finally hit on it.

"Dude, are you high or something?" Bill asked the prickly feline. Again, there was no response, only the cat rolling on its back as it stretched its paws all around, its eyes closed as it purred in pleasure. "Oh, my God, you are! You're fucking wasted!"

Bill found himself smiling and even laughing about this. That is until he saw the cactus cat completely freeze as it looked in his direction. The stoner dude tilted his head to the side at this.

I'm so confused, and I'm not even stoned yet.

That confusion turned to alarm when he saw the thorny cat roll onto its feet and take a defensive stance as it let out several low, stretched out yowls almost as if issuing a warning to an unseen presence.

Bill's eyes widened in alarm as he screamed and leaped out of the way of the charging and then pouncing cactus cat. It was at that moment that Bill heard such a terrifying, chill-inducing, near paralyzing scream of a roar. He turned around to see a most frightening sight that matched the roar it had emitted.

Struggling with the cactus cat was a six-foot-six, hairy hominid-type of beast. Bill could not tell exactly what it was because it was the middle of the night; plus, the beast was covered in wild, bushy fur that made it hard to identify. However, the strange creature seemed to stand and move mostly like a human, albeit more feral and aggressive.

"What the *actual fuck* is happening right now?" Bill exclaimed in a panicked tone.

His body language conveyed this same state of horror as he crawled and scurried back fearfully while watching the two monsters fight.

The cactus cat hissed and shrieked as it bit and clawed at incredible speeds with its razor-sharp teeth and claws against its equally strange adversary. This giant creature was obviously a bona fide specimen of the mysterious monstrosity known and feared by American loggers as a "hidebehind" since hiding behind trees and boulders *et al.* to sneak up on its human prey was what it did. True to its name, the hairy hominid had managed to hide and sneak for so long to get up to this point. But it now found itself continuously tossing the savagely attacking cactus cat away to try and get the feral feline off its hirsute hide.

But the prickly cat would always come running or jumping back to continue attacking the hidebehind. Finally, the hairy, possibly ape-like beast grabbed the cactus cat – despite how much touching its body of spine-like protrusions hurt like a 'sumbitch – and began slamming it against any nearby object.

The ground, boulders – anything and everything the hidebehind could think to smash the cactus cat into, it did so – until holding its thorny body got to be too much for the hominid's hands. Reluctantly, the hairy humanoid was forced to release the spine-covered feline, letting it drop to the ground where it landed on its feet. Instantly the cactus cat leaped back onto the hidebehind and went to work biting and clawing despite how much the moggy was hurting after being tossed and slammed around.

Bill saw this happening, saw this great battle, and knew he had to get away. "I'm out! For real this time!"

The hapless dude stumbled up to his feet and ran as fast as he could. His progress was halted when the cactus cat crashed down right next to him after having been tossed by the hidebehind. The startled stoner dude let out a shrill, girl-like scream and watched in fear as the spike-coated feline got up and jumped anew at the stealthy hairy hominid.

However, the hidebehind reacted fast, picked up a heavy boulder, and slammed it into the incoming cactus cat. Bill watched as the feline fell to the ground while the shaggy hominid lifted the large rock and smashed it down on its feline foe. Needless to say, the exotic felid squealed for several pain filled seconds after getting slammed thusly.

After five or so smashes of the boulder, the cactus cat stopped squealing or moving at all. Bill Chan looked on in horror as the bloodied and clawed up hidebehind tossed the boulder away and then lifted the defeated cat's pulverized, juice-leaking body, and released a high-pitched roar of victory.

Bill instantly ran, then jumped on his horse and rode off as fast as he could prod the animal into going.

"I'm never doing a fucking drop for Roland again!"

Cody Bratsch
Cactus Cat vs. Hidebehind: The Drop
Duel of the Monsters Volume 2

END

ABOUT THE AUTHORS

Christofer Nigro is a lifelong fan of the horror and sci-fi genres, along with comic books, superheroes, and pulp fiction. He has been running the soon-to-be-updated sites The Godzilla Saga and Warrenverse: The Amazing World of the Warren Comics Characters for years and years. He has had short stories published by Black Coat Press, Pro Se Press, Sirens Call Publications, Pulp Empire, Grinning Skull Press, Local Hero Press, and Horrified Press, with his first two novels published by Severed Press. He is the founder, owner, and editor-in-chief of Wild Hunt Press, which has a growing list of publications behind it, including the *Duel of the Monsters* anthology series and Christofer's *Nero* series of novels dealing with a certain angst-ridden teen werewolf.

Pete Rawlik is a long-time collector of Lovecraftian fiction. His first professional sale was in 1997 but he did not begin to write seriously until 2010. Since then, he has authored more than fifty short stories and the Cthulhu Mythos novels *Reanimators; The Weird Company; Reanimatrix;* and *The Peaslee Papers*. He is a frequent contributor to the *Lovecraft ezine* and the New York Review of Science Fiction. In 2014 his short story "Revenge of the Reanimator" was nominated for a New Pulp Award. In 2015 he co-edited *The Legacy of the Reanimator* for Chaosium. Somewhere along the line he became known as the Reanimator guy, but he fervently denies being obsessed with the character. His collection, Strange Company and Others, was released in 2019. His work has popped up in various Wild Hunt Press anthologies, including *Dorian Gray: Darker Shades* and *Duel of the Monsters Vol. 1*. He lives in Southern Florida where he works on Everglades environmental issues.

Matthew (Matt) Dennion lives in New Jersey with his wife, two daughters, and two dogs. Matt works primarily as a teacher of students with autism and as an SLE (Structured Learning Experience) Coordinator. He has loved giant monster and superhero stories his entire life. He began writing short stories for Black Coat Press and G-Fan magazine in 2007. In 2015 he began writing kaiju novels for Severed Press. His current works for Severed Press include *Chimera: Scourge of the Gods*; Operation ROC; *Atomic Rex; Polar Yeti*; *Atomic Rex: Wrath of the Polar Yeti*; *Kaiju Corps*; *Atomic Rex: Conquest of Chimera*; *Operation Megalodon*; and *Valley of the Dinosaurs*.

Matthew has a line of self-published novellas including *The Kaiju and the Crime Fighter and Other Tales* and *Raptor Tales: Heroes and Monsters*. He self-published the first edition of the anthology *Attack of the Kaiju Vol. 1: Age of Monsters*. He has short fiction in the anthologies *Attack of the Kaiju Vol. 2: The Next Wave* and *Duel of the Monsters Vol. 1;* and a superhero novel *Raptor: Retribution of the Revenants* from Wild Hunt Press. All of Matt's novels and comics are available on Amazon in print and digital formats and can be purchased on Amazon. Along with his friends Andres Perez and Chris Martinez, Matt has also created the charity publishing venture Kaiju vs. Cancer, through which creators use their monsters and heroes to team with St. Jude Children's Research Hospital to battle childhood cancer! The first of these anthologies to be published was *Courage on Infinite Earths: A Kaiju vs. Cancer Anthology*.

Tyler Shepard been obsessed with monsters great and small since he was two years old. It has been a life-long dream for him to become a writer. His motto: "The more blood the better, I always say!" *Duel of the Monsters Vol. 1* is Tyler's debut as a published author.

Dustin Dreyling is an avid fan of science fiction and horror, with a soft spot for all things kaiju. Originally hailing from White Bear Lake, Minnesota, he also likes proofreading novels, playing video games both old and new, and taking care of his planted freshwater aquariums. His first published story was featured in Zach Cole's linear horror anthology *The Experiment* from Wild Hunt Press, and his short fiction can also be found in Wild Hunt's anthologies *Attack of the Kaiju Vol. 2: The Next Wave* and *Duel of the Monsters Vol. 1*. His first novel, the debut of his kaiju horror series *Primordial Soup: The First Batch,* was released in early 2020 from Wild Hunt Press.

Dustin is a lifelong native of Saint Paul, Minnesota, where he lives with the love of his life, Melissa. A fan of almost all things Sci-Fi and Horror, he is a devout reader of Jeremy Robinson, Jeff Strand, Brian Keene, and Tim Curran; their work has been a large influence on him. These are in addition to horror greats like H.P. Lovecraft and Stephen King.

Cody Bratsch was born on May 15, 1991, in Washington state (where he still currently resides). From a very early age, he had a fascination with all sorts of creative ventures and forms of storytelling. Classic animation such as the *Looney Tunes* and a slew of '80s and '90s animated series. Epic sci-fi franchises like *Star Wars*, *Star Trek*, *Terminator*, and *Planet of the Apes*. Sword-and-sorcery fantasy like *Clash of the Titans*, *Conan the Barbarian*, and *Lord of the Rings*. Tough-guy action films like *Rambo, Die Hard, Commando*, and *The Expendable*. Terrifying horror found in series like *Halloween, Friday the 13th*, *A Nightmare on Elm Street*, and the *Living Dead* series by George A. Romero, among other horror franchises. Grand superhero spectacles like the long slew of *Batman* films, the offerings of the Marvel Cinematic Universe, and a great many superhero cartoons on TV throughout the decades. And especially Cody's favorite type of fiction, titanic monster battles of epic proportions find in such franchises as the *Godzilla* series (the longest continually running film series in history).

Exposure to so many different types of fictional genres and forms of storytelling on such an impressionable child made it nearly impossible that Cody would be anything other than a creative type in the wild and fascinating world of writing fiction. Larger than life, creative spectacles are the kind of things Cody lives for the most in storytelling (while still enjoying some calm downtime in his stories once in a good while). All this and more are the kind of things Cody hopes to bring to his works of literature while also hoping the public who reads them will enjoy his own spin on these elements.

Brion Halloway lives near the famed and mysterious Okanagan Lake in British Columbia, where reports of mysterious creatures lurking in its depths have abounded. He is currently at the University of British Columbia, a graduate from a local college, and an aspiring author of creature/monster fiction. Kaiju are his specialty, but cryptids and original monstrosities from his own imagination are also on the table. He is a self-made artist as well, and he is featured on the popular art-sharing site DeviantArt, which you can see for yourself at: https://www.deviantart.com/kelownazilla2017.

Aside from those things, he is also a researcher of lake monster sightings and is an eyewitness himself; he plans to continue the search for such creatures. Brion's other hobbies include drawing, camping, kayaking, reading, travelling, anthropology, and sociology, as well as learning the Spanish language. His aim in life is to become a specialist in Gothic fiction and to teach it as well. His other work, previously under the byline of Breyden Halverson, has been featured in Matthew Dennion's self-published *Attack of the Kaiju Vol. 1: Age of Monsters*; Zach Cole's linear multi-author horror anthology *The Experiment* from Wild Hunt Press; and in the horror anthology series *Duel of the Monsters Vol. 1* released by Wild Hunt Press.

Zach Cole is the author of the novella *Tsuchigumo* (his debut work), *Kaiju Epoch*, and the Jeremy Walker Thriller series (beginning with

Blue Moon: A Jeremy Walker Thriller) and is the mastermind behind the multi-author linear horror anthology *The Experiment* from Wild Hunt Press. He was born in Wooster, Ohio, beginning his love of monsters at the age of two after viewing *Mothra vs. Godzilla*. His short fiction has also appeared in *Attack of the Kaiju Vol. 2: The Next Wave* and *Duel of the Monsters Vol. 1* from Wild Hunt Press, which will soon be picking up his Jeremy Walker series, the next novel being *The Secrets of Atlantis* and due out in early 2022. He became a writer around the age of ten, penning Godzilla stories and even comics containing his own monstrous creations. His love of books started with the *Goosebumps* series, reading anything that has to do with monsters, big or small. He lives in West Salem, Ohio with his wife, son, two dogs, and an erratic lizard.

Patrick Rahall is a writer who hails from Lovecraft Country, Massachusetts, where he lives with his wife and their cats. He is the co-host of the award- winning podcasts Throwdown Thursday and Creator Spotlight on the Dorkening Podcast Network. Patrick is also a shark enthusiast and enjoys both pizza and wine. He looks forward to the collapse of civilization as a means to escape his credit card debt.

D.G. Valdron is a renegade Canadian writer, former lawyer, journalist, teacher, carpenter, car thief, ne'er do well, professional student, and breeder of mutant cats. The guy just can't hold down a job. A long-time contributor to Christofer Nigro's website The Godzilla Saga, Den has also written esoteric articles about Edgar Rice Burroughs' creations and other pulp heroes. He's the world's leading authority on the *LEXX* television series, and on *Doctor Who* Fan Films – how's that for obscure? Publications include the dark fantasy *The Mermaid's Tale*; the fantastical *Bear Cavalry - the True (Not!) History of the Icelandic Bears*; *Axis of Andes: An Alternate History* and several story collections. D.G. has previously published an essay in Wild Hunt Press's *Attack of the Kaiju Vol. 2: The Next Wave*. He is secretly working to unleash an epic kaiju throwdown novel upon the world.

Robert E. Wronski, Jr. is a life-long fan of everything the TV medium has ever had to

offer, as well as every corner of fantastic fiction and the fan favorite concept of crossovers, all of which he integrated into the popular Television Crossover Universe blog many years ago. It is chock full of his writing and that of the contributors he recruited over the years. His production outfit, Super Entertainment, brought us a memorable run of the popular Television Crossover Universe and Random Fandom podcasts, and he has taken his knowledge into book format with his independently published *Television Crossover Universe: Worlds and Mythology Volume I* and *The Horror Universe Encyclopedia* published by 18thWall Productions. His work on constructing timelines has also appeared in the horror anthology *Dorian Gray: Darker Shades* by Wild Hunt Press.

ABOUT THE ARTISTS

Elden Ardiente is an artist based in Sydney, Australia and produces graphic design, illustrations, concept art, and digital sculptures for books, games, movies, and toys. You can see his creations at LDNRDNT.COM.

Jimi Bautista is a Manila-based visual strategist/illustrator/dad who has a flair for drink and drawing, gun playing, bowling, cartooning, and guitaring when not dissecting nor posing action figures. He has done works for Ford, Toyota, Bayer, Nestle, Novartis, Servier, Otsuka, among others. He is last seen procreating on his Instagram, @jimibi.

Jim Faustino loves to draw. He also loves horror stories. He has done works for sketch card companies: Rittenhouse Archives, Upper Deck, and Cryptozoic Entertainment. When he is not doing any art – no, wait, scratch that. He is always doing art! In fact, you can see some of it on his Instagram: drawingerosijim2 and DeviantArt: humawinghangin. You can get in touch with him through Facebook: Jim Faustino, just don't mind the memes and cute cat posts.

Myke Guisinga draws for various independent comic book publishers; his most recent work appeared in Advent Comics' *Cosmos* series. His online portfolio can be viewed on https://mykeguisinga.carbonmade.com. He is based in the Philippines.

Glenn Lugapo used to work in advertising as a graphic artist and eventually as an art director. Among clients handled are Alaska, Colt 45, Unilab, and URC. Nowadays, he is usually at home with his crazy dogs. Actually, he is visually impaired (low vision), but still tries to draw as best he can.

Małgorzata Mika is a Polish artist based in Sydney, Australia. She is an alumni of CG Spectrum and has an Advanced Diploma in Concept Art. In her free time, she loves to read good Sci-Fi and history books, essays, and poetry.

Ferdie Misa is a creative with a wealth of experience ranging from advertising and branding, toys, 3D, and animation. He has worked with brands such as Reebok, Vans, Nautica, AXA, and Grand Hyatt. Ferdie lives in Rizal province, Philippines with his wife and three lovely children.

Benjo Quinajon started his career as a Final Artist for print production studios and elevated as a Senior Designer employed by reputable design shops and Ad Agencies in the Philippines. His experiences earned during years as a Designer are focused on branding, packaging, and print publication; and has handled brands such as Nestlé, Coca-Cola, McDonald's, and Proctor & Gamble. Benjo's greatest passion is doing manual and digital illustration for clients and personal projects.

213

Zach Cole – well, you already read that guy's bio in About the Authors. Yup, Zach draws too!

MONSTER CATEGORIES FOR EASY REFERENCE – Christofer Nigro

.

These classification essays describing the various types of monsters that will appear in this and subsequent volumes of *Duel of the Monsters,* and even throughout the shared Wild Hunt Universe (WHU) that we are slowly building through our publications, are slightly updated and modified versions of those that I have periodically written and posted on Wild Hunt Press's public Facebook group.

They proved somewhat popular, and I received requests to get them into print despite versions already being available for free on the group. So, never let it be said that we at WHP do not listen to our esteemed readers! More of these essays will be coming your way soon, both on the Facebook group and in future volumes of this series.

SLASHERS VS. ALPHA SERIAL KILLERS

Distinguishing between the above two categories of monster are important, especially since these are the terms we use at Wild Hunt Press (WHP) and it will aid our readers and contributors in making their reading and writing choices properly.

SLASHERS

Slashers are defined as undead or supernaturally enhanced killers that take the lives of human beings using a combination of their own enhanced strength and a great variety of natural implements – these ranging from knives, machetes, chain saws, axes, bludgeons of various sorts, and oftentimes whatever items they can get their hands on to provide a makeshift weapon in any given situation.

They come in two major sub-categories (though more may be identified upon further examination): Undead Humans and Supernaturally Enhanced Humans.

The former category are often similar to supernatural/Voodoo zombies, but they most often act on their own single-minded volition (though occasionally as pawns of others, including mystics, more powerful slashers, or liches). Some of them may be ghouls who kill to provide themselves with the flesh of the dead for sheer survival purposes.

Many others, however, are essentially self-volitional zombies who have a fast healing capacity rather than becoming increasingly necrotic beyond a certain point; and they kill based on the parameters of a supernatural curse that may have revived and empowered them. Their targets may be humans who tormented them and ultimately led to their deaths while alive; or, humans connected to or related to those who tormented them. Hence, these particular slashers are motivated by vengeance.

On the other hand, they may act as dark guardians of mystically "protected" areas, including various Native American burial grounds, in which case they will simply stalk and kill any humans who enter its boundaries (in a manner somewhat similar to that of Guardian Mummies).

Some are fully corporeal, such as Jason Vorhees and Matt Cordell (a.k.a., the "Maniac Cop," as of the third movie in his eponymous film franchise). Others are actually the ghosts of humans who were supernaturally "preserved" by dark arcane forces into a bio-ectoplasmic/etheric form that can simulate full flesh and blood solidity, such as Victor Crowley (of the *Hatchet* film franchise).

Still others, like Freddy Krueger, can simulate solidity from within the Dream Dimension by empowering himself sufficiently off the fear of his targets so that he can physically harm his victims via inflicting injuries upon the dream avatars of his targets; or, achieve full ectoplasmic corporeality by being temporarily pulled into the waking (i.e., material) world (though this form is quite resilient and resistant to pain, including even the severing of limbs; albeit not superhumanly strong or immune to being killed again).

Others, like Freddy Krueger and the Candyman, operate in otherdimensional realms where they can interact with humans and even temporarily enter the material world we know in a bio-etheric form under certain conditions.

As the varying sources make clear, some slashers are mostly mute and single-minded while displaying little signs of whatever their former human personality was like. They will nevertheless tend to be crafty and exceedingly cunning with a good ability to think strategically, as if operating on supernaturally bestowed "instincts." Others, like Krueger and Candyman, retain their full former human intelligence, personality, ability to speak, and malevolent craftiness. They seem to have a great aptitude for tracking their targets across almost any type of terrain, and they literally feed on the fear of victims and prospective victims much as ghouls do on necrotic physical flesh.

Undead slashers will oftentimes possess other supernatural powers that they can use under certain circumstances only, and their level of effectiveness or power may vary depending upon what kind of environment they are operating within (e.g., if Freddy Krueger is in the Dream Dimension or pulled into the waking world). For instance, as Stephen Smith mentioned on the public Wild Hunt Press group on

Facebook: "I would also note that supernatural slashers have a limited ability to effect their local environment. In such ways as cars not starting. Torches and other light sources not working and victims who are running away end up running in circles."

More specifically, these other attributes may also include a limited but sometimes deadly effective ability to alter probability to the "negative" for victims who are attempting to escape from or simply find quick & safe passage through such a "forbidden" area. This may manifest as making it more likely for a car that prospective victims are driving or fleeing in to suffer a seemingly inexplicable battery failure, or unexpectedly hit an impeding object; for a source of light (e.g., candle, torches, flashlight, lamp, spotlight) to go out suddenly; or, that victims will choose a wrong path when attempting to flee the slasher's pursuit or prime area of influence, whether on foot or vehicle; or, subtle mental manipulation that causes targets to make unusually poor decisions, even for people under duress. Of course, various external factors may be at work here too, and I would direct you to the film *Cabin in the Woods* (2011) to get an idea of what they are.

Sometimes this "bad luck" probability phenomenon can be due to a semi-conscious effort or "need" on the part of one of the more intelligent slashers, or externally initiated by whatever overall supernatural curse may be empowering one of the less intelligent slashers (curses are rooted in the phenomenon of negative probability effects, which is often referred to as *crossed conditions* in magick parlance). Although not a Slasher, the devil-spawn Damian Thorn of *The Omen* series of films and books is nevertheless a good example of an entity that made good use of powerful crossed conditions to eliminate targets and those who were hunting him down, including from a great distance, whereas slashers can only do this within the immediate vicinity of their targets or within a relatively small area under their "influence" (e.g., Camp Crystal Lake for Jason Vorhees; Victor Crowley's bayou).

Of course, the above-described ability or curse-initiated phenomenon is unreliable no matter who is utilizing it; and this ability can be thwarted by any person who has an unconscious psychic Death Exemption Ability or tendency towards "dumb luck" (but more on these intriguing but likewise imperfect psychic phenomena in a future section).

Slashers can be "killed" again, though this is exceedingly difficult and much more often they are rendered temporarily insensate by various conventional or mystical forces arrayed against them until another catalyst later revives them. Undead slashers can look fully human or carry the signs of various scars or mutilations they received while alive or have facial features that appear in various stages of rot.

Supernaturally enhanced slashers, on the other hand, never actually died, and hence cannot be truly classified as "undead." They will, however, display various superhuman attributes such as enhanced strength and resistance to injury & pain, healing factor, and tracking abilities, courtesy of whatever force may be empowering them. They more often than not look fully human but are often mute and every bit as relentlessly (some have described it as *inhumanely)* single-minded as their undead counterparts. Their thinking faculties seem to have been replaced by an extreme native cunning and aptitude for stealth and relentless drive, with an innate understanding on how to utilize common weapons (though rarely ever firearms for some reason).

Examples include Michael Meyers (a.k.a., The Shape) and at least one version of the various entities who took on the Jack the Ripper identity (inhabited by the demonic consciousness of the Red Jac entity, as seen in the *Star Trek: TOS* episode "Wolf in the Fold" and the episode of *Kolchak: The Night Stalker* called "The Ripper").

Interestingly, Jason Vorhees seems to have evolved over the course of his history, from a supernaturally enhanced human to a true undead slasher, becoming closer to the latter with each subsequent "death" and resurrection, with the transformation from one to the other being complete by the time of the film *Friday the 13th Part 6: Jason Lives*. As colleague Matt Hickman noted, Vorhees finally appears more like a Deadite by this point (see *The Evil Dead/Army of Darkness* series of films, comics, TV series, and video games), albeit with his original vulnerable, child-like psyche remaining alongside the demonic take-over instincts to a recessive degree (rather than being fully extricated).

ALPHA SERIAL KILLERS

These "human monsters" are actually fully human with no superhuman enhancements – though some have allegedly been goaded on, but not actually empowered, by disembodied voices that may belong to malicious ghosts, demons, djinn, or various other disembodied entities. However, they are much more cunning, dangerous, and stealthy, with a good capacity for strategic thinking, than the average serial killers. Though not superhuman, Alpha Series Killers can nevertheless temporarily display peak human strength, unusual resistance to injury, and near-indifference to pain if they are threatened, enraged, "psyched" into a killing frenzy, or under the influence of certain drugs. This is the result of an extreme adrenal flow (a.k.a., the "fight or flight" response) that often comes with a maddened frenzy, which can be prolonged and/or intensified by certain drug usage (e.g., PCP).

They are often adept at human psychology, sociology, and theology, which they readily use to their advantage to bluff and charm their way past the guard of unwary potential victims. Some are experts with certain weapons, whereas others are good at using just about any implement they can get their hands on as a deadly weapon in a pinch. Some of them are criminally insane, but others are sane though utterly evil psychopaths who lack a conscience and the ability to feel remorse for others.

Some stalk and kill other humans who fit a specific profile for the sheer sadistic pleasure of it (e.g., a combination of sexual thrill and power trip). Others stalk people – or others connected to those people – whom they feel wronged them in a serious way, i.e., vengeance. Still others target and kill certain people to satisfy what they believe to be the imperatives of a religion or cult they follow, some misguided sense of duty to something, or some sort of moral code that may or may not make sense only to them. The latter two types will often fancy themselves heroes of some sort who target and murder those whom they consider to be "undesirables" or to be "deserving" of such a fate according to whatever code they follow.

Nevertheless, all alpha aerial killers, like their less "alpha" counterparts, are fueled by a relentless psychological drive to kill people of their chosen profile and are usually unable to stop themselves (even if they periodically experience an involuntary "down" period during which they do few to no killings).

Then, finally, there is the most tragic and relatively rare of the alpha aerial killers, those that are brain-damaged from a physical injury and go about their original life's work in a twisted, homicidal way. They tend to retain enough cunning with an added relentlessness and difficulty to be put down. A good example of this sub-category is Matt Cordell, a.k.a., the "Maniac Cop," for the first two films of the *Maniac Cop* film franchise (until the third, where he is resurrected as an undead slasher). Cordell is one of those particularly physically strong and resilient, not to mention good hand-to-hand combatants, who become even stronger and more resilient with the constant adrenaline running through his system once he went mad.

Interestingly, like Matt Cordell, Freddy Krueger was likewise a fully human alpha serial killer before being killed himself and empowered by the dream demons that enabled him to become an undead slasher. Unlike Cordell, however, Krueger was not brain damaged but cunningly intelligent and committed murderous acts because he was an evil psychotic.

One trait common to almost all alpha serial killers is that they do not limit themselves to easy victims, and often have a lust for challenge that is nearly as great as their relentless desire to kill. Their lack of conscience, inability to feel empathy for others, and ruthless nature combine with their unusual innate cunning and whatever special skills they may possess to make them exceedingly dangerous foes even for monster hunters who have routinely gone up against the likes of vampires, werewolves, and zombies – not to mention conventional law enforcement officers, security guards, etc.

Examples of their number include Dr. Hannibal Lecter; Norman Bates; the Tooth Fairy Killer (from the novel *Red Dragon)*; Cletus Cassidy (before he acquired the alien symbiote to become Carnage); Matt Cordell (as noted above, prior to the third "Maniac Cop" film); Dexter Morgan; the Jigsaw Killer; Victor Zsasz (a.k.a., "Mr. Zsasz,"

Batman's foe); Roy Burns, the Jason Vorhees copycat killer from *Friday the 13th: A New Beginning*; Henry Morrison of *The Stepfather* film franchise; and Harry Warden (of the film *My Bloody Valentine*).

Also definitely included are some of the human copycat versions of Jack the Ripper – including Commissioner James Gordon's great-uncle Herbert Gordon (see the animated film version of *Batman: Gotham by Gaslight*); the physician Dr. Albert Z. Fell (see the *Fantasy Island* episode "Sincerely Yours, Jack the Ripper/Gigolo"); and Prince Albert Victor of the WHU (see the comic book mini-series *Dracula vs. Jack the Ripper: Blood of the Innocent*).

It should be noted, though, that Leatherface and the Sawyer clan and the Firefly clan of the *Firefly* film franchise beginning with Rob Zombie's *House of 1000 Corpses,* both of whom some may wish to include here, more so fall into the category of Redneck Cannibal (to be discussed another time), but the latter two killer families certainly do have many characteristics in common with alpha serial killers; and at least some of them may therefore straddle different monster categories.

MAN-BEASTS/BEAST MEN

Here we have a notable monster category that can truly vary in terms of what phenotypes & archetypes it can encompass. It does have a few specific requirements, though: 1) Humanoid shape and walking posture; 2) Fairly intelligent, though not necessarily human-level sentient; 3) A "primal" or bestial set of instincts or behavior alongside its intelligence that makes it potentially hazardous to human contact; 4) Much greater strength and agility than a normal human being, everything from manic athlete to peak human to superhuman.

Some may argue that Bigfoot belongs in this category, but this large hirsute hominid more than deserves a distinct classification of its own. Wild Men, who are not necessarily non-human or directly related to Bigfoot, can definitely straddle this category, however. The Almas of Mongolia and possibly the Orang Pendek of Sumatra, both the focus of popular cryptozoological study, can probably likewise do so.

A good example of a Man-Beast in fantastic fiction is Dr. Henry Jekyll's vile alter-ego, Edward Hyde (better known as Mr. Hyde). He started out as a brutish though somewhat diminutive human being with ugly human features who simply had manic athlete level strength (and wielded a mean whipping cane!), but eventually mutated into a brutish, hulking humanoid with truly impressive superhuman levels of strength, greater than that of a typical werewolf or vampire. He wasn't hirsute to the extent of a Bigfoot or wild man, but he did possess much more body hair than a normal human.

A similar example would be the "Jackass" entities injected with the Hyde-25 serum who appeared in the series "Night of the Jackass" from Warren's *Eerie* comic magazine in the 1970s, and again (briefly) by Harris Comics in the early '90s (see *Hyde-25* #0 and *Vengeance of Vampirella* #9-10).

Another good example of a Man-Beast who was a human that temporarily transformed into a primal hominid form was scientist Dr. Edward Jessup as a result of experiencing altered states of consciousness due to a combo of specialized drugs and immersion in a sensory deprivation tank as seen in the 1980 film *Altered States* (a rather unique use of devolution to create a Man-Beast, but any source is valid here!). Other examples include the titular entities from the vintage films *The Neanderthal Man* (1953) and *Monster on the Campus* (1958), both of whom were human subjects chemically transformed into bestial, hairy, and physically powerful hominids identified as "Neanderthals" but were likely something decidedly different.

The tele-version of a certain green-skinned goliath in *The Incredible Hulk* TV show certainly counts as a Man-Beast, thus making it clear that not all creatures in this category need be hirsute and can boast unusual skin colors with no extra-human body hair. A similar example that actually combines chartreuse skin and an excess of hair would be the bestial martial arts master Blanka from the *Street Fighter* franchise of video games (the latter was often referred to as a "Beast" for that reason). Likewise, the bluish-skinned titular Brute of the short-lived but memorable Seaboard/Atlas comic book of 1975.

Also, a Man-Beast's variable origin often means they are not a basically normal human being who was transformed into a more bestial state, either temporarily or permanently, but rather this was their natural permanent state from the get-go. Good examples of Man-Beasts who were some unidentified genus of hominid includes the titular creature from the film *Trogg;* the brutish & horned but benevolent "troglodyte" from *Sinbad and the Eye of the Tiger;* and the prehistoric hominid revival from the film *Schlock.* These three are examples of Man-Beasts who were never truly human, but alleged prehistoric relic survivors of one of the numerous unknown species of hominoid that once inhabited the Earth.

Of course, Man-Beasts can also hail from sources other than mutated humans, relic hominoid survivors, or unknown cryptozoological hominid species of man. As noted above, this category is necessarily quite broad in scope, as many of the creatures that can be included in it will straddle other monster categories as well.

KILLER/ROGUE GRIZZLIES

We have seen several examples of rogue or "killer" animal categories across myriad media in the horror and fantasy genres. The (often exceptionally large and cunning) grizzly bear on the rampage concept is rather popular, a prominent example being the classic 1976 cinematic rogue animal flick *Grizzly.*

Though *all* grizzlies are essentially very dangerous killers, and oftentimes apex predators of the woodlands they inhabit, most standard grizzlies (and other species of bears) tend to avoid humans and do not routinely attack them. They also do not normally stalk humans as a food source. But when they do break their usual behavioral protocol and become deliberate predators of humans ... well, the nightmares practically write themselves.

Enter... the Rogue or truly *Killer* Grizzlies. These are grizzlies who, for whatever reason, have "gone off the deep end" to break from their normal patterns of avoiding humans and only attacking if threatened, harassed, injured, or somehow provoked – or, in the case of a mama bear, if her litter of cubs is bothered. A killer grizzly is one that has become a man-eater and deliberately hunts humans for food. Let us keep in mind that despite their great size and bulk, grizzlies are quite fast when running, are capable of swimming, and quite good at using stealth. They are surprisingly cunning for mammals outside the *canid* genus, and they can form internal maps that enable them to memorize a vast swath of geographical territory to a degree that is daunting to humans.

In the WHU, grizzlies and other bears can become man-hunters for a variety of factors – everything from a rare genetic mutation; mental abnormalities resulting from exposure to unusual wavelengths of radiation, ultra-sound, or unusual chemicals or pathogens; psionic or mystical manipulation (deliberate or otherwise); or, even simply as an adaptation to adverse environmental conditions, such as a lack of game due to aberrant weather.

Let us keep in mind that for many reasons, a killer grizzly that feeds on humans will need to refine their stealth and cunning even further than the standard bruin. Their physical strength and the cutting power of their claws and teeth are nigh-legendary, and if one or more individuals among their number suddenly decide they are above the local humans on the food chain, then those people are in serious danger.

Since grizzlies are well-known animals fully documented by science, categorizing them as "monsters" under any circumstances may seem out of place. And normally, it is. However, when one goes rogue, and develops cunning & stealth above and beyond the norm as a side-effect, their physical formidability can easily rival that of a Bigfoot or werewolf, depending upon the size and intelligence of the individual grizzly. And killer grizzlies tend to be among the biggest and smartest of the species (albeit not to a freakish extent) almost as a rule.

SKELETOIDS

Huh? What the flark is a "skeletoid?" you may be thinking. "Well, likely something boney or looking like a skeleton, amirite?" Actually, if this is what you thought, then you are absolutely correct. In fact, the definition of this particular monster category is really that simple: any monster that resembles a walking, stalking, and (oftentimes) killing human skeleton. Some such entities, such the Lich, belongs in its own category but may straddle this one, as it can be quite inclusive.

For starters, this monster category is an integral part of folklore and actual reports of Fortean phenomena.

Among the actual reports was a skeleton-like being that allegedly made an unwelcome appearance at the wedding of one of the Kings Alexander of Scotland in the 13th century, as first mentioned by the late John Keel in his book *The Complete Guide to Mysterious Beings*.

More recently in history was an 1875 report from Croglin Hall in Cumberland, England where a woman named Miss Amelia Cromwell claimed "a horrible skeleton-like figure" broke into her bedroom through the window one summer evening and viciously attacked her, leaving bloody wounds on her face and neck. Her two adult brothers ran to her aid and broke through the locked bedroom door upon hearing her screams, and they also claimed to have seen the skeletoid figure as it retreated across the lawn outside. They gave pursuit, but the bony entity quickly outpaced them. There were allegedly other reports of a similar skeleton-like entity attacking other women in that same neighborhood.

Those above two reports, along with several others – including the Yellow Phantom of Ireland and the Borrego Phantom of the Superstition Mountains in New Mexico – were covered in Fortean researcher and experiencer Barton Nunnelly's excellent book *The Inhumanoids*, where he devotes an entire section to what he calls "Skeletoids" for obvious reasons. In fact, to my knowledge, Bart is the one who coined that term, and since that is where I picked it up from, I give full credit for its simple but very useful invention to him.

Let us also not forget that Skeletoids are very popular in horror fiction and imagery across multiple mediums. Note how popular it remains for kids and adults alike to dress as skeletons for Halloween, and how pervasive cardboard and plastic decorations of skulls and skeletons are during the Samhain season. This author once proudly wore a skeleton costume (cheap as Hel, but I loved it) for the Halloween season during my middle school years. The implication of the above imagery is that some of these skeletoid entities are mobile and capable of various levels of thought – and, more likely than not, intent upon terrifying or harming any fully fleshed human they may cross paths with.

This category is, of course, by necessity very generic. Any entity resembling an animated human or humanoid skeleton can be placed here, and they come in a variety of sizes, colors, and collection of physical attributes/powers. Some of them tend to rely on enhanced strength and or various hand-held weapons alone, whereas others can possess an array of supernatural or paranormal powers (and accompanying weaknesses). A good example of the latter is the Ghost Rider, i.e., one of the many human hosts of the personified Spirit of Vengeance, who wields hellfire, animated chains, and a dread penance stare in addition to its/his superhuman strength and penchant for hellfire-fueled vehicles (or horses, depending upon what era he/she manifests).

Another even more potent example of a Skeletoid is one of the common forms taken by Death itself, a.k.a., the Grim Reaper, a cosmic entity of truly epic power and scope in the universe entire.

Some skeletoids are nothing but animated bone, whereas others may be covered by a layer of shriveled skin that is so thin that the shape of the bones and skull are clearly defined. Some are without attire of any kind, and others may be garbed in anything from tattered clothing to the familiar hooded robe to the raiment of a pirate or the armor of a knight. Some may be glowing with supernatural (or radioactive) luminescence, whereas others will not.

The obvious connection to the Grim Reaper makes it clear that skeletoids serve as a symbol of death to pretty much all cultures in the world, and many such creatures do indeed serve as avatars or harbingers of Death itself. In some cases, actual emaciated/skeletonized human corpses can be summoned and animated to serve as soldiers and bodyguards of sorcerers, as occurred with Imhotep II in *The Mummy* film franchise of the 1990s and Sokurah against Sinbad in *The 7th Voyage of Sinbad* (1958).

Many ghosts take on a skeletal form, often for symbolic and/or terror-inducing effect. So do certain demons, e.g., Zarathos, whose possession of cyclist Johnny Blaze served as the power source for his Spirit of Vengeance manifestation. Hence, like many monster types, those counted as skeletoids can easily straddle different monster categories. Importantly, this paragraph makes it clear that skeletoids can be either incorporeal or corporeal entities, or anything in between.

Some death deities even fully or partially take on skeletal aspects, such as Hela, the Norse goddess of death. In fact, various underworld realms of a less than positive spiritual resonance are filled with this type of skeletoid, and death deities such as Hela and Hades/Pluto often use them as foot soldiers and servants. Charon, the ferryman of the river Styx leading to Hades, is another well-known skeletoid from world mythology whose appearance marks him as a representative of Death, or specifically, of one of the death dimensions.

In regards to fully corporeal Skeletoids, certain Mummies and Zombies can be placed in this second category if their appearances are cadaverous enough.

While the majority of skeletoids are supernatural/magickal in origin, this is not an absolute rule: Human skeletons in various sources have been known to become animate with varying degrees of cognition and self-motivation as a result of exposure to certain unusual wavelengths of radiation; direct psionic control by Telekinetics or Alien power sources; or, technological/cybernetic devices. Moreover, certain Human Mutants or humans suffering from bizarre diseases or afflictions have taken on a skeletal/cadaverous appearance and thus can (at least arguably) be cross-pollinated into the Skeletoid category.

SWAMP MONSTERS/BOG BEASTS

This monster category contains a good degree of leeway, but not a considerable amount. Another name for this category may be Bog Beast for obvious reasons.

These monsters, of course, all dwell in swamps/bayous, particularly those situated within one of those bothersome "window areas" where the laws of physics tend to be bent by certain unseen forces that make just about anything possible there. Just ask the residents of Citrusville, Florida or New Orleans.

However, Swamp Monsters per se can be distinguished from other monsters that often inhabit swamps or bayou areas, including Lizard Men, Skunk Apes, Voodoo Zombies, and Witch-Women; as well as non-humanoid monsters sometimes found in swamps. True Swamp Monsters (or Swamp Creatures; or Bog Beasts) as defined here are monsters that possess the two following characteristics: 1) They are humanoid or semi-humanoid and walk upright like a human; 2) They actually possess a physio-botanical nature, meaning their physical substance is either part animal organism and part plant matter, or an entirely botanical simulacrum of a humanoid being.

They can have wildly varying degrees of sentience, motivation, and attitudes towards humanity, and their level of physical solidity can also vary greatly. They can likewise possess a range of other abilities in addition to superhuman strength and being only semi-solid, ranging from esper (i.e., psychic) capabilities, to acidic secretions, to healing abilities, to a psychic rapport with plant life. Their ability to utilize these additional powers to any great effect is often dependent upon their level of sentience or the strength of said rapport with the essence of botanical life on Earth, which has often been referred to as The Green.

They can be either scientific or mystical in nature, and sometimes a combination of the two – as are likely the two most popular examples in popular fiction, Swamp Thing and the Man-Thing. The former is an example of a fully sentient swamp creature, whereas the latter is non-sentient (in most of his iterations).

Other good examples from horror fiction includes the titular monster from Theodore Sturgeon's short story "It" (the first Swamp Monster in fiction to this author's knowledge); the Heap (first published in *Air Boy Comics* during World War II and again during the 1970s by Skywald Publishing); Marvin the Dead Thing (published in *Eerie* by Warren Publishing during the '70s); the Bog Beast (published briefly by Seaboard/Atlas Comics as a feature in *Tales of Evil* #2-3); and Peremalfait from "The Spanish Moss Murders" episode of *Kolchack: The Night Stalker* TV series.

https://nightstalker.fandom.com/wiki/Peremalfait

In addition to a degree of physical strength that rivals the level possessed by Werewolves and Vampires, and sometimes Man-Made Monsters and Warrior Mummies, their semi-solidity gives them a degree of imperviousness to physical attacks. Bullets and other metal projectiles will often ooze right through them while causing minimal damage. However, explosives and fire can do a nasty number on their substance, as can using bladed weapons to gradually hack them to pieces (which is a risky way to attack them due to the very *gradual* degree of harm this inflicts). They are very resistant to force of impact attacks since they do not truly possess internal organs that can be damaged, though continual punishment inflicted upon them or extreme force such as being struck by an SUV going at high speed or a fall from a hundred feet up will likely put them out of commission, at least temporarily.

Swamp monsters can typically reconstitute themselves if smashed to pieces as long as they are in contact with the soupy substance of the swamp or very close contact with a sizable amount of botanical life so that they have a constant tether to The Green. They can also regrow severed limbs in the same manner, but this usually takes a degree of time. What they feed upon can also vary, but they tend to acquire it via photosynthesis from sunlight, absorption of organic nutrients directly from immersion in their swampy habitat, drainage of emotions from human beings – or, a combination of all of the above.

Their origins will often, though certainly not always, involve a human who is permanently transformed by either strange scientific or mystical means, or an even stranger combination thereof (as noted above *vis a vis* Swamp Thing, Man-Thing, the Heap, and Marvin the Dead Thing). Sturgeon's "It" was spawned by specially treated plant material growing around the skeleton of a murdered human. Peremalfait was actually created by the psychic emissions of a comatose man named Paul Langois who was involved in a deep sleep experiment. The Bog Beast was evidently a member of an unknown intelligent species of such creatures who dwell deep beneath the earth.

It should be noted that swamp monsters/creatures who are as powerful as Dr. Alec Holland (a.k.a., Swamp Thing) eventually became due to his powerful psychic/mystical rapport with The Green are quite rare. In regards to weaknesses for this monster category, Salvatore Cucinotta pointed out on the following on the public Facebook group for Wild Hunt Press: "I'd also recon that dehydration is a threat to this species."

Noting examples of other swamp monsters and their connections from various sources, Salvatore alluded to a Kaiju Timeline he is working on and mentioned that on it, "I linked the swamp monster to the seagoing variant, the Seaweed Monster or Zahzahn. Starting with *The Haunted Sea* pulp novel and including many other specimens.

"The most swamp monster-ish of them being *The Creature from the Haunted Sea*" [1961 film].

ALIENS VS. ALIEN MONSTERS

ALIENS

This is a relatively broad category used to define either extraterrestrial or extradimensional beings who are sentient, usually (but not always!) humanoid or semi-humanoid, wear attire of some sort (but not always), and capable of utilizing sophisticated means of communication through written & spoken language and/or via telepathy.

Most often they will use advanced technology, often more advanced than contemporary Earth tech, for purposes of detection, camouflage, misdirection, and self-defense. Those that have superior technology to humans may have traversed interstellar distances to arrive on Earth via starships or stargates; or, if extradimensional, via a temporary or permanent portal in space/time. The latter Aliens in particular need not have greater intelligence than human if they arrived here via a dimensional portal or even an active stargate they stumbled upon. Those who deliberately used advanced tech to travel here can be anywhere from on par to superior to human in cognitive ability and may or may not have the same range of emotional complexity and psychological attributes as we commonly do. They may, however, be very different in their thinking processes due to being raised in a culture considerably distinct from that of Earth's societies.

They can be larger than human or diminutive in height, with physical strength, speed, and resilience ranging from inferior to far superior to that of a normal human. Some will have cognitive capacity so advanced they can calculate equations many times the speed of humans (e.g., Coluans); have great telepathic and other psychic skills (e.g., Grays; Nordics); or outwardly resemble humans entirely but have vastly greater physical attributes (e.g., Kryptonians; Daxamites) – possibly due to generations of advanced genetic engineering. Other, more exotic sentient Aliens will be botanical (e.g., Cotati; Phylosians), or insectoid (e.g., Mantoid, Zanti), or resemble humanoid versions of Earth animals (e.g., Caitians). Some of the more exotic types could boast retractable claws, extendible limbs, or venomous bites or stings etc., natural weapons that human beings of Earth do not possess.

Some semi-humanoid aliens will have additional working limbs compared to humans as well as different skin color & certain monstrous features – not to mention a preference for utilizing primitive rather than advanced weaponry and modes of transportation – such as the Green Barsoomians. Others, like the Coluans, Red Barsoomians, and the Gamilons, may resemble human beings entirely save for their green, red, or blue skin, respectively.

Some aliens with access to advanced tech can create duplicate organic versions of themselves by injecting their DNA into humans, as seen in films like *Laserblast* and *Xtro*.

Examples of prominently known humanoid/semi-humanoid Alien phenotypes include the Grays, the Nordics, the Reptilians/Reptoids/Draco, the Mantoids, the "Roswell" type (though in at least one timeline, these were actually time-lost Ferengi from the late 24th century), the various races of Barsoom (alternate reality version of Mars), Vulcans, Klingons, the Time Lords of Gallifrey, the Yautja (Predators), Kryptonians, and Daxamites.

ALIEN MONSTERS

In contrast to the previous category, Alien Monsters tend not to be sentient entities, but rather savage beasts of an extraterrestrial or extradimensional origin that found themselves deposited upon Earth, or an Earth space vessel or space station, or an Earth colony world via a variety of means; or, encountered during an Earth exploration of an alien world in various alternate futures where space travel technology progressed to that point.

They can be roughly humanoid (albeit rarely), semi-humanoid, utterly non-humanoid; somewhat resembling certain Earth animals or utterly unlike anything that naturally evolved on Earth and living either in the past or present. Some of them may somewhat resemble Earth life due to odd forms of parallel evolution.

They can be as tiny as a microbe (though they then arguably fall into the category of Plague Horrors, like the alien microbes from *The Andromeda Strain*; or, at least skirt the two categories) to as large as Megafauna (i.e., organisms larger than all natural contemporary Earth land animals, but smaller than Daikaiju).

Some can be the creation of Alien genetic engineers, e.g., the Alien Monsters from the early 1980s films like *The Deadly Spawn* and *Night of the Creeps*; or, human scientists combining the DNA of Earth humans or animals with an alien genome, e.g., the predatory creature from the film *Species*; the monsters created by black ops government scientists at Area 51 partly utilizing recovered alien DNA as depicted in Zach Cole *et al.'s* anthology from Wild Hunt Press, *The Experiment* (shameless plug alert!).

These alien monsters can sometimes be controlled by aliens of the above sub-category or humans and can have a variety of special defensive and offensive weapons built into their biology (note the infamous acid blood of the Xenomorphs from the *Aliens* mythos; and the exotic chimeric capabilities of the Thing from Another World).

Note that some of these creatures skirt the Alien and Alien Monster categories. Examples include the savage, monstrous, but laser gun-wielding extraterrestrial being from the 1982 film *Nightbeast*; the aforementioned chimeric aliens from *Species* and *The Thing* (itself based on John W. Campbell Jr.'s 1938 novella *Who Goes There?*) – both of which can look, act, and speak like human beings in their respective "infiltration" forms; as can the savage but human-disguised extraterrestrial monster from the 1977 film *Alien Prey*. Then we have the various forms exhibited by the truly confounding category-skirting of the human/DNA combining alien entity from the 1982 film *Xtro*.

Hence, though I believe the categories of Alien and Alien Monster are distinct though obviously related, there can be clear overlap with certain sources. As a result, each instance of such an overlap should be looked at on a case-by-case basis to determine (though subjectively) which of the two categories the alien entity in question may more properly belong.

GREAT APES

Great Apes are actually a monster category that goes back well into the early days of 20th century literature, cinema, and (a bit later) television. From the get-go, this author must thank my good friend and colleague D.G. Valdron for first bringing this important but too often overlooked classification of monster to my attention.

Despite the name, the category Great Ape – when capitalized, for our purposes – is not referring to the natural category of common great apes – uncapitalized, for our purposes of distinction – that includes gorillas, orangutans, chimpanzees, and bonobos. Rather, it is referring to the variety of gorilla-like primates that have appeared throughout popular fiction with the following characteristics, all of which distinguish them from the four categories of common great apes known to real world primatologists:

1) They can usually walk around comfortably in a bipedal stance for indefinite periods, though they do sometimes go down on all fours for extra speed.

2) They are more intelligent than even chimps and bonobos, able to develop a simple but distinct form of spoken language, not merely sign lingo, when living together in a tribe.

3) They are intelligent enough to fully learn and understand human languages, not limited to signing, and can even be trained to operate certain forms of equipment and firearms. Hence, they are often used as lab assistants or henchmen in criminal ventures when captured or created (see below).

4) Their ability to speak human languages after various levels of training indicate that unlike common great apes, the "proper" Great Apes possess vocal cords capable of roughly reproducing human speech. The majority of singular specimens, however, do not seem able to replicate human speech too easily, and often prefer not to.

5) Have strength and agility at least equivalent to that of a gorilla or orangutan.

6) They somewhat resemble both gorillas and orangutans and have often been mistaken for and billed as one or the other in circuses and occasionally zoos, along with encounter reports in the wild, throughout the WHU.

7) Great Apes actually tend to have somewhat bulkier bodies than gorillas and orangutans, perhaps to accommodate their ability to routinely walk bipedally. This extra upper body musculature may serve to take a lot of stress off their spinal cord.

8) They tend to have larger jaws and elongated faces differently shaped from those of gorillas and orangutans, giving them an appearance that, while distinctly simian, is nevertheless quite distinct from that of the latter two common great apes.

9) Perhaps most interestingly, and disturbing of all, is the fact that unlike common species of great ape, the "proper" Great Apes can develop strong sexual attraction and even feelings of deep romantic love for human beings, particularly in regards to male Great Apes towards human women.

10) Individual specimens can vary in size from smaller than an adult man to larger (albeit not gigantic) but are always much bulkier and stronger than any normal human.

11) Their coat of hair also tends to be much shaggier than that of any common species of great ape, sometimes including a notable tuft of hair atop their head.

These Great Apes are distinct from the gigantic Kongoid sub-species, but likely related to them on some genetic level. Note how in the 1961 film *Konga,* its novelization, and comic book series from Charlton, a normal chimp was evolved via chemical means courtesy of scientist Dr. Chrales Decker into first a bipedal Great Ape about six feet in height and finally, after receiving an overdose of this plant-based growth serum by Decker's treacherous secretary, into a Kongoid-sized specimen.

The idea of several sub-species of Great Ape existing in the WHU can account for the notable disparities in size, as well as fur color – their coats range in hue from black, to brown, to reddish-brown, to less common colors like white and gold.

Some of the solo specimens were clearly outliers created by human scientists of the early to mid-20th century using various chemicals to stimulate the growth of chimps, gorillas, and orangutans into Great Apes for servitude or study. Again, Konga is a good example of that.

Interestingly, an arguable sub-category of Great Apes were actually shape-shifters, the result of either science or magick used to transform a Great Ape into a human-looking form, or vice versa.

Three examples of the former will suffice, the first being Paula the Ape Woman, a female Great Ape transformed into a human woman by chemical science in the trio of Universal films from the 1940s, starting with *Captive Wild Woman* (1943). We have the reverse in the next two examples, the second being a man named Dr. James Brewster, who was given some characteristics of a Great Ape via injection of hormones from one of the latter in the 1943 film *The Ape Man.* The third was entertainer Duke Mitchell who found himself transformed into a Great Ape by the chemical experiments in "evolutionary" science by the nefarious Dr. Zabor, as seen in the 1952 flick *Bela Lugosi Meets a Brooklyn Gorilla* (the ending "fever dream" sequence of the movie, by the way, was apocryphal in the WHU).

Two examples of human beings transformed into Great Apes via magick will next suffice. One was the South American plantation owner Barney Chavez, who was transformed into a particularly nasty Great Ape by the magicks of a witch doctor calling upon the powers of an ape-like demon called Sukara in the 1951 film *The Bride of the Gorilla.* The second was soldier of fortune Ken Hale, who was transformed into an apparently non-aging Great Ape that became known as "Gorilla-Man" after shooting another creature afflicted with this curse, as first seen in the 1954 Atlas comic book *Men's Adventures* #26 (he likely has a counterpart in the WHU, not just the Marvel Universe).

The examples above make it clear that there is some type of biological connection between "proper" Great Apes with both common great apes and humans that enables one to transform into the other via certain chemical stimulation. The fact that the process can also be achieved via magickal implies some overlap between the evolutionary history of humans, common great apes, and proper Great Apes.

It should be noted that the Great Apes bear no known relationship to the fully sentient gorillas or other fully cognizant apes that have developed advanced civilizations in various alternate futures, such as those seen in the *Planet of the Apes* franchise of films, TV series, and comic books.

As alluded to above, a good early example of a tribe of Great Ape sub-species is the Mangani, the fully sentient but wild-living primates that raised Tarzan and first appeared in his early novels, including the first. Others include the Great Ape species from the Valley of Diamonds that first appeared in the Tarzan novel *Tarzan and the Golden Lion,* which actually enslaved a group of primitive humans in a manner very similar to the apparent common great apes that evolved in the alternate timelines of the *Planet of the Apes* franchises.

The type of evolutionary quirk that resulted in the Great Apes evolving naturally within the WHU and many other alternate Earths, but not the more mundane world outside our window is not fully known, but this author theorizes that it is likely not the result not of natural evolution. One possibility is that of ancient Lemurian and Atlantean genetic experimentation on great apes of the common species. Another may be the exposure of common great apes in ancient history to radioactive meteor landings, possibly similar to those that created the human meteor mutants comprising the Wold Newton Family; or, similar to the one whose otherworldly energies are credited with creating the advanced apes inhabiting Gorilla City in the Africa of the DC Universe.

Notably, in the world outside our window, the Great Apes were depicted in early cinema and TV sources via just two or three suits from the 1930s to the 1950s worn by a few costume actors to depict "movie gorillas."

As D.G. Valdron pointed out via personal correspondence, these thespians were, "… guys like Charles Gemorrah, Ray Corrigan, George Barrows, Bob Baker. These guys wore custom made suits, often with prosthetic extensions for forearms, and extensions for the faces to [provide] them muzzles and jaws that could move. The suits were sometimes handed down from one generation to the next. They'd go to zoos, watch real gorillas, chimps, orangs, and monkeys, and try and develop a language of physicality. Call their creations Mangani, I think the pretend apes of the movies were fairly influential."

Their story is told on the informative website Hollywood Gorilla Men, which can he found at **hollywoodgorillamen.com**. These costumes create the distinct look of Great Apes as seen and described in the screen sources that distinguish them from the four species of naturally occurring great apes.

Of course, Great Apes are rare in the WHU and other similar realities but can be found living in small tribes (e.g., the Mangani) or solo (depending on sub-species) in certain sparsely inhabited jungle areas of Africa; and in even smaller numbers on the South American continent and various uncharted islands located all over the tropics. Of course, they also sometimes turn up in laboratories – these being the creations of scientists using the methods described above, or captives acquired by them. Great Apes either captured in the wild or created via chemical alteration of common great apes in laboratories are why these unusual primates have turned up in urban areas in the past, often wreaking great havoc on human lives and property in the process.

A few final film sources prominently featuring Great Apes include Erik the Great Ape from Universal's 1932 film version of *Murders in the Rue Morgue* (Erik was a rather diminutive specimen of Great Ape, but still far exceeding a human in strength and agility); and some of the "gorillas" that appeared on memorable episodes of the sitcoms *The Abbott and Costello Show* and *Gilligan's Island.*

LICHES

A lich is, basically speaking, an undead entity whose creation generally results from a sorcerer or someone using sorcerous means to deliberately prolong their own life indefinitely via spellwork. Unlike a zombie in the great majority of cases, a lich will retain a full level of sentience and mobility.

Oftentimes, their physical body will wither like a true corpse while remaining sentient and fully mobile, taking on a skeletal state (where they arguably straddle categories with a Skeletoid entity). They will often possess considerably greater than human strength in this undead state, much like supernatural zombies created by Voodoo mysticism. Many forms of magick can be used by mystics to transform themselves (or sometimes others) into a lich, however.

In some cases, a sorcerer will become a lich by projecting his/her soul into the body of a corpse after they have expired, thus taking possession of and animating it, much as Deadite demons of *The Evil Dead/Army of Darkness* franchise do; or, they will take possession of an already living person's body.

A lich will retain the full use of their sorcerous powers in that form, though the degree of their mystical abilities will vary according to what they possessed as a human. They will often use weapons they were expert in while alive, be they medieval armaments like swords and daggers, modern firearms, or mystical artifacts. They often possess the power to control other, lesser undead creatures created by magick. The retention of a physical body is often dependent upon a small glass jar or leather box covered in sigils known as a phylactery.

Liches of various sorts are most prominent in the sword and sorcery genre of fictional literature, including the tales of Clark Ashton Smith and Robert E. Howard, e.g., his novella *Skull-Face* and his short story "Scarlet Tears"; as well as H.P. Lovecraft ("The Thing on the

239

Doorstep"), Gardner Fox ("The Sword of the Sorcerer"), and Karl Edward Wagner ("Sticks").

However, they are perhaps most well-known from the *Dungeons and Dragons* RPGs that originated in the 1970s, which generally take place in myriad mystical realms resembling Earth's medieval era but are much more prominently governed by laws of sorcery and magick.

A good example of a lich is Acererak from Gary Grygox's *D&D* module "Tomb of Horrors," and the character also appeared as the guardian of the mystical object known as the Copper Key in Ernest Cline's book *Ready Player One.* Others are the Lich King from Fred Perry's comic book *Gold Digger* published by Antarctic Press; Queen Necrafa from the animated TV series *Mysticons;* and the main antagonist from the episode of the TV series *Lost Girl* entitled "Death Didn't Become Him." My friend and colleague Robert E. Wronski, Jr. noted at the public Wild Hunt Press group on Facebook that Billy Butcherson, the "zombie" from the 1993 Disney flick *Hocus Pocus,* was much more likely a lich than a zombie (albeit a benevolent one who did not initiate his rise from the dead himself).

One sub-category of lich (of which there are likely several) includes *demiliches,* which would be a sorcerer causing their soul to remain in his/her skull or some other bone from his/her corpse following their physical demise, where it can remain conscious and magickally active despite the body not being independently mobile. An example would be the jeweled skull in Fritz Leiber's short story "Thieves' House."

The name "lich" is an old English word meaning "corpse," a term taken from the lich gate, which was the gate located at the lowest end of a cemetery where the funeral procession normally entered.

FEARSOME CRITTERS

This massively varied category from the realm of folklore refers to the myriad strange, wondrous, and outright oddball creatures exchanged in (mostly) tall tales between North American loggers of the lumberwoods between the 19th and early 20th century, particularly (but far from exclusively) in the Great Lakes region of the continent.

This diverse assemblage of critters ranges from silly oddities like the goofus bird, teakettler, squidgicum-squee, jackalope, and fur-bearing trout; to the dangerous beasts like the hoop snake, wampus cat, hidebehind, hodag, cactus cat, whirling whimpus, and snallygaster – the latter sometimes spelled "snoligoster" and God knows how many other ways depending on region and source. A few of these entities may roughly qualify as cryptids with actual sighting reports behind them, albeit often as generic names for entities whose appearance, behavior, and intrinsic nature seems to regionally vary – this is especially the case with the wampus cat and the snallygaster. Most, however, are likely just a combo of elaborate storytelling to pass the time and exaggerations of real animals often sighted in the woods. A few were likely adapted from local Native American lore, and this is probably the case with the wampus cat, which may be a variant of the water panther.

What is the "reality" of this motley lot in the WHU? Some are likely types of nature spirits (e.g., wampus cat), genetic mutations, sub-species of dragons (e.g., snallygaster), variants of the hairy hominid species (e.g., hidebehind), and the result of human shapeshifters. The majority of the more absurd and physics-challenging critters are theoretically residents of one or more alternate planes of reality with a different set of rules concerning biology, physics, and spatial relations. They likely temporarily arrive here ("here" being the Earth of the WHU) when portals occasionally open in the North American woodlands due to phenomena ranging from rare but naturally occurring electromagnetic disturbances to deliberate magickal practices from human mystics.

The best source of info on these creepy creatures is the 1939 book *Fearsome Critters* by Henry H. Tryon with some terrific illustrations from Margaret Ramsay Tryon, which can be read for free on the Lumberwoods site located at **www.lumberwoods.com;** and an early chapter of the late Daniel Cohen's terrific 1975 book on cryptids, *Monsters, Giants, and Little Men from Mars: An Unnatural History of the Americas,* which was the nostalgic introduction of fearsome critters to this author. A notable horror-oriented source of creative fiction featuring these critters is the 2017 anthology *Fearsome Critters of the*

Lumberwoods: 20 Chilling Tales from the Wilderness by Hal Johnson. Another such source, which features 25 cool figurines of various fearsome critters, is Matt Cross's 2020 cooperative board game *Fearsome Wilderness*.

I hope you enjoyed *Duel of the Monsters Volume 2!* If you did, then please strongly consider saying so with a nice rating and review on Amazon, Goodreads, your personal blog, or anywhere else that allows and encourages such reviews! The more positive reviews we get, the more books we sell, the more visible we get on Amazon, and the more we can afford to bring you quality books of horror like this one at very affordable prices! I know we can count on you, the readers, and know that you can also count on us to deliver without breaking your bank!

Coming soon: *Duel of the Monsters Volume 3!*

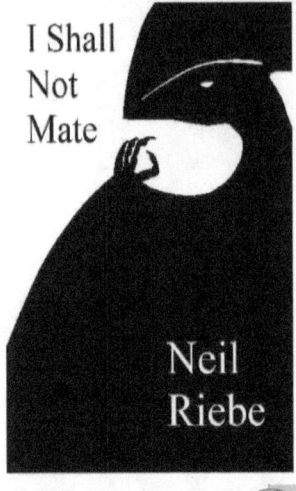